Melina Marchetta was born in 1965. She currently lives with her family in Sydney and is attending university. *Looking for Alibrandi* is her first book.

'a novel to rejoice in, a story from the heart'
Australian Bookseller & Publisher

'a sensational debut'
Herald-Sun

'so fresh and strong it bounces off the page'
Andrea Stretton, *The Bookshow*, SBS

Looking for Alibrandi continues to be enormously popular and has won many awards, including the 1993 Children's Book of the Year Award for Older Readers, the 1993 Multi-cultural Book of the Year Award and the 1993 Variety Club Young People's Category of the 3M Talking Book of the Year Award, as well as several children's choice awards. It is the winner of the 2000 Fairlight Talking Book Awards most outstanding talking book for the past 10 years in the Young People's category.

Melina's most recent book, *Saving Francesca* is the winner of the 2004 Children's Book Council of Australia Book of the Year for Older Readers.

Also by Melina Marchetta

LOOKING FOR ALIBRANDI
Melina Marchetta

Puffin Books

PUFFIN BOOKS

Published by the Penguin Group
Penguin Group (Australia)
250 Camberwell Road, Camberwell, Victoria 3124, Australia
(a division of Pearson Australia Group Pty Ltd)
Penguin Group (USA) Inc.
375 Hudson Street, New York, New York 10014, USA
Penguin Group (Canada)
90 Eglinton Avenue East, Suite 700, Toronto, ON M4P 2Y3, Canada
(a division of Pearson Penguin Canada Inc.)
Penguin Books Ltd
80 Strand, London WC2R 0RL, England
Penguin Ireland
25 St Stephen's Green, Dublin 2, Ireland
(a division of Penguin Books Ltd)
Penguin Books India Pvt Ltd
11, Community Centre, Panchsheel Park, New Delhi-110 017, India
Penguin Group (NZ)
67 Apollo Drive, Mairangi Bay, Auckland 1310, New Zealand
(a division of Pearson New Zealand Ltd)
Penguin Books (South Africa) (Pty) Ltd
24 Sturdee Avenue, Rosebank, Johannesburg 2196, South Africa

Penguin Books Ltd, Registered Offices: 80 Strand, London WC2R 0RL, England

First published by Penguin Books Australia, 1992
50 49 48 47
Copyright © Melina Marchetta, 1992

Typeset in 12/13.5 Goudy Old Style by Midland Typesetters, Maryborough, Victoria
Printed in Australia by McPherson's Printing Group, Maryborough, Victoria

National Library of Australia
Cataloguing-in-Publication data:

Marchetta, Melina, 1965–
Looking for Alibrandi.
ISBN 978 0 14 036046 2.
I. Title.
A823.3

www.puffin.com.au

This publication is assisted by the Australia Council, the Australian Government's arts funding and
advisory body.

The publisher gratefully acknowledges Anastasia Kipriotis for the use of her poem,
'Can you see what I see?' on p 237–238.

To Mummy and Daddy
    Marisa and Daniela –
    Life is good because of you

Also for my grandparents
    Salvatore, Carmela and Maria

In memory of
    Giovanni Marchetta, 1910–1991
    Nonno, when are we ever going to
    stop missing you?

1

Panic was my first reaction to the multiple choice options which lay on my desk in front of me. I glanced at the students around me before turning back to question three. I hated multiple choice. Yet I didn't want to get question three wrong. I didn't want to get any of them wrong. The outcome would be too devastating for my sense of being.

So I began with elimination. 'D' was completely out of the question as was 'A', so that left 'B' and 'C'. I pondered both for quite a while and just as I was about to make my final decision I heard my name being called.

'Josephine?'

'Huh?'

'I think you mean "I beg your pardon" don't you, dear?'

'I beg your pardon, Sister.'

'What are you doing? You're reading, aren't you, young lady?'

'Um . . . yeah.'

'Um, yeah? Excellent, Josephine. I can see you walking away with the English prize this year. *Now stand up.*'

■

So my final school year began. I had promised myself that I would be a saint for this year alone. I would make the greatest impression on my teachers and become the model student. I knew it would all fail. But just not on the first day.'

Sister Gregory walked towards me and when she was so close that I could see her moustache, she held out her hand.

'Show me what you're reading.'

I handed it to her and watched her mouth purse itself together and her nostrils flare in triumph because she knew she was going to get me.

She skimmed it and then handed it back to me. I could feel my heart beating fast.

'Read from where you were up to.'

I picked up the magazine and cleared my throat.

' "What kind of a friend are you?" ' I read from *Hot Pants* magazine.

She looked at me pointedly.

' "You are at a party", ' I began with a sigh, ' "and your best friend's good-looking, wealthy and successful boy-friend tries to make a pass. Do you: A – Smile obligingly and steal away into the night via the back door; B – Throw your cocktail all over his Country Road suit; C – Quietly explain the loyalty you have towards your friend; D – Tell your friend instantly, knowing that she will make a scene".'

You can understand, now, why I found it hard to pick between 'B' and 'C'.

'May I ask what this magazine has to do with my religion class, Miss?'

'Religion?'

'Yes, dear,' she continued in her sickeningly sarcastic tone. 'The one we are in now.'

'Well . . . quite a lot, Sister.'

I heard snickers around me as I tried to make up as much as I could along the way.

Religion class, first period Monday morning, is the place to try to pull the wool over the eyes of Sister Gregory. (She kept her male saint's name although the custom went out years ago. She probably thinks it will get her into heaven. I don't think she realises that feminism has hit religion and that the female saints in heaven are probably also in revolt.)

'Would you like to explain yourself, Josephine?'

I looked around the classroom watching everyone shrugging almost sympathetically.

They thought I was beaten.

'We were talking about the Bible, right?'

'I personally think that you don't know what we've been talking about, Josephine. I think you're trying to fool me.'

The nostrils flared again.

Sister Gregory is famous for nostril-flaring. Once I commented to someone that she must have been a horse in another life. She overheard and scolded me, saying that, as a Catholic, I shouldn't believe in reincarnation.

'Fool you, Sister? Oh, no. It's just that while you were speaking I remembered the magazine. You were talking about today's influences that affect our Christian lives, right?'

Anna, one of my best friends, turned to face me and nodded slightly.

'And?'

'Well, Sister, this magazine is a common example,' I said, picking it up and showing everyone. 'It's full of rubbish. It's full of questionnaires that insult our intelligence. Do you think they have articles titled "Are you a good Christian?" or "Do you love your neighbour?".

No. They have articles titled "Do you love your sex life?" knowing quite well that the average age of the reader is fourteen. Or "Does size count?" and let me assure you, Sister, they are not referring to his height.

'I brought this magazine in today, Sister, to speak to everyone about how insulted we are as teenagers and how important it is that we think for ourselves and not through magazines that exploit us under the guise of educating us.'

Sera, another friend of mine, poked her fingers down her mouth as if she was going to vomit.

Sister and I stared at each other for a long time before she held out her hand again. I passed the magazine to her knowing she hadn't been fooled.

'You can pick it up from Sister Louise,' she said, referring to the principal.

The bell rang and I packed my books quickly, wanting to escape her icy look.

'You're full of it,' Sera said as we walked out. 'And you owe me a magazine.'

I threw my books into my locker and ignored everyone's sarcasm.

'Well, what was it?' Lee grinned. 'A, B, C, or D?'

'I would have gone with him,' Sera said, spraying half a can of hairspray around her gelled hair.

'Sera, if they jailed people for ruining the ozone layer, you'd get life,' I told her, turning back to Lee. 'I was going to go for the cocktail on the Country Road suit.'

The second bell for our next class rang and with a sigh I made another pledge to myself that I would be a saint. On the whole I make plenty of pledges that I don't keep.

■

My name, by the way, is Josephine Alibrandi and I

turned seventeen a few months ago. (The seventeen that Janis Ian sang about where one learns the truth.) I'm in my last year of high school at St Martha's, which is situated in the eastern suburbs, and next year I plan to study law.

For the last five years we have been geared for this year. The year of the HSC (the Higher School Certificate), where one's whole future can skyrocket or go through the toilet, or so they tell us. Personally I feel that the HSC is the least of my problems. Believe me, I could write a book about problems. Yet my mother says that as long as we have a roof over our head we have nothing to worry about. Her naivety really scares me.

We live in Glebe, a suburb just outside the city centre of Sydney and ten minutes away from the harbour. Glebe has two façades. One is of beautiful tree-lined streets with gorgeous old homes and the other, which is supposed to be trendy, has old terraces with views of outhouses and clothes-lines. I belong to the latter. Our house is an old terrace. We, my mother Christina and I, live on the top. We were actually renting the place till I was twelve but the owner sold it to us for a great price and although I've calculated that Mama will have it paid off when I'm thirty-two, it's good not to be renting in these days of housing problems.

My mother and I have a pretty good relationship, if a bit erratic. One minute we love each other to bits and spend hours in deep and meaningful conversation and next minute we'll be screeching at each other about the most ridiculous thing, from my room being in a state of chaos to the fact that she won't let me stay overnight at a friend's home.

She works as a secretary and translator for a few doctors in Leichhardt, a suburb unfortunately close to my grandmother's home, which means I have to go straight to Nonna's in the afternoon and wait for her. That really gets on my nerves. Firstly, the best-looking guys in the world take the bus to Glebe while the worst take the bus to where my grandmother lives. Secondly, if I go straight home in the afternoon I can play music full volume whereas if I go to Nonna's the only music she has is *Mario Lanza's Greatest Hits*.

My mother is pretty strict with me. My grandmother tries to put her two cents worth in as well, but Mama hates her butting in. The two of them are forever at loggerheads with each other. Like whenever school camp comes along, it's fights galore. My grandmother thinks that if a member of our family isn't looking after me I'll get raped or murdered. She accuses my mother of being a bad mother for not caring enough and letting me go. Mama almost gives in to her each time, and some days when the three of us are together it's World War Three.

So not being able to go out a lot is one of my many problems. My biggest, though, is being stuck at a school dominated by rich people. Rich parents, rich grandparents. Mostly Anglo-Saxon Australians, who I can't see having a problem in the world.

Then there are the rich Europeans. They're the ones who haven't had a holiday for twenty years just so their children can go to expensive schools and get the proper education which they missed out on. These people might have money, but they're grocers or builders, mainly labourers. However, they were smart. They moved out of the inner west and inner city and became 'respectable'. Being respectable has made them acceptable.

I come under the 'scholarship' category, and when I say that, I would rather be the daughter of a labourer.

I felt disadvantaged from the beginning. Maybe because I hadn't gone to the same primary school as them. Or maybe because I received the six-year English scholarship. I don't know why I tried so hard to win it. But it back-fired on me because I ended up going to a school I didn't like. I wanted to go to a school in the inner west where all my friends had gone. They were Italian and Greek and we ruled primary school. They were on my level. I related to them. They knew what it meant not to be allowed to do something. They knew what it meant to have a grandmother dressed in black for forty years. I looked like them. Dark hair, dark eyes, olive skin. We sounded alike as well. It felt good being with other confused beings. We were all caught up in the middle of two societies.

I think I had it worst. My mother was born here so as far as the Italians were concerned we weren't completely one of them. Yet because my grandparents were born in Italy we weren't completely Australian. Despite that, primary school was the only time I was with people I could compare notes with and find a comfortable place alongside. We'd slip our Italian and Greek into our English and swap salami and prosciutto sandwiches at lunch-time and life was good in the school-yard. Life outside school, though, was a different story.

The reaction of the Italian mothers to my mother being unmarried drove me crazy at times. There is nothing terribly romantic about my mother's supposed fall from grace. She slept with the boy next door when they were sixteen and before anything could be decided his family moved to Adelaide. Although he knew she was pregnant he never bothered to contact her again. We do know that he's alive and is a barrister in Adelaide, but that's about it. I don't know where the logic is but back then no one was allowed to come and stay at my house. I knew they wanted to, yet I never understood why they couldn't. God knows what their parents thought my mother would do or say to their children.

I think things got worse when I started at St Martha's because I began to understand what the absence of a father meant. Also there were no Europeans like me. No Europeans who didn't have money to back them up. The ones like me didn't belong in the eastern and northern suburbs.

I used to hear my illegitimacy mentioned during the first years at St Martha's, but nobody has spoken about it for ages. Still I wish someone else at school had a Bohemian mother who believed in free love back then. It's an embarrassing contradiction when your mother gets pregnant out of wedlock because her Catholic upbringing prohibits contraception.

Even though the girls at St Martha's don't mention it, I bet you they're talking about me behind my back. I can feel it in my bones. It makes me feel I will never be part of their society and I hate that because I'm just as smart as they are.

Anyway, the other day, after the magazine incident, I couldn't wait to get out of St Martha's. When I went to see Sister Louise, she handed me back the magazine and asked me to write a two-thousand word conversation between myself and the editor of *Hot Pants* magazine.

I took the bus straight home instead of going to see my grandmother, deciding that I'd use the HSC as an excuse not to see her for most of this year.

I was relieved to be going home because it was so hot. The temperature must have been in the high thirties. I just wanted to put on my shorts and sunbake on the balcony.

I could see the English guys who live on the bottom floor of our terrace sitting on the front verandah, stripped to the waist and drinking beer. They used to be backpackers, living in the youth hostel up the road, before deciding they wanted more privacy. I get on really well with one of them. His name is Gary and he's from a place called Brighton in England. He always invites me in for a cup of tea, which is so strange. I mean Australian guys don't really sit around drinking tea, yet he seems as comfortable sipping his tea and talking about his mother as he does drinking his beer and chanting Tottenham soccer songs.

'My mother wants to know when you're going to mow this lawn,' I asked them, taking the mail out of the box.

Our front lawn is tiny. The deal is that my mother tends the garden and the guys look after the lawn. They're usually pretty good about it. They even painted the wooden fence and front door a beautiful deep green which looks great because the outside of the terrace is yellow.

'How can you bear that uniform in this heat, Jose?' Gary asked, handing me his can of beer.

I took a sip and handed it back.

'Believe me, I'm melting.'

Later on, when I was down to a T-shirt and shorts I made myself a sandwich. I didn't hear Mama when she came in. She could have been standing at the kitchen door for at least five minutes before I noticed her.

She looked worried.

'You okay?' I asked.

She nodded.

'Let me guess? You're wondering how a beautiful specimen like me could have an ugly mother like you,' I said, putting the butter back into the fridge.

9

That is a joke because my mother is absolutely gorgeous. She has a beautiful olive complexion. I have a few blemishes. (I hate using the word 'pimple'.)

She's tall and slender with very manageable hair. I'm average height and probably will never be able to get away with wearing a bikini in this lifetime, and my hair is a legacy from my father. It's curly and needs restraining at all times.

People say I look like Mama and Nonna, yet somehow I missed out on the beautiful part.

'No, I was just wondering how someone as tidy as your mother could rear a child as untidy as you.'

'I tidied up, thank you very much,' I said, walking past her into the lounge room where my school books were scattered all over the dining table.

Because the terrace is so small, the dining room and lounge room are all in one. It's not squashy though. It just means that you can eat in front of the television, study in front of the television and do anything recreational in front of the television. Suits me fine.

The room isn't like the living rooms of my friends. There aren't any wedding photos of my parents. The only photo of someone dressed in frilly white is my communion photo. There aren't any pieces of china that were wedding presents. No ugly vase that you have to keep on the mantelpiece because your great aunt gave it to your mother for an engagement present. No masculinity. No old jocks to keep the furniture clean. But I like it. Because my mother and I are stamped all over it. I just have to walk into the house and I smell her even though she's not there. The pictures or tapestries on the walls are done by us. The photos on the mantelpiece are of us, give or take a few of my cousin Robert's family.

On the wall near the television there's a poster we

had done at a Saint Alfio's feast when I was seven. It reads 'Josephine and Christina's Place'. It's a bit worn at the sides but I know that it'll have to fall off the wall in tatters before we ever get rid of it.

Mama was poking round in the kitchenette.

'And I suppose you couldn't cook anything?' she asked, looking into the oven.

'Maaaa,' I wailed. 'I am studying, or has that escaped your attention?'

She opened one of the top cupboards and I closed my eyes knowing that the pots and pans I had crammed in there were going to fall out.

'All I ask is that you have something ready in the afternoons. Even something defrosted,' she snapped, placing them back tidily.

'Yeah, yeah.'

'Don't "yeah, yeah" me, Miss. Now clear that table and set it.'

'You went to Nonna's, didn't you? You're always in a crappy mood when you go to your mother's.'

'Yes, I went to Nonna's, Josephine, and what's this about you and your friends driving around Bondi Junction half-dressed last week?'

'Who told you that?'

'Signora Formosa saw you. She said you and your friends almost ran her over. She told Zia Patrizia's next-door neighbour and it got back to Nonna.'

Telecom would go broke if it weren't for the Italians.

'She's exaggerating. We'd just come from the beach and Sera was driving us home.'

'How many times have I told you that I don't want you riding around in Sera's car.'

'The same amount of times that Nonna has told you to tell me that.'

'Don't answer back, and clear the table,' she snapped.

'Now. This very minute. This very second.'

'Are you sure you don't mean in an hour?'

'Josephine, you are not too old to be slapped.'

It mostly ends up that way in the afternoons. My grandmother's meddling could put Mother Theresa in a bad mood. As much as Mama says that she doesn't care what Nonna says, she takes every word to heart.

I don't exactly help out much, but sometimes I do decide to start anew and do the right thing with her. Though just when I want to sit down and have my time with Mama, she'll be too tired or she'll want to go to bed or worse still she'll want to spring-clean the terrace. Sometimes I wonder if my mother loves housework more than me.

'Don't open that cupboard,' I said, too late. Tea-bags, onions and potatoes came tumbling out.

So we've got a tiny kitchenette. Is it my fault?

We were pretty quiet as we ate that night. I could hear the guys downstairs playing some crazy music and the cicadas outside. I desperately wanted to open a window because it was sweltering inside, but there's always the threat of a cockroach or some horrific insect flying in and until we buy screens we can't really have the windows open at night.

I didn't feel like eating. It was too hot for potato bake.

While we were sitting there I felt Mama looking at me again.

'What are you looking at, Ma?'

'Nothing.'

'What else did Nonna have to say?'

'She . . . she had guests.'

I eyed her for a while before I picked up a bread-roll and toyed with it.

'How was your day?' she asked.

I shrugged, rolling my eyes. 'Reasonable. Father

Stephen came in for religion class. The attention span was unbelievable. If he was a teacher he could do heaps for HSC results. Pity he's a priest.'

'He'd probably make a horrible husband.'

'Well, he decided to ask questions. Picked on me of course because he sees me at church. He wanted to know what we think of when we come back from communion and kneel down. Like do we pray or what. I told him that I check out any good-looking guys in church.'

'You did not?' she asked, horrified, looking up at me.

'Did so. He laughed. Sister told me I was a pagan.'

'Oh, Jose. Couldn't you just have lied and told him you pray for your poor mother, or something?'

'Lie to a priest. Sure, Mum.'

She grabbed the bread-roll from me and I watched her butter it, noticing her hands trembling.

'Something's worrying you. I can tell.'

'I'm getting old,' she shrugged, dramatically.

'You only say that to cover some horrible truth,' I said.

'Really?'

'And truly.'

She leaned forward and tucked a piece of hair behind my ear.

'How would you like to go away for Easter? Just the two of us. Cairns or some place.'

I don't know why I got scared then. Something had to be wrong for her to suggest that. I had begged for a holiday for years. There had always been some excuse.

'I don't want to go anywhere at all for Easter,' I shouted at her.

'Why are you shouting?'

'Because.'

'Great defence. I can see you in a court room one

day, Jose,' she laughed. 'I thought you'd *want* to go on holidays. Remember how you used to go on when you were young?'

'I've got homework to do,' I said, picking up my books.

As I lay in bed that night, I tried to keep the worries about Mama at the back of my mind. I knew something was worrying her. She seemed upset and preoccupied. We're pretty good that way. We tune into each other very well. Maybe because it's always just been the two of us.

Just lying there gave me an uneasy feeling. Night-time scares me. I hate the complete silence of it, especially when I can't sleep. I feel as if everyone could be dead and I would never find out until morning. When I was young I would stand by my mother's door to make sure she was breathing. Sometimes now I pretend to get a glass of water and do the same.

The worst thought struck me as I lay awake.

I leapt out of bed and ran to her room, yanking open the door.

'It's cancer, isn't it?'

'*What?*' she asked, sitting up in bed.

'Don't hide it from me, Mama. I'll be strong for you.'

I burst out crying then. I didn't know what I would do without her.

'Come here, you silly girl. I have *not* got cancer and I'm not dying,' she said.

I threw myself on her bed and lay beside her.

'Where do you get these silly ideas from?' she asked, kissing my brow.

'Holidays at Easter.'

'Whatever happened to those great speeches after watching "Lost in Space"? If Will Robinson's father could take him to space, I could take you on a short holiday.'

14

'I was young and foolish then. Anyway, his dumb father never did find Alpha Centauri and they're still floating around because they can't find Earth.'

'Well, I do not have cancer.'

'You've been staring all evening and your attitude has been weird. It's something terrible, isn't it?'

She shrugged and looked away and then glanced up at me again with a sigh.

'Your grandmother went to the Fiorentino wedding.'

'Yeah, I heard the bride wore a pink dress and now everyone is going on about how she wasn't a virgin.'

She laughed and then sobered up quickly.

'The groom's cousin is Michael Andretti. He and his sister's family were at your grandmother's.'

I was shocked. Dumbfounded. My mother had told me about him once and once only. I'd never heard his name mentioned since. Just 'your father' or 'he'.

But for her to actually see him and worse, for him to actually exist, was mindboggling. Sometimes I think he is a myth. My mother told absolutely nobody except me. As far as the world is concerned, Michael Andretti was just the guy next door.

But for him to be a myth means that I'm a figment of the imagination.

I touched Mama's hand.

'How did it feel? To see him, I mean. Did you hate him? Love him? Anything?'

'Nothing.'

'Nothing?'

'No . . . that's a lie.' She sighed, lying on her back and looking at the ceiling. 'I did hate him sometimes. When he was in Adelaide I could forget he existed. But now . . . can you believe it, Josie? He's going to live in Sydney for a year. To work in some law chamber here. MacMichael and Sons, I think. Your socialite grandmother will make sure we see plenty of him. She'll be his surrogate mother.'

'But we can handle it, Ma,' I said shaking her. 'There's no big deal.'

'Josephine, you can't handle it. You think you can, but I know you.'

'That's bull,' I exploded angrily. 'I don't care about him. I wouldn't care if he was sitting in this room with us now. I'd look straight through him.'

'He asked me how life was. When we were alone he even told me he had no regrets.'

'What did you say?'

She turned to me and smiled. My worry lifted then. My mother may look like a delicate soft woman but the strength in her eyes is such a comfort to me when I'm scared. She would never ever fall to pieces on me.

'I said I had no regrets either.'

'Did he ask if you were married?'

'He asked if I had a family. I said yes.' She laughed bitterly. 'His sister said that Michael is great with her kids. He loves kids, she said. He'd love to have some of his very own. I wanted to spit in his face.'

'Spitting? Very impressive. My serene lovable mother has become aggressive.'

'I don't know what I'm scared of, Josie. Maybe I forgot he existed after all this time.'

'We don't need him.'

'What we don't need and what we get are two very different stories.'

'Well, I've got a wonderful idea. How about we never go over to Nonna's place again so we can't ever bump into him?'

'You'll have to meet him sooner or later, Miss, and you'll go to your grandmother as per normal.'

'Maaaa,' I groaned. 'She drives me crazy. She's

starting to tell me all those boring Sicily stories. If she tells me one more time she was beautiful, I'll puke.'

'I want you to try and get on with her more.'

'Why? *You* don't. It's not fair to expect me to.'

'Our circumstances are different, Josephine. I've never got on with her. When I was young she used to keep me at such a distance that I used to wonder what I could possibly have done wrong. My father was much worse and it was only after he died that she took a step towards me. By then I kept *my* distance. With you, it's different. She's always wanted to be close to you.'

Mama looked at me and shrugged.

'I envied you that.'

'Five, Jozzie,' I mimicked. 'Five men came to ask for my hand in marriage when I was your age.'

Mama laughed and I lay back content. I like to make her laugh. It's weird that I've spent my whole life trying to impress her and out of everyone I know she's the only person who loves me the way I am.

'What does *he* look like?' I asked later, trying to act uninterested.

She thought for a moment and then looked over at me, amusement lurking in her eyes. 'He looks like a male Josephine Alibrandi.'

Because it was the easiest thing to do, we both began to laugh.

2

——— Spending half your morning trying to pull Sera away from a mirror is one of life's mundane tasks.

Thankfully I don't have to go through it every morning, but two days after Mama told me she'd met Michael Andretti, we had the annual 'Have a Say Day' in Martin Place. Sera volunteered to drive. She and Anna are the only ones of us who have a licence.

For two days I just couldn't help thinking about my father. I felt sick at the idea of meeting him, though at the same time I desperately wanted to. But I couldn't tell my friends about it yet. I just wanted to keep it to myself until I figured out how I felt.

There are four of us who hang out together and we make the most unlikely group. Most of the other students in the school are in clone groups. They all look similar. Either blond yuppies or European trendies. Either intellectuals or 'the beautiful people'.

Our group represents all types, yet we hadn't fitted into any of them in Year 7.

Anna Selicic is your typical Slavic-looking girl. Long blonde hair and blue eyes and that healthy red-cheek look. She's the most nervous person I have ever known. She puts her hand up in class and whispers the answer with dread. It's as if she thinks that if she whispers the wrong answer a blade will come hurtling across the room and decapitate her. She stands like a stunned mullet if guys approach us and still hasn't been kissed, despite her good looks.

At fifteen, she was the last of us to get her period. I remember the three of us standing outside the toilet cubicle instructing her on how to put in a tampon. She went through two packets of Carefree 20s before she was successful.

We tend to mother her a lot, and if we're ever in a risky situation, like being squashed at a concert or terrorised by the students of Cook High, she's the first person we try to protect.

Then there's Seraphina. It's pretty difficult describing her. She has to be the most brazen person I've ever met. She can look a person straight in the eye and lie her heart out. She can bitch about a person for three hours straight and then turn around and crawl to them. Winning them over with what they see as sincerity. The three of us tend to look on in disgusted fascination. She has black roots and blonde hair teased from here to eternity. She's skinny yet voluptuous and tends to dress in whatever the latest rock or pop star is wearing. Since she was fourteen she has never been without a boyfriend for more than a week and she's the only one of us who's slept with a guy. Her father, like most Italian fathers, thinks she's the Virgin Mary and like most Italian fathers is dead-set wrong.

I have a funny relationship with Sera. As the only two of Italian ancestry in the group we have a thin bond and I find that when I'm in her home I crawl more to her parents than to anyone in the world. I'm charming and kiss them on both cheeks, knowing deep down as they kiss me back that they'd think nothing of tearing my family or myself to shreds. I'm not sure why I put up with it. Maybe for acceptance, because I think that if you're an outcast with your own kind you'll never be accepted by anyone.

Sometimes I really don't like her. But other times she makes me laugh more than anyone I know. Those times are mostly in church or class or places where you have to control yourself but can't. I envy her, I think. People really bitch about her at St Martha's. She's a yuppie's nightmare. Her father's a fruit grocer. She's the stereotype of a wog yet she doesn't give a damn. She just gives the finger.

And last, but never least, is Lee Taylor, whose main objective in life is to hang out with wax-heads down at the southern beaches and who thinks it's cool to come to school with a hangover.

God knows why, because her father is an alcoholic. That's why she's with us and not 'them'. Because she went to primary school with 'them' and her father came to pick her up from a birthday party once, blind drunk. Nobody was allowed to go to her place after that.

Lee and I have a weird relationship. We pretend we have nothing in common, yet we can talk for hours on any subject. We pretend we come from two different parts of society, yet both of us are middle-class scholarship students. We pretend that our families have nothing in common because people in her family use words like 'wogs' and mine happen to be 'wogs'. Yet I respect her more than any of my friends, although I couldn't tell her that because we both pretend we don't know the meaning of the word.

One day we'll pass each other in the street, pretending our lives have gone in different directions, but I can guarantee that our adult lives will be as identical as our school lives have been.

Guys go for her a lot. My cousin Robert, though he won't admit it, has had a crush on her for six years. She's one of those people you think is quite plain until you're sitting in front of her and realise just how attractive she is. Straight brown hair streaked gold by the sun, freckles on her nose and hazel eyes which never look directly at you when she speaks. Yet you can't call her a coward. I think she has so much emotion she doesn't want to show, she makes sure nobody sees it.

We grew up in the midst of the snobs of St Martha's and discovered that somehow brains didn't count that much. Money, prestige and what your father did for a living counted. If your hair wasn't in a bob or if your mother didn't drive a Volvo you were a nobody.

That's where the problem lies between myself and our school captain, Ivy Lloyd, who we call Poison Ivy. I was awarded the insulting task of being her deputy. We hate each other's guts, probably because we've been competitive all our lives. She's one of those girls with perfect white skin and not one split end in her strawberry-blonde hair. She's a bore though. She's obsessed with school-work and whenever we get assignments back she looks over to me to try to find out how well I went. Sometimes when she's looking and I know that I've probably received the highest mark, I shake my head in a sorrowful way as if I'm devastated. Then as we're walking out of the classroom and she has an ecstatic grin on her face, I'll show Sera my mark and she'll scream it out hysterically.

Yes, I know. I'm immature and vain about my brains, but you can't imagine how wonderful it is to beat Poison Ivy. It doesn't happen very often. I remember the first day of school in Year 7. She walked up to me in a really snotty way and said 'I hear you're the recipient of the English scholarship'. I remember thinking that she wanted to be my friend. I was so thrilled, imagining the slumber parties and holidays we'd be spending together.

But I was only given ten seconds to dream, because she looked me up and down and then walked away. The look kind of said it all.

So I sat with Sera, who no one else would go near. Lee joined us so it wouldn't seem as if she didn't have friends and the three of us later rescued Anna from vomiting to death, due to nerves, in the toilet. We actually didn't have our first conversation for a week. We just needed each other's presence.

I suppose we've done well for a group which the elite of St Martha's believed shouldn't be at the school, but I only wish we could have been the best or the worst in the form. Not just somewhere in between.

Purgatory. I hate it so much that when I die, and if God sends me there, I'll beg him to send me to hell instead.

'You guys ready?' Sera asked, breezing past us.

'I read in a book that your hair can fall out if you put too much hairspray in it, Sera,' Lee laughed as we walked out of the house with her.

'A book?'

'Yeah, you know those things they lend you in libraries,' Anna said seriously.

'Very funny, smart ass. If you'd like to know, I'm reading a very good mystery at the moment.'

'Let me guess? *The Mystery of the Missing Disco Lights?*' I asked, grabbing her arm.

'Not all people are intellectuals like you, Josie,' she said, shaking me off.

'I know. Isn't life tragic?'

Anna, Lee and I stood at her car and she avoided looking at us.

'We're not taking my car.'

We exchanged looks.

'What are you talking about, Sera? We discussed this

yesterday,' Anna said patiently.

'We're getting a lift. All right?' she sniffed, walking down the street.

'No way,' I shouted. 'No way, Sera. I'm not getting into Angelo Pezzini's car.'

'Good, Josie. Walk to Martin Place,' she yelled back.

'Sera, someone will see us,' I shouted. 'The whole school will be down there.' She shrugged and walked on.

You'd understand my reluctance if you'd met the guy.

He picked us up at the top of Sera's street. Remember when I mentioned that Sera's never been more than a week without a boyfriend since she was fourteen? Well, her parents have never known about them. She's never been picked up at home.

Angelo Pezzini's one of those guys who can't drive a car without sharing his love of bad-taste music with the rest of the suburb he's driving through. He sped through Randwick with the latest night-club music blaring from a set of speakers which were best suited to a dance hall. Sera danced, while seated in the front, and the three of us clutched on to each other in the back seat, ignoring filthy looks from passing motorists and pedestrians. Angelo Pezzini is a spray painter. The car is black and red with wheels that probably came from an eighteen-wheeler truck and an engine that is certainly eligible for a noise pollution fine.

I had visions of being in a horrific road accident and our photos being on the front page of the local newspapers. 'Four St Martha's schoolgirls found in Angelo Pezzini's Valiant' the headlines would scream.

My mother would have to move to Perth. Mainly to get away from my grandmother's hysteria. Nonna is convinced that Angelo Pezzini's mother put the evil eye on her once.

As he drove along Angelo turned around, grinning at us.

The three of us in the back pointed to the road begging him to turn around. Anna was grasping at her asthma inhaler for dear life.

'Hey, my cousin said he'd like to go out with you, Jose. How about it, huh?'

I'd been roped into going out with Sera, Angelo and his cousin, Dino, once before. We went to the cinema and watched a blood-and-guts violent movie where everyone shot each other dead at the end. Angelo and Dino managed to get into a fight with the people sitting in front of us. Later on at a café they fought with the waiter and we were eventually asked to leave. To top off the night they picked a fight with the driver of the car next to us and I found myself in a drag-racing competition all the way home.

'Yeah, we'll go to the movies,' Sera said.

Anna took my hand in sympathy and squeezed it.

'I'll see,' I whispered quietly, knowing I couldn't get out of it without having a fight with Sera.

As we approached Martin Place he crossed three lanes of traffic and came to a heart-shattering stop behind a mini-bus. We heard shouts of abuse, honking of horns and explicit threats from all around.

After five minutes of passion we managed to drag Sera out and she made kissing sounds to the back of his car as he drove away.

'Isn't he hot?'

Lee looked at me, shaking her head sadly.

'You are a dick, Sera,' she pointed out.

Anna tapped me on the shoulder and turned me round.

Sister Louise and Poison Ivy were striding towards us. I knew they had seen us getting out of the car. I hadn't prepared any explanation for Angelo Pezzini or the fact we were late. But I could tell by the look on her face that she would accept no excuse.

'What time did I request you to be here, Josie?'

Why is it that teachers ask questions they already know the answers to?

'Nine o'clock, Sister.'

'And what time is it now?'

'Nine-thirty.'

Then she said nothing. Just looked at me with ice-cold blue eyes and her head tilted back in disgust.

I looked at Ivy who had a 'try getting out of this one' look.

'Sister, I . . .'

'I don't want to hear it,' she snapped. 'The Catholic Education Office has requested that one of our students make a speech. An oratory speech on any subject you prefer. Ivy will be having discussions with other school leaders. Josephine, you will make that speech.'

'Have a Say Day' takes place every year at Martin Place, a walkway in the middle of the city where people sit and have lunch. It has a war memorial and an ampitheatre and houses most of the major bank buildings as well as the General Post Office. It runs horizontally across three major streets.

On 'Have a Say Day', schools from all over Sydney come together and do just that. Have a say. It's something that was organised about ten years ago by some students from a school out west. They came to Martin Place and stood up at the ampitheatre and griped about the state of their school due to lack of government funding.

Because it gets too packed with people, only the Year 12 students can attend from our school, so this year was our year.

'But, Sister, I don't have anything prepared,' I whined.

'Josephine, you are so wonderful at making up stories, I'm sure you can handle it. Now come along all of you and, Seraphina, take off that ridiculous bolero. You are not going to a fashion parade.'

She stalked off with Poison Ivy in tow and I groaned in dismay.

'She's just jealous because she can't wear trendy clothes,' Sera sneered, making rude signs at Sister's back.

Anna grabbed Sera's hands, giggling.

It was stiflingly hot sitting on the stage of the ampitheatre. I managed to make a fan for myself out of the program and tried, at one stage, to take off my blazer. However, Sister Louise saw me and the look in her eyes clearly said 'leave it on'.

I looked out at the crowd which was mostly made up of students in uniform. There were a lot of business people as well who had stopped to take a look, but most of them were rushing off to work. Everyone seemed to be having a fun time. I saw my friends talking to some gorgeous guys from St Anthony's and cursed Sister Louise over and over again.

So I sat there next to a Jewish hunk, wishing he believed in Jesus so we could get married, and behind a girl resembling Poison Ivy who belonged to a Presbyterian school. Seated on my other side was Jacob Coote from Cook High.

Cook High is a public school in the city area. Because it's the closest school to us we don't get on well with them. We think we're better than them. They think we're the biggest dags in the world.

When we were young, they would throw things out of their bus windows at us and in Year 10, on the last day of school, Jacob Coote and about ten of his friends, male and female, blocked both entrances of a lane we cut through to get to our bus-stop. Twelve of us were bombarded with eggs, rotten fruit and vegetables. Everyone said that one day we would look back on the occasion and laugh.

Very unlikely.

'What are you going to talk about?' he whispered in my ear.

I moved away hoping nobody had seen him speaking to me. My friends think he's gorgeous. His hair is brown, shoulder-length, not cut into any particular style and his eyes are green and they always seem to be laughing at you.

He grinned and by the way his lips were twitching he looked like he was trying to control a laugh. I knew he recognised me from the lane.

'Didn't I once squash two eggs against your glasses?' he asked.

'I'm flattered you remember. I tripped over a rubbish can, you know, and cut my hand on some broken glass.'

'Oh, come on. We were suspended for that. We didn't go to school for six weeks.'

'Very funny. We had six weeks holiday after that.'

He tapped the Presbyterian girl in front of us and asked her what she was going to speak about.

'University careers,' she smiled, flirting before turning around.

'Great choice,' he said looking at me and making a face at her back.

Some people spoke about the government's school cuts, others about careers. The environment was spoken about, as well as the homeless.

I decided to speak about sex education in our schools due to the AIDS issue. I had used it as an oratory speech before and had won, so I knew I couldn't go wrong.

I spoke for five minutes and accepted the Jewish hunk's hand when he offered it to me, and the nod of approval from the Presbyterian girl when I sat down. Jacob Coote nudged me, almost sending me sprawling over my neighbour.

'Great speech. Only the seniors have AIDS talks at our school, which is a waste because by that stage most of us have had sex for years.'

I nodded vaguely in agreement, embarrassed that he had divulged that information to me.

'What are you going to talk about?'

He dug into his pocket and pulled out a condom.

'I'm going to show these people how to put one on,' he said seriously, standing up.

I was horrified. I knew he wasn't a debater and that he probably didn't have a speech prepared. I was also worried that by sitting behind him I wouldn't see anything and was ashamed of myself for thinking it. Until he stood in front of the microphone and spoke.

'I'm speaking about the vote today,' he said, digging his fingers into his pockets.

I sighed in relief but was disappointed by his boring topic.

'I think that all political parties are the same,' he began, sounding a bit stilted. He had taken his fingers out of his pockets by then and was kneading his neck with one. His white sleeves were rolled up to his elbow and I could see that he was tanned. Not a beach tan though. More like a working, outdoor tan.

'These politicians, they make the same promises. They tell the same lies and frankly, I can't understand why normal voters get influenced by a political campaign. We all know that what they're gonna say is what we wanna hear.'

I could feel my Jewish neighbour cringing at the 'gonna' and 'wanna'.

'I used to think that when it came time for me to vote,' he said, knocking his fist to his chest, 'I'd put no effort into it. Maybe I would put in a dummy vote. Maybe I wouldn't even bother registering at all.

'Probably because until recently I wondered what the big deal was. *What's* great about our political system here? *Why* do we call ourselves the lucky country when half of us can't afford housing payments?'

He was pointing his finger now and I could feel my neighbour sitting up and taking notice.

Jacob Coote shrugged. 'You know, I didn't know what to talk about today, because I was only told an hour ago that I had to say something. I was gonna speak about the freedom you feel when you ride a motor bike, but that has nothing to do with having a say. When my neighbour up here was talking about ignorance when it came to sex education I was worried. I couldn't think of anything to say that was as worthwhile as her speech. Until I looked out and saw everyone.'

He shook his head and gave a little laugh.

'And I felt lucky. Because we have a choice, and I think that we vote, not to get the *best* party in, but to keep the *worst* party out. Because we can stand here and protest. We can get all riled up about the Premier's ideas. We can say he's a dickhead even. We can call the Prime Minister and the Leader of the Opposition one as well.

'We can scream and shout and protest and even burn our flag if we want to. Because we're free to do whatever we want to do and if we break the law we get a fair trial.

'But in some countries, people can't do that. They can't go out into places like Martin Place and protest. In some countries people our age can't concentrate on their schoolwork or their lives because of the sound of gun-fire.

'In some countries they have one-party systems and they have things called the People's Army and when the people come out and have a say like we're doing today – scream and shout and voice their opinion – the People's Army shoots the people. Young people like us,' he added in almost a whisper.

'So, great. Let's be apathetic. Let's not vote. Let's let anyone run this country. Let's all be ignorant and let's all be proud of that ignorance. And maybe we'll have a People's Army one day too.'

He sat down next to me and everyone in our row leaned forward to stare at him before they clapped. I could sense where his friends were standing because of the shouting and whistling that was coming from their direction.

I was stunned. Not about what he'd said, but the way he'd said it. I would never have thought that Jacob Coote would be passionate like that.

The Jewish guy leaned across me and clasped Jacob Coote's wrist in a 'brothers-in-arms' grip.

'I'm impressed,' I whispered.

'You didn't think I watched the news, did you?' he laughed.

'No, I didn't.'

'Well, I used to watch "Hinch", anyway.'

'You're kidding me? My mother always says that if any current affairs team came to our door she'd slam it shut even though we have nothing to hide. She reckons they'd find something.'

'Yeah, every time I get drunk I wake up the next morning afraid, because I've had a nightmare that I was on the "Shame" file.'

I laughed and shook my head.

'How come you got picked for this?'

'One-party voting system. If they didn't vote me school captain I was going to break all their legs.'

'You're school captain?'

'Unfortunately. You?'

'Vice.'

'Too bad. It could have been beautiful between us.'

I opened my mouth to say something, but nothing came out. I wondered if he meant it. As we sat back to listen to the next speech I couldn't help being aware of his rolled-up sleeves and tanned arms.

That's when all the great come-back lines to what he had said came to mind. But like always, with come-back lines, it's too late.

There were a few more speeches after that. Great speeches made by the best orators in our schools, but nothing compared to his. Ours were all polished. We didn't say ours with passion. We had lost that passion after winning our first few debates. It was all so clinical for us now.

But his speech was said brashly and from the heart.

'I'm in love,' Lee stated, matter-of-factly, when I stood down. 'How could you have sat next to him without throwing yourself on him? He even spoke to you.'

'He's not my type.'

'Why?' she shouted, incredulously.

I shrugged.

'Because . . . I don't know.'

'Because he's not Italian, he's not going to be a solicitor and he goes to a public school, right?'

'I'm not a snob,' I shouted.

'You are so. You might have one hundred hang-ups, but you still think you're better than the average person.'

'He cracked two eggs on my glasses once.'

'Out of twelve girls in that alley, he picked you to do that to. I think he likes you.'

I laughed, grabbing her hand and pulling her towards the TV cameras.

We weren't on the news that night. Poison Ivy was, because she was in the group that threw questions at the Premier. As usual she was there in technicolour, sitting on top of the world. No matter how much I hate Poison Ivy, I want to belong to her world. The world of sleek haircuts and upper-class privileges. People who know famous people and lead educated lives. A world where I can be accepted.

Please, God, let me be accepted by someone other than the underdog.

3

Rituals. They come and they go, but the ritual of having to see my grandmother every afternoon drives me absolutely insane. So I dawdle, because I know it gets on her nerves and my main objective in life at the moment is to get on my grandmother's nerves. I swear to God that if there is something I am going to escape in this life of rules and regulations it will be my dreaded rituals.

It's almost the end of February and instead of getting cooler the weather gets more humid as the days go by. Because of the heat, the only thing I was looking forward to at Nonna's place was the swimming-pool. I crossed the road as soon as I reached her street to try to avoid old Mr Catanzaro who lives on the corner. As much as I love him, he has this habit of grabbing me by the skin under my chin and pinching me affectionately. It's very hard to smile when tears of pain are welling up in my eyes.

He tends to live in his garden. I've never seen him anywhere else. Whenever we go to Nonna's place, whether it's seven in the morning or seven in the evening, Mr Catanzaro is in his garden. His lawn is usually covered with bread because he loves to feed the birds.

That day, though, I managed to escape with a wave

and raced into Nonna's house. I was force-fed when I arrived. Force-fed like every afternoon of my life.

'Eat, Jozzie, eat. Oh, Jozzie, Jozzie. Look at your hair. Why, Jozzie? Why can you not look tidy?'

My grandmother says that to me every afternoon. She says it with a painful cry in her voice as if she is dying. I'm not sure if anyone has ever died of the fact that their granddaughter looks untidy, but I'm sure my grandmother will one day because she'll strain her voice so much she'll choke.

'It's the fashion.'

I say that to her every afternoon because I know it gets on her nerves.

On Wednesday, she was wearing a woollen jumper. It was thirty degrees outside and the woman was wearing wool on her skin.

Nonna tends to believe that the more you suffer on earth the better the reward is in heaven. Wearing wool in summer must be one of the suffering requisites. It gets on my nerves that she won't let me sit in the good living room where the air-conditioner is. That room is reserved for visitors she hates but wants to impress with her good Italian furniture. The granddaughter she supposedly loves gets to sit in the boiling hot TV room on a torn sofa.

I walked into the kitchen to see if she had any junk food, trying to block out her rambling about how she wants us to live with her.

Nonna has tried, unsuccessfully, to convince us to move in with her. She can't understand why my mother says no every single time. She tends to forget that all she does to Mama when they're together is nag her about the way she's bringing me up or how she's disrespectful by not visiting our relatives. She tends to forget that most of her relatives gave my mother a bad time when she had me.

My mother had been estranged from her family for years after my birth. It was only after my grandfather died that we were welcomed back into the fold.

I remember on one occasion playing hide and seek with my cousin Robert, who's the same age as me. We were both huddled behind the laundry door when my grandmother's cousin and her daughter walked into the room. They spat out my mother's name in disgust repeatedly and all I remember hearing was 'they don't even know who he is' in Italian, over and over again.

I didn't understand what it all meant at the time. Until a bully called Greg Sims, who lived next door to us when I was ten, called me a bastard. When I asked him what it meant he told me that it was when you didn't know who your father was. I remembered what I had heard in the laundry that day and how they had mentioned the word '*bastarda*'.

Illegitimacy isn't a big deal any more. But it was back then and I remember the lies my grandmother would tell me. That I did have a father who had died. My mother never lied to me that way. Maybe that's what I dislike about Nonna. That she couldn't accept things the way they were. That she probably would have been spitting out some girl's name and saying 'they don't even know who he is' if it wasn't her daughter.

Sometimes I feel really sorry for her. I think that my birth must have cut her like a knife and I feel as if she's never forgiven Mama. But she loves us, even if it is in a suffocating way, and that makes me feel very guilty.

'What were you talking about with Giovanni Gilberti's boy at the baptism the other night?' she asked, trying to pin back my hair with a comb.

'We were discussing his perm, Nonna. He was

contemplating blond streaks and I was advising him against it.'

'Did I tell you that he was a mechanic and owned his own house?'

'About one million times,' I said, escaping her clutches.

'He asks me about you all the time, Jozzie. "How is Jozzie, Signora?" he asks. "Is she good?"'

'"No, she's bad" you answer,' I said, eating some Nutella out of the jar.

'He is a very well-manner boy.'

'Mannered,' I corrected, knowing that it irritated her, although I'm pretty proud of the way she speaks English.

'He is like your cousin Roberto. He loves his nonna, Roberto does.'

'Meaning I don't love you, right?'

'I did not say that, Jozzie,' she said angrily. 'You always try to put the words into my mouth.'

'You mean it,' I sighed, throwing myself on the couch in front of her.

'You misintrepid everyting, Jozzie.'

'It's "mis-interpret everything",' I corrected, rolling my eyes.

'You are without respect, Jozzie. Just like your mother. Always wit no respect.'

'Mama is good to you, Nonna,' I shouted angrily. 'If she is ever rude to you it's because you pester her about every single thing possible.'

'Don't you talk to me like that, Jozzie.'

'Why? You sit there and pick a fight deliberately and then you wonder why I argue back?'

'I did not pick a fight, Jozzie. I just said that you and Christina are rude and should treat me better. I am an old woman now and I deserve respect.'

'Yes, Nonna,' I muttered, bored.

'Now see if you can find my tablets. I have a migraine

now,' she said touching her forehead dramatically.

She drives me crazy. Sometimes I have to grit my teeth to control myself. She wants to know why other Italian girls have Italian boyfriends and I don't. If I want to go out with Australians, she objects. 'What do they know about culture?' she asks. 'Do they understand the way we live?'

The way we live?

You would think we had a totally different lifestyle like the Amish or something.

Then she tells me about Eleanora Castano who married Bob Jones and now they're divorced.

Why? Because he's Australian and she's Italian, of course. Not because she's a flibbertigibbet and he's an idiot.

'No manners, Jozzie,' I heard her say. 'That is Christina's fault because if she was a good mother, you would be a good daughter and granddaughter and respect me. But there is no respect left wit the youth of today.'

I gave her a glass of water and tablets and picked up my bag.

'It's not the youth of today, Nonna,' I said angrily. 'It's you and people like you. Always worrying about what other people think. Always talking about other people. Well, we get spoken about as well, Nonna, and that's your fault because you have no respect for other people's privacy, including your daughter's and granddaughter's.'

'It is Christina's fault that you are speaking to me like this. A daughter's behaviour always reflects on how good a mother is.'

'Well, I guess that means you did a pretty hopeless job as a mother because look at the life your daughter ended up with.'

We looked at each other coldly for a long time. I knew I had gone too far. Maybe, by the look on her face, she knew that I had hit the truth.

It scared me looking at her so close. I don't do that too often and I realised that she was getting old. Because of her vanity and the fact that she constantly dyes her hair black she can get away with looking like a woman ten years younger. But today she looked like a woman in her sixties. She looked tired and I realised that I loved her as much as I disliked her.

'Go home, Jozzie,' she said icily. 'I do not want you here.'

The doorbell rang and we both ignored it for a few seconds. I tried hard not to think of the trouble I would be in with my mother. Nonna went to answer it and I stayed in the TV room wondering whether I should go home. I heard her call my name, so picking up my bag I walked into the corridor where she was standing with a man.

'This is my granddaughter Jozzie, Michael.'

Michael! My heart began to pound at one hundred miles per hour and I could feel the hairs at the back of my head standing on end.

'I will just go and get that address, Michael,' she said walking up the stairs. 'Jozzie, show Michael to the lounge room and turn on the air-conditioning. It is boiling hot.'

I looked at him and at that moment every image I had of my father flew out the window.

I had thought he'd be tall.

He wasn't.

I thought he'd be good-looking.

He wasn't.

I thought he'd look like a weakling.

He didn't.

He had a sense of strength about him. A kind of tilt

to his head when he looked at me. He looked like an intellectual and so sure of himself. Somehow I figured that women would really go for him. He was very solid and when I looked into his eyes I saw an obvious resemblance.

'You're Christina's daughter?'

He had a deep articulate voice, which was cool and very impersonal.

'Yes.' I watched him tilt his head even more and I slowly began to enjoy his oncoming discomfort.

'I didn't expect you to be so old.'

I picked up my school-bag and walked past him, opening the door.

'My mother had me young,' I said, turning around to face him.

His face kind of fell. It went pale. I had never seen anything like it before. He looked at me in absolute shock and if I had it in me I would have said more to make him feel even worse.

'Goodbye, Mr Andretti.'

I walked down the steps of the house and along the pathway and only when I reached the road did I turn around. He was still watching.

■

Before I could even walk through the door, my grandmother had rung my mother recounting every single word of our conversation. I was ordered to apologise. Wouldn't you love to receive an apology from someone because they were ordered to?

I was so stressed out about the whole affair. I couldn't believe that I had stood so close to this man who I have spent all of my life slotting into the furthest part of mind. I wanted to go to Mama and tell her how I felt. I wanted to ring up Sera or Lee or Anna. Anyone. Just to tell them how I felt. Except I knew that if I walked into Mama's room or rang up one of my friends I would open my mouth and nothing would come out. Nothing right, anyway.

I had a one hour 'hating Nonna' session. I hated her because she never had anything nice to say about Mama. I hated her because she'd never let my mother forget the past. I hated her because I had to go to her place in the afternoons. I hated her because she tried to act like my mother. I hated her because she was being friendly to Michael Andretti. I hated her because she rang up Mama to keep her up-to-date on everything I said and did wrong so she could say 'You're a bad mother, Christina'.

I vowed like I do every time we have a fight that when I turn eighteen I'll leave and never have anything to do with my family again. Not with my grandmother or meddling great aunts or cousins or gossiping family friends. I want to run from all of them.

They stifle me with ridiculous rules and regulations they have bought with them from Europe, but they haven't changed with the times like the Europeans have. There's always something that shouldn't be said or done. There are always jobs I have to learn because all good Italian girls know how to do them and one day I'll need them to look after my chauvinistic husband. There's always someone I have to respect.

I hate the word 'respect'. It makes me sick to my stomach.

I'll run one day. Run for my life. To be free and think for myself. Not as an Australian and not as an Italian and not as an in-between. I'll run to be emancipated.

If my society will let me.

4

It's debating time again. The only time when Poison Ivy and I are on the same side of life, agreeing on the same thing. It begins each year in March and this year the competition began for us at our school, against St Anthony's.

Have I ever told you about John 'love of my life' Barton?

Picture this. School captain of St Anthony's. Son of a member of parliament. Greatest debater who ever lived. Good-looking. Popular. Tell me, what more could I want out of life?

For him to be equally in love with me, that's what.

St Anthony's beat us on Friday night. Due to the fact that it was an argument about politics, I feel that John Barton's team had a certain advantage.

When it was over I rushed to the classroom where they were serving coffee and biscuits. I was hoping to salvage the last piece of cake or maybe a chocolate biscuit but discovered I was too late when I found a girl taking the last four.

'I bet she was the type who hogged the potato chips at parties when she was young,' I heard someone whisper in my ear.

I turned to face John Barton and laughed, nodding my head.

It had been three months since I last saw him and he was looking even better. Not that he's a 'pretty boy' or even bursting with sex-appeal, come to think about it. It's the honesty and realness about him that I love. It's written on his face like a script.

If he was a woman he would never need to wear rouge. He has that natural redness on his cheekbones. Although he's a bit on the thin side, it's his height that I like and the way his hazel eyes smile and change so instantly with his moods.

'I'm left with the Scotch Finger biscuits as usual,' I told him.

He grinned mischievously and held out his hand, holding two Tim Tams.

'I was a fairy-bread hogger at parties,' he told me seriously, his eyes immediately changing. 'I used to put them in my pockets or hide them wherever I could, until one day I was exposed when my host handed me my parka and four slices of fairy bread fell out. I was seven years old and up till this day if I ever see fairy bread I palpitate and realise that pyschologically I will never be cured.'

I laughed at his theatrics and took the Tim Tam he offered me.

'So what deep, dark secret do you have to tell me about your party days?' he asked.

'Well, I was one of those "pass-the-parcel" hoggers. I used to hold on to the parcel for five seconds more in case the music stopped. The same for "musical chairs". I'd stand in front of the chair and not move. I was banned from parties after that.'

'Yeah,' he said, narrowing his eyes in mock suspicion. 'You look the type.'

Mama came up and gave me a kiss and then made a bee-line for Sister Louise before I could stop her.

'She's very natural. She looks more real than anyone else in this room,' he observed, his hazel eyes following her.

'I know,' I said, watching her talking to Sister. 'I'm just worried about what Sister Louise is telling her. I've been in trouble lately.'

'You were very good at Martin Place the other day. I recognised your speech.'

I looked at him and frowned. 'I didn't see you there.'

'I was with Ivy and some others talking to the Premier.'

I nodded, thinking how perfectly suited his family was to Poison Ivy's. I wished like crazy that he hadn't mentioned her name. How could I compete with someone whose father was one of Sydney's top heart surgeons and whose photo was in the *Australian* when she was elected school captain. I could picture her parents at dinner with his. They'd talk about politics, the arts and world affairs. Then I tried to picture them at dinner with Nonna and Mama. Not that I have ever been ashamed of them, by any means. But what would they talk about? The best way of making lasagna? Our families had nothing in common.

'That Cook High guy was pretty impressive. I mean he wouldn't make a great debater, but he was a surprise.'

'Jacob Coote,' I murmured as he grabbed some biscuits and we walked outside.

I tried to picture John Barton terrorising girls in alley ways or Jacob Coote being able to converse with the Premier. It made me so much more aware of the social and cultural differences around me.

We ended up sitting on cane chairs on the verandah looking up at the sky. It was a beautiful, balmy night.

'Heard about the regional dance?'

I didn't want to look at him because I would have

seemed too eager. To walk into the regional dance with John Barton would make me the envy of every snob at St Martha's.

'It's all we talk about. Can you imagine five different schools in one room? There's either going to be heaps of fights or the beginning of mixed relationships.'

'I'm just glad St Joan's isn't going to be there. We get stuck with them every time,' he complained. 'We detest them.'

'We detest St Francis' guys. We were invited to their formal in Year 10. They grouped together and sang "rah rah" songs all night. For their football team and cricket team and basketball team and God knows what else.'

'All those guys know how to do is play sport,' he said. 'The Marist Brothers are obsessed.'

'Slaughtered by them, right?'

'Embarrassing. The day after election day, actually. My father came to watch and said he was humiliated. The press were there of course. I pointed out that academically the St Francis guys were inept, but it still took me days to live it down.'

We sat alongside each other without speaking for a while. He's the type of person you can do that with. It wasn't an embarrassing silence, just a comfortable one. As if we both respected each other's private thoughts.

'So what are you going to do next year?' he asked, offering me his last biscuit.

'I want to be a barrister.'

'If you couldn't beat me back there with your clever conversation, you'll never make it,' he teased.

I hit him and shrugged.

'Your father would have been humiliated if you'd lost the argument tonight so I allowed you to win.'

He gave me a side-long look and we laughed.

'What about you?' I asked.

He looked at me in mock horror.

'Could you imagine me not going into law and then politics?'

'Yeah. I reckon you'd make a great teacher. I watched the little debaters come up to you. You're very patient with them.'

'My father would have a stroke.'

'You're a snob.'

He shook his head. 'No, I'm a realist. My father is a politician, my grandfather was a politician and my great grandfather was a backer of the first Liberal prime minister. My father believes that we have the breeding to one day give this country the best prime minister it has ever had. It was something his father told him and something his father's father told him. On my birthday, every year, he stands on a soap box.'

John stood on the chair and pulled his fringe back, imitating his father's receding hair-line.

'One of my sons,' he began in a droning voice, 'will one day lead this country back into the path of glory and I feel it can easily be John. Forget the incidents of the past. He did his stint at FBA and is now on the road to recovery.'

'FBA?'

'Fairy Bread Anonymous. My parents even went to the organisation that helped the family members of addicts.'

'You're crazy.'

'I've slightly exaggerated the case, but how can you escape his type of thinking and tradition?'

'Easy,' I shrugged. 'My great grandmother dressed the dead in Sicily, my grandmother worked on a farm in Queensland and my mother is a medical secretary in Leichhardt. I'm not going to follow their footsteps and

I know more than you about escaping tradition. You kind of just pave your own path.'

'It's different for you,' he sighed. 'You haven't got any pressures in life. I've always had to be the best because it's been expected of me. Do you think they voted me school captain because they wanted me? Get real. They knew I was going to be school captain when I was in Year 7 because every other Barton has been one. It's got nothing to do with popularity. The guys don't even know me.'

I was surprised at his bitterness and tried to cut the mood.

'I haven't got any pressures?' I asked, grabbing his sleeves dramatically. 'I could write a book about them.'

'You always seem so in control.'

'And you don't?'

He laughed, but somehow not humorously. There was a darkness in his eyes that had nothing to do with colour.

'I'll let you in on a secret. I'm not. Sometimes I think that this life is shit. I mean, don't you find it pathetic?'

I had never seen John like that before. I wondered if it was something new or if he hid those moods well. Whatever it was I found it a bit freaky. My friends and I always muck around that life is shit, but none of us actually believe it.

I looked at him for a moment, finding his copper cowlick irritating and wanting to hand him a comb.

'Only when my mother comes up with excuses on why I can't go out. Or when I feel that I'll be a nothing because socially I haven't got a foot in the door,' I answered as truthfully as I could.

'Well, as I'm allowed to go out whenever I want to and socially I have got a foot in the door, I can't really understand your problem.'

'So what's your problem, John?'

'I don't know what I want out of my life, but I know what I don't want. I don't want to make promises I can't keep. I don't want my children embarrassed every time I make the wrong decision and some journalist shits all over me in the paper. I don't want a lot of responsibility in life. Does that sound weak and unambitious? Well, that must mean that I am weak and unambitious. I don't want to climb to the top, Josephine. I'm comfortable enough where I'm standing. But when you have a father who is a minister in parliament, you are expected to have ambition. And when you can't work out your ambition, good old Dad does.'

'Then tell him what you told me.'

'Okay, I'll just go find him. I'll be back in a minute,' he said standing up.

I grabbed his arm and we both burst into laughter.

'It's obvious that you don't know my father, Josephine.'

I heard a noise behind me and winced when I saw Ivy approaching us.

'I've been looking all over for you,' she told John, smiling. I rarely see Poison Ivy smiling unless she's crawling to Sister.

'Just appreciating the presence of a beautiful, fascinating, exotic woman,' he said.

'Oh, really, where did she go?' she asked, giving me a sweet, insincere smile.

'So you've found me, you parasite. I bet it's for a lift home.'

'You bet right, and in the meantime think of Sarah Spencer's party. I'm not going alone.'

'I will not associate with pretentious people with nothing constructive to discuss except what kind of car they're getting for their eighteenth birthday,' he said, looking at her with a raised eyebrow.

'Come on, John. She's Doctor Spencer's daughter. He's my father's best friend. I have to go,' she begged.

He thought about it for a moment and then shrugged. 'I'll keep it in mind. Bribes over two dollars are tax deductible.'

'Thank you,' she said victoriously. 'I'll meet you outside in five minutes.'

We watched her walk away and then he turned and smiled at me.

'Are you going to go to that party?' I asked.

He gave me a mock horrified look. 'Dr Spencer is my father's biggest backer. Of course I'll go to that party. I'll even be charming to Sarah Spencer and try not to froth at the mouth when her father presents her with the keys to the Ferrari.'

'A Ferrari?' I asked, shocked. 'I'd kiss the dirtiest part of the ground just for a second-hand Mini.'

'On the North Shore, in our circle of friends, the fathers all try to outdo each other. Ever since we were young. If Ivy got a ten-speed bike for her tenth birthday, my father would get me a better one. We got to the stage that if I wanted something really badly I'd tell Ivy and she'd get her father to buy it for her and I was guaranteed to get it next birthday and vice versa.'

'I didn't realise you and Ivy were such close family friends.'

'We had no choice, but it's worked out well because we get on,' he said, sighing and standing up. He extended his hand and we made our way back into the building.

'What do you think of the English texts?' he asked.

'*Macbeth* is all right. They're going to be playing the Zeffirelli version at the cinema just for all the HSC students.'

'Would you like to go see it with me?'

I smiled up at him and nodded. 'I'd like that.'

People began to file out and I spotted my mother and Sister Louise looking at me and shaking their heads. Trouble as usual.

'That nun hates me.'

'Ivy reckons she's a living doll.'

'Yeah, a voodoo one,' I said. 'I'm going to grab my mother before Sister finds something else to complain about.'

'I'll leave you to it. It was great beating you tonight.'

'You won't be so lucky next time,' I called out after him.

I thought about his mood swing all weekend. It depressed me for a while because I was suddenly faced with a John that I really didn't know.

The first time I ever saw him was about two years ago during a debate. One of the girls in the debating team left to be an exchange student and I was asked to fill her place. We were both third speakers and the topic was so boring that I can't even remember it. But I do remember him looking over at me and mouthing the words 'I'm bored'.

From that minute on I begged to stay on the debating team and I haven't regretted a minute of it. Every time we debate at the same venue we race off alone afterwards and talk. It's kind of the highlight of my boring social life.

Another interesting thing that happened over the weekend was that I got a job at McDonald's. Anna and I had seen the advertisement in our local paper and decided to go for it.

McDonald's is not the most glamorous job to have, but living on five dollars pocket money a week is like something out of 'The Brady Bunch'. I didn't tell

Mama that because she'd have a complex.

We had a big fight after I told her about the job. She eventually backed down when I explained to her that Anna's father would let her have the car for the two nights a week we work.

Anna and I spoke on the phone for an hour about how disgusting the McDonald's uniform was, about all the guys from St Anthony's who go to that particular outlet, and especially what we'd be doing with the money.

Sportsgirl, Country Road and Esprit, here we come.

5

I looked at myself in the mirror for the billionth time and teased my fringe for the zillionth wishing that my neckline wasn't so high.

My grandmother had volunteered to make my dress. Short, black and velvet with a nice neckline, I had told her. Instead it was emerald green, (because only people in mourning wear black, she informed me), it came to my knees, and the neckline was almost choking me.

'Josephine, why do you have to wear those low medical shoes?' Mama asked from the door.

'Maaa, they're Doc Martens,' I informed her.

'Well, pardon my ignorance.'

'It's the fashion.'

'You would look much lovelier if you wore your flat black shoes. It's not that important to look like everyone else.'

I looked over to her with little patience. 'I feel like the Virgin Mary with this neckline.'

'I don't think the Virgin Mary ever wore a velvet dress to her knees. Now do something to please me and change the shoes.'

'Just say nobody asks me to dance,' I asked, getting flustered.

'Because you're not wearing those doctor shoes?'

'No,' I said. 'Because they might find me unattractive.

Just say the music starts and every girl is dancing with a boy, except me.'

'For the one-hundredth time, Josie, you look beautiful. You should wear your hair out more often. I can't believe that you were lucky enough to have beautiful curly hair and you don't appreciate it.'

'You're just saying that because you're my mother.'

The doorbell rang and she pulled me away from the mirror. 'Go get your shoes and I'll let the girls in.'

I hugged her hard and laughed.

'Thanks for letting me go tonight, Mama. I'll never ask for anything again.'

'I want you home at twelve on the dot,' she ordered.

'Cross my heart and hope to die.'

'And don't let me hear any stories and don't be influenced by that silly Sera.'

'Okay, okay.'

■

It was the first school regional dance in order to bring the school community together. Apart from St Martha's and St Anthony's, Cook High was included and a Presbyterian co-ed private school.

'It's beautiful,' Anna kept on saying, referring to my dress. She was wearing a white smock and blue-spotted pants and her long hair was up in a high ponytail.

'The neckline looks like it's choking her,' Sera said as I climbed into her father's car.

I grabbed the compact mirror from her and fixed up my hair.

'I thought you were wearing your Docs,' Lee said, looking at my shoes.

'My mother's introducing me to individuality,' I said, fixing up her ear-ring.

Lee has always had this sixties fetish. She wore opaque

tights and a short orange dress and shoes which would have to have belonged to her mother who was a model in the sixties.

Sera wore a tight black lycra dress and enough make-up to supply a complete cast on a soap opera. She never wears anything that's not short and tight except for her school uniform. She has two wardrobes. The one in her cupboard and the one under her bed. The latter is the one she changes into when she's out of her parent's sight.

The town hall was lit up and decorated and the crowd was cosmopolitan. Some classical, others mod. Some trendy, others casual.

I looked around for John Barton, making every deal with God so he would ask me for the first dance. Yet when I saw him standing with Poison Ivy, I wanted to tear my hair out with rage, except I'd spent so long fixing it up. It seemed as if it had been all for nothing.

'Who is this sexy woman?'

I looked up at my cousin Robert, who goes to St Anthony's, and he feigned shock.

'Oh my God, it's Josie.'

'Thanks a lot, Robert.'

He kissed my cheek loudly. 'You look gorgeous, woman, and don't let anyone tell you otherwise.'

'You reckon.'

He leaned forward and smiled.

'He couldn't get out of it,' he whispered. 'She lives in the same street.'

I knew he was talking about John Barton and I hugged him.

The music started soon after.

'If we don't get asked to dance, pretend that we're talking about something interesting,' Anna whispered to me as soon as Lee and Sera were asked.

53

I nodded and then she nudged me hard in the ribs. Both Jacob Coote and a tall, well-built boy stood in front of us.

'Would you like to dance?' the tall guy asked Anna. She nodded shyly and grinned at me.

'Take off your glasses,' she hissed.

Jacob Coote was smiling with his usual closed-mouth twitch.

'My friend is besotted by your friend.'

'He's got good taste.'

'So how about dancing with me, Miss Vice Captain of St Martyr's?'

'It's St Martha's, Mr Captain of Crook High.'

So we danced to 'Crocodile Rock' while I looked at everyone but him and when the disc jockey played a slow Elvis song, we fumbled around a bit before we were in the waltz position.

'Funny song to be following a fast one.'

'The disc jockey is the Presbyterian minister. A bit of a romantic perhaps,' I tried to joke.

He nodded and drew me closer.

We didn't talk for the rest of the song. Nor through the third or fourth.

I wondered why he had danced with me when there were girls more suited to him in the room. I wondered if it was a dare or something equally hideous. Because boys like Jacob Coote, who would easily be the most popular guy in his school, didn't ask girls like me to dance.

But we danced to the point of exhaustion and it gave me the opportunity to look at him properly for the first time. His eyes weren't a bluey green or hazelly green or of a mixed colour. They were just green.

He didn't look trendy or casual. He just looked like himself. All things aside, my mother would probably love this guy. He was the epitome of individuality. I wondered what he was doing at this dance. Jacob Coote and company weren't the regional dance type, and when he caught my curious look he smiled knowingly.

'I was ordered to come tonight. Setting a good example you know. I was promised that if I went tonight I'd never have to go again.'

'And what Jacob Coote does, everyone does at Crook High,' I mocked.

'I have that effect on people.'

'I still find it hard to believe that you'd turn up to one of these things. It's not you.'

'You don't know what "me" is all about.'

I excused myself after the next dance and went to the ladies room.

'The one dancing with Coote,' I heard one girl say.

So they stared and rolled their eyes and I tried to ignore them all.

'Seven dances, Jose. Marriage next, eh?' Sera said, spraying her hair as well as the faces of people around her.

Anna grabbed my arm, shaking it hysterically. 'I'm in love,' she said through her teeth.

'Did you all follow me into the ladies?'

'He is the man of my dreams. I want to marry him.'

'You dance with him once and you decide that he will be the person to spend the rest of your life with?'

'I know it in my heart.'

'Try dancing with a few other guys and then tell me how you feel at the end of the night.'

Poison Ivy walked in and stood at the mirror next to me fixing her hair. God knows why a person with a straight, shoulder-length, flawless bob would need to fix her hair, but that's vanity for you.

'Are you and John Barton an item?' Felicity Singer

asked her. 'I saw you guys pulling up in his car.'

'His father's car,' she said. 'How many seventeen-year-olds do you know with a BMW, Felicity?'

'He's a great catch, Ivy. Think about it, captain of St John's with captain of St Martha's,' Felicity went on.

'We're just friends,' she said in an almost patronising, smug tone, looking at me and then back to the mirror. 'We're in the same circle of friends.'

We went back into the hall after that and danced some more and surprisingly enough I wasn't left without a partner all night.

I saw Jacob Coote a few times, but he only stood around talking. I couldn't bear looking over at John Barton in case Poison Ivy caught me, so I always kept to the other side of the hall. I even danced with Anton Valavic, Anna's future husband, and almost fell in love with him myself.

But when the dance ended at eleven-thirty and everyone decided to go for pizza and coffee, I felt disappointment settle in.

My mother's twelve o'clock time limit meant not a second after and I didn't want to push it this time.

'Robert, I have to be home by twelve,' I told him as a large group gathered around outside.

'I'll take a taxi with you, Jose,' Lee volunteered half-heartedly.

'Lee, I'll really be miserable if you have to miss out too.'

'Well, what is she going to do?' Sera asked. I knew she was hoping that nobody would volunteer her because she had a car. 'Her mother will go crazy if she's not home by twelve, although I can understand why. She's a bit paranoid about what people say.'

'Shut up, Sera,' Lee snapped.

'I'll take her.'

Jacob Coote seemed to be looming behind us and I could see Sera gasping and palpitating at the gossip that would be created.

So out of spite, I found myself trailing after Jacob Coote, wishing I was with the rest.

When we reached the road, I spotted John Barton and Poison Ivy and cringed inwardly, wondering what I was going to say.

'Good dance, wasn't it?'

I nodded, knowing that both boys were sizing each other up.

I didn't want John thinking that I had been picked up at the dance by just anyone and I could almost hear his mind ticking.

'This is Jacob Coote. Remember, you saw him at Martin Place,' I swallowed. 'Jacob, this is John Barton and Ivy Lloyd.'

'Yeah, I've seen you around,' Jacob Coote said looking out on to the road. We were standing on George Street, the main road in the city. It was packed with people streaming out of the Hoyts and Village cinema centres which were situated down the road. Most of them were heading for Town Hall station which was beneath us.

'Are you from St Anthony's as well?' Ivy asked politely.

'Nope. I'm a Cook man.'

Ivy, John and I looked at each other nodding in silence, as if we had plenty to say. Jacob Coote seemed to be preoccupied elsewhere.

'I'll drive,' Ivy said, taking John's keys and waving goodbye to us.

John and I continued looking at each other and turning his back to Jacob Coote, he took my hand.

'Wished we would have danced tonight,' he said quietly. 'I meant to ask, but I could never get away and before I knew it, the night was over.'

I looked at his face which, although not as attractive as Jacob Coote's, was so earnest and honest.

His copper hair was slicked back with gel, making his cow-lick obscure. He was beautifully dressed in baggy beige pants and a paisley shirt. Compared to Jacob Coote's black jeans, white shirt and what looked like his school tie, he looked like a million dollars.

'Maybe next time,' I said.

He nodded and looked back to where Ivy was walking towards the car.

'You want a lift? I could drop Ivy off first and we could go for a coffee.'

I looked at Jacob Coote's back wishing John had come along sooner.

I shook my head and shrugged apologetically.

'I've already got a lift.'

He leaned over and kissed me on the cheek softly and let go of my hand, walking away. I stood looking at him for a while before I noticed that Jacob Coote had walked away as well.

'Hold on,' I yelled, trying to catch up.

'You like him or something?'

'He's a very nice boy.'

'Ah, come on. He's the type of guy who goes to uni and decides to be gay because it's trendy.'

'That's not true,' I snapped back. 'John Barton is very intelligent and he's going to do law at university with me. He's Robert Barton's son actually.'

'Whoever *he* is when he's at home,' he snapped sarcastically.

'Can you stop being so rude? Didn't your mother teach you any manners?'

'For your information, my mother is dead.'

I stopped, in embarrassment and shame, not knowing

what to say. 'I'm sorry. I shouldn't have said that.'

He waved away the apology and allowed me to catch up and we crossed George Street without using the traffic lights. Cars zoomed by us, beeping their horns. A car-load of hoods screamed obscenities out the window and Jacob Coote waved at them.

'My friends,' he explained.

'Charming.'

'What's your name by the way? I know it's long and complicated.'

I couldn't believe it. He had thrown eggs at me, sat next to me at Martin Place and danced with me for seven songs and hadn't even asked anyone my name.

'Josephine Alibrandi.'

'I'm Jacob Coote.'

'Oh, is that who you are,' I said, feigning vagueness. 'Which one is your car?'

'Which one do you think is my car?'

I folded my arms, trying to keep warm. Although the days were mostly still warm, the nights were cool and my dress had short sleeves.

I surveyed the ten or so cars in front of us and then looked at him.

'It's the panel van, isn't it,' I groaned. 'Oh God, I knew you'd be the type to have one of those. My reputation is ruined.'

'Wrong guess,' he said, stopping beside a motor bike and leaning on it.

I shook my head while he slowly nodded.

'Want to take a taxi? I'll pay,' I volunteered, swallowing hard.

He unlocked the case at the back and pulled out two helmets.

'I am wearing a good velvet dress, thank you very much. It's the best thing I own so it'll probably be a family heirloom one day. How could you suggest I sit on that bike with my family heirloom on?'

'Velvet and bikes? You might start a trend.'

'My mother will murder me.'

'Your mother need never know. I'll drop you off around the corner.'

'She'll find out all right. Who do you think will identify me at the morgue?'

'Get on the bike,' he said pushing the helmet down on my head.

'Turn around while I get on. It's bad enough that the whole of George Street is going to get a glimpse of my undies.'

'You're denying me that honour?' he asked, wounded as he turned around.

I pulled up my dress and climbed on to the bike, self-consciously.

'Ready?'

'Let me check my bag for ID. I don't want to be named something as plain as Jane Doe in the hospital.'

'You are one morbid chick,' he groaned, stepping on the bike to start it.

I screamed. A long piercing scream in his ear from George Street to Broadway. Give or take about five traffic lights, that's five minutes of screaming.

As we sat at the lights on Broadway, waiting to turn into Glebe Point Road, I felt strange being so exposed. I mean we were unprotected from all those weird people who walk around after midnight. Anyone could have just come up to us and knocked us out. I noticed the middle-aged couple in the car next to us staring. I tried to stretch my dress to my knees but was unsuccessful. Maybe they were saying things like 'Thank God that's not our daughter sitting on that bike'.

A car-load of guys pulled up behind us and honked their horns. I think I heard one call out 'Show us your legs' amongst other things. My face burnt with embarrassment. I just felt as if the whole world was watching me and I couldn't hide behind a car window. I just knew in my heart that someone in a car around me knew my grandmother and this would get back to her via the Italian phone system.

On St John's Road I came face to face with the gravel on the road as we took a tight corner, and it was only thirty seconds away from my street that I began to enjoy it. I tapped his shoulder and yelled for him to stop, trying to grab my glasses from around my mouth. My eyes smarted from the wind and my skin felt tight, not to mention my throat hurting from all the screaming.

'It's this street,' I croaked.

'I'm sorry, I'm deaf. I can hardly hear you. A hysterical girl screamed in my ear and busted my ear-drum,' he said, slowing down and touching his ears.

I pulled up my dress again quickly, trying to get off before he turned around, but when I stood up after adjusting it around my knees, I knew he had seen every movement.

'I'll walk you.'

I shrugged and handed him the helmet.

He was quiet as we walked down the street. Almost in his own world, and I wondered what boys like Jacob Coote thought about.

'How did your mother die?' I asked him quietly.

'Cancer, about five years ago,' he said.

'I'd die if my mother died.'

He shook his head and looked at me almost gently.

'You don't die. You just . . . get really angry and then after you're angry you hurt a lot and then the best thing is that one day you remember something she said or did and you laugh instead of crying.' He smiled at the thought.

I shook my head. 'I'd run you know. It's like when you're really busy doing something and you don't have time to think about things. Well, I'd run and run and run so I couldn't think.'

'And when you'd finished running you'd be thousands of miles away from people who love you and your problem would still be there except you'd have nobody to help you,' he said with a shrug.

I tried not to think about my mother dying.

'I'm really sorry, you know. For mentioning your mother the way I did,' I said as humbly as I could.

'No big deal.'

I stopped in front of the terrace and he looked at it shaking his head.

'We're the same, you know. You're middle-class and I'm middle-class, except you're a middle-class snob who goes to an upper-class school.'

'I am not a snob. My mother is a single parent and we don't have a lot of money, but I'm on a scholarship with the school.'

'So if it weren't for the scholarship, you'd be at Cook High,' he shrugged. 'Like me.'

'I would be at a Catholic school still, thank you very much.'

'Yeah, a middle-class Catholic school equivalent to Cook High.'

'Well, yes I would and I wouldn't be ashamed of it either.'

He looked at me and leaned forward and I knew his intentions so I leaned back. But just looking at him made me want to lean forward.

'Forget it,' he muttered, turning away. 'Listen, you're not my type, you know.'

'I know.'

'Not as an insult or anything.'

'No, of course not.'

We looked at each other uncomfortably for a few more seconds before he gave a final shrug.

'Got to go.'

'Are you going to meet the others wherever they were going?' I asked curiously.

He shrugged. 'Naw. That red cordial they served tonight really did me in. It was too strong. Don't want to be drinking and driving too much.'

I smiled and nodded. 'Where do you live?'

'Redfern.'

'Redfern? Do you know that I've been in this country all my life and I've never spoken to an Aboriginal person.'

He shrugged. 'Come to Redfern. I'll introduce you to a few. I don't know much about Italians either.'

'There's not much to know except that they're the best cooks, best lovers and a highly intelligent race,' I said seriously.

He laughed and shook his head and with a wave he turned to walk back to his motor cycle.

6

My second encounter with Michael Andretti happened today at my grandmother's house. She had a family barbecue and because it was hot we were able to go swimming in the pool.

I spent the whole morning looking at him. He looked at Mama. Mama looked at me. Then he would look at me. I would look at Mama. She would look at him.

In different circumstances, I'd be amused.

I was in the water at one stage when Robert came from behind and shook my shoulders, pushing me down under the water. We struggled for a while until my grandmother told us to behave.

While we were splashing water into each other's faces I saw Mama go inside and two minutes later Michael Andretti followed. I pushed Robert down and managed to crawl out.

'Jozzie, grow up,' Nonna Katia instructed.

'Oh, great. He tries to drown me and I have to grow up,' I said trying to wrestle the towel from her as she tried to dry me. Robert followed me out of the water and gave Nonna Katia a smacking kiss before running away. I watched her beam after him.

'Don't tell me. He's a good boy,' I said, walking away.

They were in the kitchen. I stood outside the door

with the towel and sat on the step. I felt guilty listening to the conversation, but personally I don't know anyone who'd walk away if someone was discussing them.

'What do you think I'll do, Christina?' I heard him ask. 'Fly into a rage and demand to see her? Do you think everyone wants a son or daughter? Do you think I'll pretend that I wanted her from the beginning?'

'I'll think and pretend no such thing,' I heard her say frankly, before she turned on the tap.

'I don't want her,' he said flatly.

I cringed and wanted to walk away then, but couldn't.

'I do not want to see her. I do not want to love her. I do not want a complication in my life, Christina. I've worked for fifteen years to get where I am and now I don't want this in my life,' he stated in a clear no-nonsense tone.

'Don't you dare call my daughter a complication,' she said coldly. 'Because we have nothing to do with you, Michael. It's *us* who don't want *you* complicating our lives, so stop implying that we're out to ruin everything for you. Get married, Michael. Forget Josie and have other kids. Ten of them if that will make you happy. Forget everything that happened eighteen years ago, but the fact that it was your choice.'

I could hear the tremble in her voice. Not that it was so noticeable, but I know Mama's normal voice so well that any change is noticeable. I stood up and looked in to see her holding a shaking hand to her head. He was rubbing his face as if to wipe away the problem. Somehow I knew I was the problem.

'Just don't come back here one day wanting to get to know your daughter, because you won't be allowed,' she added quietly, as I sat back outside.

'What does your mother know about this?' he said.

I figured out that I was supposed to be the 'this'. I

had been called worse in my life so I tried not to let it offend me.

'She doesn't know who Josie's father is. Maybe I should tell her who you are, Michael. Then you'd really have something to be paranoid about.'

I heard him sigh, and somehow I felt sorry for him.

'What do you want from me, Christina?' he asked in a tired voice.

'Nothing. All I can say is I'm glad that your family moved away, Michael. I'm glad you left me high and dry. I'm glad you were a coward, because if you hadn't run I wouldn't have a daughter today.'

'So I'm a monster now?'

'You're the father of the person who is my life. You can't possibly be a monster. I just pity you because you haven't been able to share that.'

'Do me a favour, Christina,' he said. 'Don't pity me. My life lacks nothing.'

'Then go, Michael. Forget you ever spoke to me. Forget you ever saw her. You did it once. I'm sure you can do it again.'

There was silence and then a sigh. I don't know whose.

'Do you need money?'

'I beg your pardon?'

'I can set up a fund for her.'

'I needed money eighteen years ago, Michael. Today I need nothing but peace of mind,' I heard her say in an angry tone.

'It's too late. Seventeen-year-olds don't need fathers.'

'Oh God, Michael. I'm thirty-four years old and I need a father. I can't even begin to think of what my daughter needs.'

I didn't want to listen any more. I walked back to the pool and sat on the side with my young cousin.

Mama came out a few minutes later carrying a tray

of coffee. He followed a few minutes later. That's when I discovered the fourth member of our staring act.

Nonna.

I saw her look from Michael Andretti to Mama. Then she looked over at me. Her mouth was open in surprise and her eyes had narrowed, and at that moment I knew that she knew.

Later, he went back inside.

I don't know what possessed me to walk in after him. I wasn't sure what I was going to say to him either. He had poured himself a glass of water and was walking around the lounge room, where he touched the photo frames perched on the cabinet.

Nonna's lounge room cabinet is cluttered with photos of the family, including ancient ones from Sicily. I can hardly remember posing for the half a million she has of me.

He looked up at the tapestry on the wall and then over to the other side of the room where there was another cabinet of ornaments. He touched everything he passed, almost like one of those people who test for dust. He sat down on one of the black leather chairs and closed his eyes.

His hair was cut extremely short and around the ears. I suspected that if I took after him in the hair department he would have to keep it that confined. My type of hair on a man would look chaotic, especially on a barrister. He had dimples, which really pisses me off because my mother has high cheek bones and I've inherited neither. But he wasn't smiling, the dimples were part of a grimace.

It was his build that impressed me most. Because he was stocky. Not round or anything. Just very sturdy and no taller than five foot ten. But he looked so strong and I actually pictured him picking me up as a child and that really got on my nerves, because I didn't want to picture him in such an affectionate way.

'My grandmother doesn't like people in the living room when she's having a barbecue outside.'

He looked around in surprise and then nodded, standing up and moving towards the door. Intending to walk past me without a word.

'Oh, get real,' I said scornfully.

'I beg your pardon?'

'Say something to me.'

He stopped and gave me that tilted head look again.

'What would you like me to say to you, Josie?'

'I don't know,' I said confused. 'Just something. But I don't expect you to walk past me as if I don't exist.'

'I've spoken to your mother about this situation . . .'

'Stop being polite. You're making me puke. Be angry or be rude to me, but don't be polite,' I said angrily.

'Okay then, what do you want from me?' he asked, adopting my attitude of confusion.

I shook my head and we both looked ridiculously confused.

'I never thought meeting you would be this boring. I thought we'd put our Italian emotion into gear and scream the place down. I never expected indifference.'

'I hate to tell you, Josie, but I wasn't aware of your existence until very recently so I haven't had time to think about this.'

'Firstly, my name is Josephine. Only people close to me call me Josie, and secondly, I've known about you for a lifetime, so I have had plenty of time to think about this.'

'And what do you think about it, Josephine?'

'I think you got off too easy. Nobody gets to yell at you and call you names or kick you out of the house. My grandmother thinks you're the second coming of

Christ. But if Robert or my uncle knew about you, they'd smash your head in for what you did to my mother. Maybe I should tell them all who you really are so you won't be Mr Wonderful any more.'

'And you? Are you going to smash my head in?'

'Don't you mock me. Don't you dare make fun of the way I feel about my mother.'

'I have no intention of making fun of the way you feel, Josephine. But what happened between your mother and I was a very sad situation eighteen years ago and I think considering the circumstances things turned out pretty well.'

'You should be a politician. They're all full of crap too.'

'I think we should both go outside before we say something we regret.'

'You're a liar,' I whispered angrily. 'You said you haven't a thing to say, but I reckon you've planned out everything you've said so far. You're full of bullshit clichés.'

'And I think you're going too far.'

'Who cares?' I shrugged. 'I can go as far as I like with you and there is nothing you can do. I mean, are you going to act all fatherly and discipline me?'

He was angry now. I could see it in his eyes and the way his mouth tightened.

'Listen, I have the right to think this out clearly before I let you into my life.'

'How dare you think that I want to be in your life! I don't want you anywhere near us, especially my mother. If she cries in the next couple of weeks and I find out it's because you've hurt her you're in big trouble.'

'Okay,' he snapped back. 'A promise. You keep out of my life, I keep out of yours.'

'Let's shake on it.'

He had a hard handshake, yet very shaky and I could see that he was upset and again I felt sorry for him. At that moment we were both unrealistic, because I honestly wanted to see him again. But then again I didn't.

'Have a good life, Mr Andretti,' I said to him.

He nodded and we tried avoiding each other's eyes for a while, before he walked out.

∎

Mama asked me about him that night.

We were sitting in front of the television pretending to watch the news. We were still in the same clothes from the barbecue and I noticed that her nose was sunburnt.

I ignored her when she first asked me about him.

'Come here,' she said, patting the carpet between her outspread legs.

I sat between them and she wrapped her arms around me. We seemed all brown legs and brown arms.

'If you want to know what I think of Michael Andretti, I think he's a lovely man. Very talented by the looks of things and he should go far,' I said, stiffly.

'Oh, really?'

'You don't believe me?'

'You spoke to him today, didn't you?'

'You did too, didn't you?'

'I asked first.'

I shrugged. 'We made our positions clear.'

'Knowing Michael's tact, he told you he was glad you weren't in his life.'

'I told him the same.'

'Are you upset?'

'Don't be silly, Mama. I just hope he doesn't go around upsetting you.'

I pretended to be interested in the scene on television.

She pulled me back and held her cheek against mine.

'You're not so tough, Alibrandi. I can see through you.'

'I can see through you too, Alibrandi. I'm thinking the shithead is probably going to want kids now and why not then and you're thinking he will marry someone else one day and why didn't he come back to marry you?' I said. 'All I can come up with is that women keep their brains in their heads and men keep theirs in their pants.'

She laughed and hugged me closer. 'It's his loss, kiddo.'

I turned around to try and look at her.

'It was so weird, Mama. I had it planned out so differently in my mind. I think it was too neat and tidy.'

'Things don't turn out the way you expect them to.'

I took her hand which was around my chest and played with the ringless fingers. 'Can you answer something for me. The truth. By eliminating me out of the picture you won't hurt me, okay? I just want you to tell me how you wanted your life to turn out when you were seventeen.'

'Josie, I like my life . . .'

'Mama,' I sighed, closing my eyes. 'I'm not saying that you don't. I just want to know what you dreamt of when you were seventeen. I dream of being successful and of falling in love with someone with money. Of someone loving me. Of having two children. One boy and one girl. What did you dream of?'

She smiled and sat back. She kind of reminded me of Anna. Such pensive, peaceful people. How Mama could have come from Nonna Katia and Nonno Francesco and borne a child with my personality confuses me.

'I dreamt of marrying a man who didn't necessarily have to have money, but who would take care of me. We'd talk a lot. Talk so much. We'd have four children. I wanted lots of girls. I love little girls.' She smiled. 'The most important thing was that he would like me and my children would like me. That's what I dreamt of, Josie.'

'Was the man Michael Andretti?'

She nodded.

'What a simple dream.'

'Simple dreams are the hardest to come true.'

I shrugged and she entwined her fingers in mine.

'How about pizza?'

'Pan-fried,' I insisted.

'Supreme with pineapple.'

'Mama, we're Italians. Italians don't have pineapple on their pizza,' I said in disgust.

She laughed and reached across for the phone while we continued arguing about the pizza.

7

We never did go away at Easter. We did the same old thing that we do every year and spent the day with my grandmother's family at Robert's place. I didn't even get any Easter eggs. Just stuff for my glory box. It's so exciting receiving table-cloths and crocheted doilies while everyone else is eating chocolate bunnies.

I thought about the glory box while I was sitting on the verandah on Wednesday night. The way my mother's relatives had looked at me pointedly when they told her how grown-up I was now.

If life was a silent movie I'd be able to see the captions under their faces. 'A boyfriend next,' Cousin Maria's pointed look would say. 'Yes, then a three-year court-ship,' Cousin Camela would indicate by nodding her head. 'On her twenty-first she could have her engage-ment party as well,' Zia Patrizia would display with a proud smile. Mama and I would be the heroines who gasp in dismay.

Sitting outside with the sun going down, amongst the changing colours of autumn leaves and feeling the breeze on my face, made it all seem so frivolous and unthreatening. It was easy to slip away from the problems in my mind. Until my mother came out to tell me that she had to keep her Cousin Camela company overnight while her husband was in hospital. I was going to Nonna's.

Penance to me isn't saying a few Hail Marys and Our Fathers. It's sleeping at my grandmother's house.

'I'm seventeen, Mama. I can look after myself,' I argued as I followed her into the house.

'Iron your school shirt before you go, so you won't have to iron it in the morning,' was her answer. 'And pack your jumper.'

'Oh God, Ma, I have to sleep in the same bed as her. She doesn't shave her legs.'

'I'm leaving in five minutes. Be ready.'

'She's old.'

'You cannot catch old age by sleeping with your grandmother, Josie.'

Somehow, lying beside Nonna that night made me wonder if that was true. The curlers she vainly insisted on putting in her hair made a rattling noise every time she moved. Her vanity really got on my nerves. I mean, why would a woman in her sixties want to look good and who cares?

She asked me one hundred times if I wanted to see some old photos.

'No, I'm tired,' I explained to her.

'You look just like I did, Jozzie. Just like Christina as well.'

'Really?' I said looking at her. I must admit she has beautiful olive skin like Mama. Every day, because of the curlers, her hair looks as if it's been done at a hairdresser's. She doesn't wear make-up because she's natural-looking like Mama, but I have caught her on odd occasions bleaching her upper lip. One of the curses of being European is facial hair.

'Oh, Jozzie, Jozzie, when I was your age I ran around my *paese* like a gypsy. A gypsy, Jozzie. People would say, look at that *zingara*, Katia Torello.'

I sighed, knowing that unless I gave her my full attention she wouldn't stop.

'Mama and Papa, they used to tear out their hair. "What are we going to do wit you?" they would say to me. Oh, Jozzie, tings these days are so bad because you can get away with anyting. But tings those days were so bad because you got away wit nuting. Nuting.'

'What did you do that was so bad?'

'I wanted to talk to the boys.'

I laughed and she joined in.

'My cousin Adrianna and I, we used to talk all the time while we washed our clothes. By hand, Jozzie. The old women would yell at us to be quiet and we'd laugh at them. Stupid old people, we would say. But look at me now,' she said with that famous cry in her voice. 'I'm a stupid old woman.'

'You aren't old, Nonna,' I said rolling my eyes at her vanity.

'Anyway, my Zio Alfredo, who was my father's oldest brother, decided that I should marry. He found a husband for Adrianna first and then me.

'Francesco Alibrandi was fifteen years older than me, but he was established and promised to treat me well. So my parents agreed. It would be good for me, they said, to marry an older man. I remember walking down the road in my town on my wedding day. People came out and followed me in a procession. I was very happy.

'Another girl, Teresa Morelli, had been engaged to a boy, but her father found out that he had been with another woman. So they finished it with him and she became engaged to someone else. But on the day before her wedding she was walking down to wash her clothes and the first boy took her. Eloped, Jozzie.'

'Did she want to elope?'

'Oh, no, no. Not Teresa, poor girl. But he took her

away for a night and that was it, Jozzie.'

Nonna Katia wiped her hands clean in the air.

'He did not want her any more and returned her to her family and she never married again. No man would have her.'

'But that's not fair. She didn't want to go,' I said, indignantly. 'That makes me so furious.'

'So many times that happened, Jozzie, so many times. Anyway my cousin Adrianna was going to America with her husband. America, Jozzie. Back then it was like going to heaven. You were going to be rich if you went to America. We were going some place too. All the time I would hear Francesco talk to his friends. Never to me. I thought we were going to America too. I was sad to leave my family, but happy because Adrianna would be there.

'But when he told me that we were going to Australia, oh my God, I didn't know what to do. Who knew back then, Jozzie? Who knew where this Australia was? Under Africa people would say.'

'Africa?'

'*Madonna mia*,' she said fanning herself.

I almost laughed at her theatrics.

'I cried and cried. I begged him. "Please, Francesco, please." My mother even begged him not to take me away, but my father shook his head and shrugged. "What can I do?" he said. "She is his wife. She goes where he goes." So I will always remember that day in Messina waving to my mother. She fainted, Jozzie, because it is not like these days where you wave to your mother and know that you will take a Qantas flight the next year to see her. You sometimes never see these people again. These people who are your family. Yet we all did because it was our husbands' will.'

Such self-sacrifice is very hard for me to understand.

'For half the journey I cried. I stayed in my cabin and cried. I was sick. All I could think of was my mama fainting in Messina. Then one day I heard the music. The Tarantella. Oh, Jozzie, I loved to dance. I remember going up on that deck and dancing. People clapped as I danced. I took off my shoes and my hair was down. Like yours, Jozzie, when it is out. Long and wavy. I saw the way the men would look at me, Jozzie. Pooh, I was better looking than any of their wives.'

'And modest, of course.'

As beautiful as the photos are of her, I doubt they do her justice. I looked at her sitting there, excitement in her eyes, large and dark, as she told her stories. All I could think of was that she must have been the most beautiful woman around. It's funny that everything has aged. Her face, her hair, and her hands. But her eyes haven't. Her eyes that night were identical and as youthful as her eyes in the photos.

'But when Francesco saw me out there he was red in the face,' she continued. 'He grabbed my arm and pulled me down to the cabin and I was never allowed up there again.

'When we arrived in Sydney, I saw the Sydney Harbour Bridge and they let us get off and walk across it. Sydney, of course, wasn't anyting like it is today. There was no Opera House or skyscrapers, no beautiful boats in the harbour and no beautiful houses and worse still, Jozzie, nobody spoke Italian.

'In my whole life I had never been out of Sicily so I had never heard a language apart from Sicilian. The people, they dressed different to us. A lot of us were from small villages in Sicily and there we were in a city where the women were painted up wit red lipstick. Your nonno went to a pub, Jozzie, and there was a woman working in there. A woman, Jozzie. The Australian men

77

would call out to us and whistle. In Sicily men did not call out and whistle to a woman that belonged to somebody else. Oh, no,' she said, shaking her head and finger, 'I tell you, Jozzie, it was like going to another world.

'We boarded the boat again and finished in Brisbane and from there we took a train to Ingham. Ingham was even worse, Jozzie. It was bare. Where we lived out in the bush there was nuting but us and the snakes. I did not see anyone but your nonno for six months. It was so hot, Jozzie, that I would wash myself and two minutes later I would need to wash again, but I couldn't because we could not waste water. There was no air-conditioning then. No tiles on the floor to keep the house cool. No room I could go to, to cool down. The house was a shack. One room and a dirt floor.'

I looked around at the room we were in and it amazed me how far they had come from being penniless immigrants from Sicily.

Over forty years ago she had a one-room shack and today she was living in a double-storey house with Italian furniture, carpet, air-conditioning, a swimming-pool and many other luxuries. Nonna's house is tasteful and I somehow had the feeling that her one-room shack would have been as tasteful as she could make it.

'The Australians knew nuting about us. We were ignorant. They were ignorant. Jozzie, you wonder why some people my age cannot speak English well. It is because nobody would talk to them and worse still they did not want to talk to anyone.

'We lived in our own little world and as more relatives and friends from the same town came out to Australia, the bigger our Italian community became, to the point where we didn't need to make friends with the Australians.'

She went on, telling me more, and as I lay back I thought it was ironic that the same ignorance that was around back then is still here now. An ignorance that will live in this country for many years to come, I think.

When I hear Nonna Katia tell me about how life was forty-odd years ago, I find it hard to believe that she was just seventeen, my age now, when she was married and taken halfway across the world. But then again, Mama was just seventeen when she gave birth to me so it makes me realise how young we youth of today really are.

Maybe we know more or think we know more, or do a lot more, but we haven't been through as much. We'd never be able to cope with the pressures our mothers and grandmothers went through.

But I wonder about that seventeen-year-old girl back then. I wonder what really happened to her. I wonder what she used to dream about if she ever did dream and how she turned out to be a person I really don't like. And worst of all I wonder if I'll turn out to be just like her when I turn sixty-five.

I wanted to ask her more, but I didn't want to give her that satisfaction. So I decided to leave it for another day. Another day when I would see the photos and look for that young seventeen-year-old, boy-crazy gypsy named Katia Torello.

8

The time before class starts in the morning is the most exciting. Because we haven't seen each other for *sixteen* hours, it's gossip galore.

What happened on TV. What happened at work if one worked. What happened on the way from or to school. What good-looking guy spoke to you. What ideas you came up with during the night. What kind of nagging your parents did. What magazine you bought on the way from or to school. Who was the best-looking guy in the magazine. Why he was the best-looking guy in the magazine.

The list goes on. By the end of the day we've heard it all. We're sick of each other and look forward to getting away. But those first ten minutes are the very reason you come to school. Miss out on them and you are behind with the times.

This morning, amidst all this excitement, I was unpacking my satchel and listening to the gossip.

Standing in front of me, flicking untied masses of hair all over my desk, was Carly Bishop. Carly Bishop belongs to the 'beautiful people' previously mentioned. The 'beautiful people' are the ones who have the most modern hairstyles. If long hair is in, they've got it. If one gets her hair cropped, so do the others. If one comes to school and announces she'll be growing her hair, so do the rest of them.

The 'beautiful people' aren't dumb. Their marks are usually average. They do just about what they need to. They don't complain about their marks or stress. The 'beautiful people' don't need to.

Carly is a part-time model. She was in *Hot Pants* once. We have a few models in the school. The others, though, are not vain, nor are they coy about it. To them it's a job. A better one than most of us have, but just a job that one never boasts about.

Except Carly.

Carly is the type of person who is constantly in the Sunday society pages of the paper. She's the one with her mouth open, always laughing in a fake way, surrounded by great-looking people who could have different colour hair, eyes and skin, but look exactly like her.

She sits in front of me in our home room as well as in English.

Only a few people can stand Carly and her group. They're the most pretentious try-hards in the world, but they seem to survive somehow. No matter how much we all say we detest them though, we kind of perk up a bit when they speak to us. If one of them tells you that your hair looks good, then you feel vain for the rest of the day. To us mortals who are dags or brains they represent that limited part of society we will never be a part of.

Carly's already eighteen so she spends most of her evenings night-clubbing.

'The night-club was the pits,' I heard her say.

'How come?' Bettina Sanders asked.

'They were all wogs. They seem to be everywhere,' she snickered.

'I beg your pardon, Carly?' I asked, sick of her daily racist remarks.

She looked at me slightly embarrassed, scooping her fringe back between her fingers.

'Oh, not you, Josie. I didn't mean you. You're not a wog.'

'Well, what did you mean?'

'I mean . . . just those other people. But you're different.'

'No, I'm not. How am I different? Do I look different to them?'

'Well, no . . . but I know you're different.'

Her friends began to look uncomfortable and resentful.

'I'm just the same as them and I'd appreciate you not going on about wogs every day. It offends me.'

'Well, I'm sorry,' she said, sounding anything but.

'No, you're not. You're just sorry that I heard you and that you're forced to say you're sorry.'

'Well, you shouldn't be listening to my conversations anyway. This is a free country. I have the right to say whatever I want.'

'And so do I, you racist pig.'

'How dare you, you wog,' she said standing up.

'But I thought you said I wasn't one.'

'And you're more than a wog, if you know what I mean.'

I had a very strong feeling that she meant my illegitimacy. God knows what possessed me, but having that science book in my hand propelled me to immediate action. So I hit her with it.

Next thing I knew I was in Sister Louise's office with Carly's father bellowing at me. Between his shouting, Carly's snivelling and Sister Louise's nervous reassurances, mostly to herself, that everything was all right, I was becoming extremely tense. I wanted desperately to faint or something, just to get out of the hysterical environment in there. I focused my attention on the picture of St Martha on the wall.

'Are you happy you broke my daughter's nose?' he bellowed.

Carly's father is a morning-talk-show host. Carly never lets anyone forget that. But he looks different in real life. His skin is paler and blotchier. His eyes aren't as warm and humorous as they seem on television and there hadn't been a hairdresser that morning to hide his receding hair-line. Sister Louise continued to look pretty distressed and tried to calm him down, but he seemed to get more furious by the minute.

'I advise you, young lady, to call your lawyer.'

I almost snickered aloud. I would have liked to explain to him that some people on the other side of the bridge didn't have solicitors and that solicitors weren't called 'lawyers' in this country. But I didn't. I think I had said and done enough.

'Josephine, tell us what happened.'

'She hit me with her science book,' Carly wailed.

Ron Bishop grabbed the science book out of my hand and waved it under my nose.

'We'll need this as evidence in court.'

'Mr Bishop, I don't think that's really necessary,' Sister Louise said, sending me a sharp look that begged me to defend myself.

But how could I tell these people that I'd hit someone in the nose because she'd called me a wog, and made a slur about my illegitimacy? Sister would probably recite 'sticks and stones' to me.

'I might settle this out of court if the circumstances satisfy me,' he said glaring at me. 'If not . . .'

'Josephine, explain what happened,' Sister Louise ordered, looking as though she was getting very fed up with both myself and the Bishops.

'She hit my daughter with her history book.'

'Science,' I corrected.

'Josephine, we require an explanation,' Sister Louise snapped sharply.

'I want this young lady to call her lawyer.'

'She doesn't have one, Dad,' Carly sneered nastily.

'Josephine does not have a solicitor,' Sister said trying to keep calm. 'I hope we can settle this without a solicitor.'

'I don't think that's feasible, Sister. She'll have to find herself one,' Ron Bishop stated finally.

'She can hardly afford . . . '

'My father is a barrister. I'll call him,' I said calmly.

Three heads swung around to face me in shock.

'You don't have a father!' Carly yelled.

'Yeah, sure. My mother's the Virgin Mary and I'm the Immaculate Conception.'

'She's lying, Dad.'

Ron Bishop glared at Sister Louise.

'Is this girl lying?'

I don't think Sister exactly wanted to call me a liar because she was giving me a pleading look.

'Could you ring him, Josie?'

'I'll have to look up his number.'

'Oh sure,' Carly scoffed. 'She doesn't know her father's phone number.'

'He's just moved from Adelaide. I know his Adelaide one off by heart. 5516922,' I lied, making one up.

'Well, then, find the number and ring him.'

I looked nervously at them and took the phone book from Sister Louise, thankful that Mama had mentioned the name of his firm to me.

Michael Andretti was on the phone, so in the bravest tone I could use I told his secretary that Josephine needed him at school. Knowing he wouldn't know which school and not wanting the room's occupants to know that he didn't know, I told the secretary to remind him it was St Martha's Darlinghurst and not St Matilda's at Darling Point.

When I hung up I was shaking like a leaf. If I'd had a gun I would have shot myself. I knew that Michael Andretti would never come to my rescue, but I prayed all the same. Because I was about to be made into a liar, probably be expelled, and become the laughing stock of the school.

I listened to Carly sobbing about her nose and complaining that she would never model again while her father comforted her.

Sick people, I thought. How long could these people survive in the real world?

St Martha on the wall and I became very well acquainted during the next half hour. I wondered what type of problems teenagers had in her days. I figured that things must have been much easier. I mean all she had to do was pray and her brother, Lazarus, rose from the dead. What kind of miracles do teenagers get these days?

Nobody was more surprised than me when Michael Andretti walked in. He looked business-like and cool, but he was also glaring at me so sharply that I felt no need for celebration.

'Alibrandi,' Ron Bishop said, coming forward.

'Andretti,' he corrected, extending a hand which was ignored.

'Your daughter has broken my daughter's nose with her science book.'

'My daughter . . .'

He caught the pleading look in my eye and rolled his.

'My daughter inherited my quick temper.'

Sister Louise seemed to sigh with relief and showed Michael Andretti a seat.

'We're suing.'

'How interesting. What's the story, Josephine?'

I mouthed 'Josie' and stood up. 'Can I see you in private, Dad?'

He nodded and Sister Louise showed us into the secretary's office, closing the door behind us.

'What the hell is going on?' he asked through clenched teeth.

'I can explain.'

'Tell me what happened to your passionate speech the other day about keeping out of each other's lives?' he asked, standing in front of me.

'I was desperate,' I said. 'They're going to expel me. I can't afford to be expelled. A suspension is fine. It'll be a great holiday, but not expulsion.'

'You hit someone. What did your mother bring you up to be? A boxer?'

'Carly made me angry.'

'I get angry every day in court, Josephine. I don't hit people because of it.'

'Yeah, well, I'm not you,' I snapped. 'Listen, if you get me out of this I'll never approach you again. Cross my heart.'

He looked stern and I felt about ten years old. His mouth was tight with anger, but I could see him weakening slightly.

'What did she say to you?'

'Nothing.'

'Oh, great. I have to try to get you out of this mess after you hit a girl for nothing,' he whispered angrily. 'Josephine, don't waste my time. You don't seem like a violent type. She had to have said something to rile you.'

'I just don't like her. She's vain. She puts her hair all over my books when she sits in front of me in class.'

'So you hit her?'

'No . . . yes.'

'A girl puts her hair all over your books, so you break her nose?'

'Well, I don't think it's broken, personally.'

'Doctor Kildare, we are not here to give a medical opinion. I want to know what she said to you.'

'God,' I yelled exasperated. 'She said something to upset me, okay?'

'What? That you were ugly? That you smell? What?' I looked horrified.

'I'm not ugly. I don't smell.'

He sighed and took off his glasses, sitting down in front of me and pulling my chair towards him.

'I was just asking for a reason.'

I had never seen him so close before. The dimples were back because he was grimacing again. I could see the outline where he had shaved that morning. I could smell him so vividly. I had never smelt my father before. I knew Mama's smell. She likes musk perfume. Yet this was the first time my father had a scent.

'Never mind,' I said.

'That creep out there wants you to pay for his daughter's nose-job. Because of that nose-job she will be a famous model one day and you'll be working in a fast-food chain because you couldn't finish your Higher School Certificate due to expulsion. Now tell me what she said.'

'There's nothing wrong with a fast-food chain,' I said, thinking of my McDonald's job.

'I'm really getting pissed off now, Josephine. You called me out of work for this and you won't tell me why.'

'Just go,' I said, as he stood up and paced the room. 'I'll defend myself in court.'

He groaned and looked up to the ceiling pulling his hair.

'God save me from days like this,' he begged.

'Go,' I yelled.

'Okay. Let him win. He's a creep. Creeps always win,' he said walking to the door. 'But don't think you're going to make it in a court room, young lady. If you can't be honest, don't expect to stand up in a court room and defend honesty.'

'She called me a wog, amongst other things,' I said, finally. 'I haven't been called one for so long. It offended me. It made me feel pathetic.'

'You are a wog, Josie. Does it offend you to be one?'

'I'm an Italian. I'm of European descent. When an Italian or another person of European descent calls me a wog it's done in good warm humour. When the word "wog" comes out of the mouth of an Australian it's not done in good humour unless they're a good friend. It makes me feel pathetic and it makes me remember that I live in a small-minded world and that makes me so furious.'

'Did you provoke her.'

'Yes. I called her a racist pig due to some things she was saying.'

'Is she one?'

'God, yes. The biggest.'

He sighed and stood up. 'As long as it doesn't offend you to be a wog,' he said. 'Come on, let's go.'

We walked out and stood facing the others.

'Sorry, I didn't catch your name,' he said to Mr Bishop.

'My father is Ron Bishop,' Carly said, horrified that someone didn't recognise him.

'My father doesn't believe in commercial TV,' I informed her as both Michael and Ron Bishop walked into the secretary's office. 'He's an intellectual. He watches SBS or the ABC.'

After I sat down, I didn't look at Sister Louise or Carly during our fathers' absence. I didn't want to read what was on their faces. I was scared that it would be victory or sympathy or something equally pathetic.

But all the same my heart was beating fast at the thought of Michael Andretti coming to defend me. He hadn't needed to. He had said once before that he owed me nothing. But whether he did or not, he had come through.

When the door opened, Ron Bishop walked out first, looking red-faced and defensive.

'Well, I think we've got that settled,' Michael Andretti said, putting his glasses back on.

'Get your things, Carly,' her father ordered.

'Are we suing, Dad?'

'Get your things.'

I looked at them both and then up to Michael.

'Anything else?' he asked.

I nodded.

'He has my *Concepts of Science*.'

'My daughter's book, thank you,' he said briskly.

When the Bishops left, Sister Louise adjusted the chairs and gave us room.

'It was a pleasure meeting you, Mr Andretti.'

'Likewise,' he said with a smile. For once his dimples served the right purpose. 'By the way, Josie informed me she was looking forward to suspension so she could have a holiday. I hope you won't give her that satisfaction.'

I seethed with embarrassment and avoided looking at both of them.

'Josephine, dear, come here.'

I wonder why nuns always sound so sarcastic when they say 'dear'.

Sister Louise opened a drawer and I looked in.

'What do you see?'

'Applications.'

'Yes, dear. Dating back to 1980. Every lunch-time till the job is complete you'll come in and put them into alphabetical order. You'll find it good for the soul, dear.'

'Thank you, Sister.'

'You are suspended for the rest of the day, though.'

I nodded and walked out with Michael Andretti at the same time that the bell rang.

Everyone walked past me taking great interest.

'So how was court today?' I asked at the top of my voice.

Michael Andretti looked around, seeming uncomfortable with the attention and gave me a great spiel about his day in court. I heard the whispers of excitement, knowing how impressive he sounded.

I walked past my class-mates with Michael Andretti beside me and for a few minutes I knew how it felt walking alongside one's father.

It was a great feeling.

9

Usually on Fridays Sister Louise calls Poison Ivy and myself into her office to keep us up-to-date with what's going on. Sister Louise and I don't get on very well as you've probably worked out. Nothing verbal though. That's the trouble I suppose. We just look at each other untrustingly and don't say a thing. But I do respect her.

She's not like the nuns we had in primary school. I don't think any nun is like that any more. We call them the penguins because of them wearing wimples and all that *Sound of Music* gear. Except they really don't look like that any more. They're liberated. I think that during the seventies when women were burning their bras, nuns were burning their habits.

They no longer go around saying 'Bless you, my child' or 'God will punish you for your sinful ways' like the nuns of my kindergarten year did. I mean how can a five-year-old have 'sinful' ways?

I remember when I was young I used to wonder if they had parents like us or if they'd hatched out of some church. I wondered all kinds of crazy things, like did they go to the bathroom or did they think bad thoughts.

The first time I saw a nun without a habit, I prayed for her, thinking that she'd go to hell. But I think Sister Louise made me change my mind. I've never met a more liberated woman in my life and I realise now that these women do not live in cloistered worlds far away from reality. They know reality better than we do. I just wonder whether she was ever boy-crazy.

After our usual boring discussion during which Poison Ivy crawled to Sister and Sister took it all in, Ivy was excused and I wasn't. I sat there for five minutes trying to work out what I had done wrong since punching Carly the week before.

'Josie, Josie, Josie.'

I looked up at her and then it clicked.

'Sister, I only got on that bike because I needed to get home. I also think that my private life is my own.'

'I beg your pardon?'

'What are you talking about?'

'Certainly not a motor cycle.'

'Oh.'

'And for your information, young lady, I used to own a motor bike myself when I was your age.'

I almost laughed aloud.

'Then what was the "Josie, Josie, Josie" about?'

'I heard your father is defending a very prominent business man.'

I rolled my eyes and shook my head.

I don't know what it is with that woman. She finds out every single thing about us. She knows who we go out with, what we did over the weekend, if we're on diets. Probably even who sleeps with their boyfriends.

'It's not a rumour. It's the truth.'

'I'm sure it is.'

'Does that mean I'm off my scholarship because my father holds such a high position?'

'No, it only means that I'd like to know how you're coping with the situation.'

She made me feel ashamed that she cared after I was being so catty.

'I'm coping pretty well.'

'I hope there are no hostilities between your parents that affect you, Josephine. I know that you hadn't been in contact with your father when he lived in Adelaide. Your mother told me.'

I sighed, looking out the window.

'I found it very necessary to lie last week, Sister. I gambled and I won.'

'I'm sure of it.'

'I don't know him well, but he seems like a nice person.'

'Good,' she nodded. 'And this job at McDonald's?'

'Sister,' I said, exasperated. 'Is there anything we do that you don't know about?'

'Of course there is, Josephine,' she said, annoyed. 'I only know minor details about you girls.'

'Well, the job is going fine and I'm going fine.'

'Any sign of your marks going down and I'll speak to your mother.'

'Sister, I'm aggregating As.'

'Well, after six years of promise it's about time, isn't it, young lady?'

I looked sheepish and nodded.

'You can go. I just wanted to check up on you, that's all.'

'Thank you for the concern,' I said, picking up my bag and walking to the door.

'And I hope that if you decide to go out with the captain of Cook High, you'll behave in a Christian way.'

I gritted my teeth and walked out. Forget what I said earlier about nuns changing. They're the same old tyrants who terrorised children in the sixties.

'Christian way?'

That means when the Romans feed us to the lions we sit around with passive looks on our faces and smile. Like hell I will.

■

'Don't hover by the doorway, Mother. It makes me nervous,' I said, helping Nonna Katia set the table in the lounge room that afternoon.

'You nervous?'

'And check out the oven, Queen Christina. I actually made dinner. Meatloaf, which I might add is your favourite,' I went on in a smug tone.

Nonna Katia was beaming proudly. She thinks it reflects on her how well I cook.

'I showed her, Christina. Jozzie said she wanted to cook for you, so I came over.'

Mama seemed to look from Nonna to myself with dread and I began to wonder what we had done wrong.

'Mama, could you look after Josie tonight?'

Nonna Katia looked up in surprise and wiped her forehead with the back of her hand.

'You are going to one of Jozzie's parent-teacher nights?'

'No. I'm just going out.'

'I do not understand, Christina,' Nonna said shaking her head. 'Where are you going?'

I shut the oven door and waited for her answer.

'Just out, Mama,' she snapped, both nervously and angrily. 'I'm just going out with a man at work.'

'Do not yell at me, Christina. Jozzie yells at me enough.'

Mama was holding a shaking hand to her forehead. She always does that when she's upset about something.

'Well, if you didn't have to ask so many questions

I wouldn't yell. If you didn't have to treat me like a baby, I wouldn't yell,' Mama argued.

Nonna Katia was shaking her head.

'Well, I do not like it when you neglect Jozzie.'

'Neglect,' Mama shouted incredulously, clenching her fist. 'You have the hide to say that I have neglected Josie? I have devoted my whole life to her and the one day that I want to go out with people my age, you tell me I'm neglecting her?'

She looked at me, shaking with rage. It was as if she had worked herself up for a fight before she even got home.

'Have I ever neglected you, Josie?'

I looked bewildered and shook my head.

'Are you going out with a man?' I asked.

'People will talk, you know,' Nonna Katia said angrily. 'They always talk and it is always me who suffers because of their talk, Christina. Always me.'

'Forget it,' Mama sighed, shaking her head. 'Just forget I asked, Mama.'

'No, I will not forget it, Christina. Why do we always have to fight? All the time we fight and fight and fight,' Nonna Katia cried. 'I am an old woman and I am tired of fighting.'

'And I am a young woman and I'm tired of being old,' Mama cried back. 'I don't need your permission to go out, Mama, but it'd be so good one day to do something without you making me feel as if it was wrong.'

'You are Jozzie's mother. How do you tink Jozzie will feel that people are talking about her mother gallivanting around the place?'

'People? What people? Italians? Mama, I have already disgraced myself in their eyes and there will never be anything to change that, so who cares if they talk about me?'

'Christina, you always had to make tings more

difficult for all of us. For once, tink of me.'

Mama walked into her room and Nonna Katia quickly followed.

'Don't make tings worse, Christina. Do you tink I don't know?'

'Know what?' Mama asked, swinging around.

'Michael Andretti, Christina. Do you tink I didn't see what happened at my house the other day? I know who he is, Christina. I know it was him.'

'"It was him" *what*, Mama? Say it. You know that he's Josephine's father. Why can't you say it?'

'Why? Why, him?' Nonna pleaded. 'Why Pia Maria Andretti's son? Why did you have to disgrace me with Pia Maria Andretti's son?'

I thanked God at that moment that I wasn't named after my paternal grandmother.

'Does it matter whose son fathered Josephine seventeen years ago, Mama? Does it?' my mother yelled.

'I will never, ever have him in my house again,' Nonna spat out.

'Good, Mama. Now let me get dressed.'

'People will talk. They will talk for sure.'

'You know what I think?' Mama shouted. 'I think you're jealous, Mama. I think you're jealous because you didn't go out there and make anything of your life when Papa died. Because you didn't mix and you wanted to so much but you were scared that people would talk. Well, I'm not going to run my life by their rules. Things have changed. I remember when I gave birth to Josie you told me that I would never get married because no respectable man would marry a girl with a baby. Well, you're wrong, Mama. Women with babies do get married these days. Women who are widows do go out and have better lives.'

'You don't understand,' Nonna said.

'No. It's you who doesn't understand,' said Mama. 'You never have understood what I feel or want in my life. Everyone's opinion has always come before mine. Why can't you understand how I feel for once, Mama? Just once.'

Nonna Katia had this strange, tired look on her face. She shook her head in despair.

'I understand, Christina, more than you think I do.'

They didn't say a word after that and Nonna Katia drove home leaving Mama looking at me as if I was a dragon to slay.

'I'm going out tonight, Jose,' she swallowed.

'I heard. What's got into you?' I asked curiously.

'Well, Paul Presilio . . . '

'I hate that man. He always stares when I walk into the surgery. I don't like the fact that you're going out with him again. The Christmas party was one thing, but I don't understand this, Mama.'

I began to get really edgy and scared. Although Mama had gone out with a few guys in the past, this man seemed different. I'd seen the way he looked at her. It was the look of a man who didn't want to play games with women any more. The look of a man who wanted to settle down. Mama and I had always sat around talking about why she never married. It was always because she hadn't met the right man and I was always so relieved. Yet now, things seemed to be changing so fast.

'He is a very nice man and . . . '

'I don't care,' I shouted. 'Since when have you become so social, anyway?'

'Since tonight, young lady, and don't you dare speak to me in that tone,' she said stiffly, walking back into her bedroom.

I followed at her heels, not quite sure why I was so furious.

'Is it a work thing? Is it a going-away party for anyone? Are other people going to be there?'

'No. No. No. I am a single woman, Josie. Socially it is very acceptable to go out with men.'

'Socially it's bullshit. You have never been very interested in going out with men and the only reason you probably are going out with this Paul Presley shithead is because Michael Andretti is back on the scene.'

'Don't you speak in that bad language, Josephine, and if you have nothing nice to say, get out.'

'*No*. This is my house.'

'This is *my* house. You live here because you are my daughter. This is also my room.'

'Oh, great. She starts going out with men on a regular basis and she's ready to kick me out.'

'*Get out*,' she said, pushing me out the bedroom door.

'I'm not going anywhere.'

'Go next door and stay with Mrs Sahd.'

'Are you kidding? What, and tell her that my mother is on a date?' I spat out.

'Does me being your mother make me less human, Josie?' she yelled, grabbing hold of my shoulder. 'I have needs like other people and once in a while I like being with people my age.'

'Oh, great. So now I find out she regrets having me and I've stopped her from being human,' I yelled, walking to the kitchen and opening the oven.

'Well, just remember that he won't just want to hold your hand,' I said, throwing the meatloaf down the sink.

'How dare you say that to me?' she said, shaking her head almost sadly.

I stood by my desk and stuck my fingers in my ears so I could ignore her but she walked over and pushed me back.

'You are such a selfish, unreasonable child, Josephine. One day you'll understand.'

'Screw your understanding,' I yelled, throwing my books across the room angrily. 'Why should I understand you when you've never understood what I've gone through? I've suffered in my life, you know, and you've never understood.'

She walked away in disgust.

'I hope I die during the night and you regret it for the rest of your life,' I yelled.

'I don't know what I did to deserve you,' she said, shaking her head.

'I can tell you what you did with . . . '

She pointed a finger at me, furiously. 'Don't-you-dare-say-another-word.'

We stood staring at each other, but neither of us would look away.

'You break my heart, Josie.'

She left me at home alone. I hated her for that. I'm not sure why. All I know is that I never ever want my mother to marry anybody. I never want it to be anything but her and me and I'm angry that she's even thinking of letting anyone else in.

She came home at twelve-thirty-nine and opened my door.

I pretended I was asleep and she knew that I wasn't.

'I had a good time tonight,' she told me. 'I realised that I knew more than I thought I did. I have a know-it-all daughter and that's made me a know-it-all mother. He's attracted to me and for once someone found me interesting, not because I was Josie's mother or Katia's daughter but because I was me, and there is *nothing*, Josie, *nothing* you can do to take that away from me.'

She slammed my door and I wanted to cry. Because I didn't want to take that feeling away from Mama. I just didn't want him to give it to her.

10

I've been working at McDonald's for the last few weeks now. Because it's on Parramatta Road it always seems to be packed with people. Whoever thought of building it there was smart because not only is it situated on the route into the city, it's also close to Sydney University and the hospitals in Misseden Road. That also means that it's the hang-out for every hood in the inner west and inner city. Just walking into the place through the car-park is a nightmare. Nobody hangs out inside except for the families. All the teenagers are out in the car-park competing for who can play the loudest music or rev their car the most.

Yesterday made me realise that it mightn't be exactly what I want at the moment, but I don't want to admit that to Mama because we're not talking.

I'll be the first to admit that I over-reacted the other night. But fighting and yelling and screaming feels healthy, and apologising and being humble feels embarrassing. I've tried to apologise during the week but the words haven't come out. I know I shouldn't have said what I did. My life isn't as bad as I make out and sometimes I think it's all in my head, but I can't help it. I'm beginning to realise that I can be a little selfish and I'm trying to find the words to apologise to Mama and to understand Nonna just a little bit more.

Anyway, yesterday at McDonald's, Anna and I were serving and we had the whole of hood city in there including Jacob Coote, Anton Valavic and a bunch of their noisy friends. I ignore Jacob Coote when I see him. I'm not sure why. It's not as if I dislike him or anything. I think I ignore him because if I look at him I might find that he's looking at me and I'm not sure where that would lead us.

At about ten-thirty a group of loud-mouthed creeps came in and I recognised their leader as a boy who used to live next door to us. I think I've mentioned Greg Sims before. He was the one who called me a bastard when I was ten.

He's a bully like you would never believe. I once saw him hit someone from behind with a brick and he was only a kid at the time.

Greg Sims, I think, will end up in jail and if not in jail he'll end up dying in some pitiful alley from an overdose. I thought that the moment I first saw him and I still feel that now.

Mama and I called our time of living next door to the Simses the 'horror years'. Mr Sims would get drunk constantly and yell out suggestive things to my mother. I remember the nights we'd lock the doors, petrified that he'd come bursting in. Sometimes we'd wake up in the morning and there would be beer cans all over our backyard. Screaming and yelling could be heard coming from their house at any given time. Once Mama called the police in the middle of the night because she could hear loud crying. The next day Mr Sims dragged the whole family over and they all told us to mind our own business. Another time he was so drunk that he backed his car into our fence. We called the police again and he had his licence suspended and he ended up losing his job because he was a driver for a delivery company.

It became very hostile after that. Greg Sims kept on calling me names and because I was just begining to understand what they all meant, I'd cry every time. So knowing it would make me cry, he'd go on and on. Nonna kept on saying that if we had a man around the house it wouldn't be happening and that would really rile Mama and they'd end up fighting. I was absolutely relieved when we moved to Glebe.

I could tell that Greg Sims knew who I was. He gave it away by the look in his eyes. The worst eyes you could possibly ever look into. All bloodshot and so cold. I think that when the light goes off in your eyes then there is no hope for you.

'Hi, Josie,' he said in a sing-song voice, leaning on the counter an inch away from my face.

I stepped back because his bad breath mingled with alcohol made me want to puke.

'Josie and I are old friends,' he explained to his friends, inching closer to me.

He burped loudly and I could see Anna's horrified glance in my direction, as well as looks of distaste on the faces of the people waiting to be served.

'What would you like to eat?' I asked angrily.

'Not quite sure yet.'

I looked past him to the people waiting behind but he stepped directly in my path and gave me no choice but to wait for him to decide. I knew that he wouldn't pay for the food after I put it on the tray. Anna went to call the trainee manager but Greg Sims looked straight through him as if to ask what he was going to do about it, and at that moment I thanked God that cops are fanatical about McDonald's.

'That'll be nine dollars and thirty cents,' I said, loud enough for the cops who'd just walked in to hear. Greg Sims and his friends looked around before they reluctantly gave me the money and my big mistake was grinning in victory. Because it didn't end there.

Anna and I were on the late shift which meant we had to scrub the place from top to toe, but we got paid double-time for it.

Anna's car was parked at the back of the building, facing the fence rather than Parramatta Road. When we reached it we found Greg Sims and friends sitting on it, drinking and carrying on and when they spotted us, I knew there was no turning back.

'Just get in the car and ignore them,' I whispered to Anna who looked pretty scared.

'We're going to get raped,' she said breathlessly.

'Oh, look who it is. What are you going to do without the pigs around to help you now, Josie?' Greg Sims snarled, jumping off.

Anna fumbled with the keys and one of the guys grabbed them off her, as well as her McDonald's hat which he perched on his head and danced around with.

'Let me introduce you, guys,' Sims went on, leaning forward to grab my glasses, 'to the kid who thought she was God's gift to the world.'

'Give her back the keys,' I said in a wobbly voice.

'Or what?' he mocked, looking me up and down.

I looked down. Anywhere but at him, but he grabbed my face and made me look straight at him.

'How about a quickie in the back, Josie,' he whispered.

'Her father could put you away for the rest of your life,' Anna yelled hysterically.

Remember how I mentioned that Anna when peaceful is a calming influence? Well, a hysterical Anna is what nightmares are made of.

The guy who'd taken Anna's keys feigned terror and grabbed her around the waist.

'Don't touch her,' I yelled, pulling free of Greg Sims to stand next to her.

'Come on, Josie,' Greg Sims continued in a repulsive voice. 'Let's take turns in the back. I know you're dying to. It's in your blood, you know.'

I spat at him. Something I had never done in my whole life, but at that moment I hated him so much that spitting was the least of offences. He grabbed me by the front of the uniform and slobbered all over my mouth and I could hear Anna scream and pull me away while the bile rose in my throat.

Before I knew what was happening he was pulled away from me and I wondered for a second where Anna had got such strength from. But it wasn't Anna who was bashing Greg Sims's face on the ground.

It was Jacob Coote.

Being an eyewitness to violence is a truly horrible experience. It's not like the movies where everything seems so gallant and romantic. It's savage and bloody and I cried because I felt that I would never see anything so ugly again.

'Stop it, Jacob,' I sobbed, grabbing his arm while the rest of the guys were threatening each other over my head.

I saw blood on his fists and on Greg Sims's face but still he didn't stop until I grabbed his arm again and pulled him away.

'Just stop, Jacob.'

He looked at me, heaving with fury, and stood up slowly.

'She's a slut,' Greg Sims yelled, getting up savagely. 'Like her mother. Bet she'd let anyone fuck her.'

I hit him with everything I had as fast as I could and as much as I could. Because he hadn't regained his balance yet, he seemed to topple, but I kept on hitting him. I'm not sure what possessed me. I remember once reading that there is a killer in all of us. If I'd had a gun, I know I would have killed him.

Jacob grabbed me away and pushed me towards Anna who was clutching Anton Valavic's arm for dear life.

'You ever touch her again or even talk to her, I'll come after you,' he said quietly, but in a tone so icy it shook me.

The hoods left after that. Slithered away like snakes more like it.

Anna picked up her keys with shaking hands and dropped them three times before Jacob picked them up for her.

'Take her home, Anton. I'll take Josephine. They might follow them,' Jacob said finally, walking me away from the others.

I didn't argue. Not because I saw him as my protector or anything like that. I think, deep down, I just wanted to be with him.

'Get on the bike,' he snapped.

'Don't yell at me.'

'You're stupid,' he yelled.

'Don't call me stupid,' I cried back.

'What was all that about? You tell me?' he kept up in the same tone.

He put the helmet on my head and I got on behind him as he started the bike. I cried all the way home. Howled. Sobbed. Whatever you want to call it. Because a bunch of grotty junkies had said horrible things about my mother, who I had treated so badly.

Jacob stopped the bike where he had the last time and we sat there for a while before he looked back at me and took off my helmet.

'Are you going to tell me what happened back there?' he asked gruffly.

'I spat at him.'

'What?' he spluttered. 'Do you know what used to happen to me when I spat at people? My mother gave me a fat lip. Is that how your mother brought you up?'

'Don't you say anything bad about my mother,' I yelled, getting off the bike quickly. 'She's a good mother.'

He sat there for a while watching me before he sighed and got off.

'Here's a hanky. Your nose is running.'

I ignored him and wiped my nose with my sleeve pathetically.

'Classy.'

'Go away,' I mumbled.

He lifted up my face and handed me the hanky.

'I hope you haven't blown your nose on this,' I said, embarrassed.

'My mother always taught me to walk out of the house with a clean hanky.'

'Well, your mother must have been quite a lady.'

'She was,' he said softly.

I looked up at him for a while and he shrugged.

'Listen . . . you wanna go out?'

'Me?' I asked, shocked. 'I thought I wouldn't be your type.'

'Well, I would have thought that you'd think someone who spits at people and punches them in car-parks and wipes her nose with her sleeve and so on and so forth would be just my type,' he said sarcastically.

'I broke a girl's nose with a science book as well,' I added quickly.

He looked like he was trying to hide a grin and shook his head.

'Not as meek as I thought.'

'You'd have to meet my mother,' I said, surprising

myself that I would even contemplate it.

'No way, mate,' he said, shaking his head. 'I don't meet mothers.'

'Well, you can't go out with me if you don't meet my mother,' I said angrily.

'Well, good. I won't go out with you. It was a stupid suggestion anyway.'

He got on to the motor bike and slammed the helmet on his head.

'I probably would never be allowed out with you anyway,' I continued to yell.

'Oh, does Mummy only let you out with bores like Barton?' he sneered sarcastically.

'So all well-mannered boys are bores now, right?'

'I'm not meeting your mother, so that's that. I suppose you'll expect marriage next? I heard all you ethnic girls get married young.'

'You're nothing but an ignorant Australian,' I said angrily, walking away.

'And what are you?'

'I certainly don't go around generalising. Goodbye, Jacob.'

'Okay okay, I'll meet her,' he said.

'Well, I probably won't be able to go out anyway,' I argued.

I could just imagine the look on my mother's face if she saw Jacob Coote and his friends hanging out in car-parks, draped all over their bikes; the boys wearing T-shirts which read 'Put something between your legs, buy a bike' and the girls wearing clothing that my mother believes should only be worn in aerobics classes. I looked down at my McDonald's uniform which was so far removed from his heavy-metal T-shirt.

'Go to hell, Alibrandi. I don't need this shit.'

He stepped on the pedal of his bike and started it

up, but as he rode past me I yelled out his name.

'Okay, I'll ask.'

'Don't do me any favours.'

'Listen, you don't understand a lot of things about the way I was brought up,' I tried to explain.

'I'll be here seven-thirty Saturday night. We'll see a movie,' he sighed. 'If you can't make it I'm in the book. Only Coote in Redfern.'

He rode away as I yelled 'Try to wear a tie'. Somehow, whether he heard it or not, I knew he wouldn't.

11

Mama parked in front of the terrace and turned to me questioningly. Mainly because I was brooding, leaning against the car window, not saying a word.

'Apart from the fact that you're not talking to me, are you okay?'

I shrugged with a sigh.

'Is it that bad?'

'Yes.'

'I went out with the man, Josie. I am not going to marry him.'

It was a week since our fight.

'Oh, Ma, it's not that,' I said facing her. 'How do you put up with me when I treat you so bad?'

'Oh my God, is this my daughter talking?' she laughed.

'No, I mean it. God, you spend all your life bringing me up, wasting your youth on a selfish person, yet you never complain.'

'Josie, are you possessed? I've never heard you being this humble.'

'I wasn't worth it, Mama. You should have gone through with the abortion.'

'Oh, stop it, for God's sake! I had you, Josephine, because I wanted to. I have never ever regretted having you, except when you threw that meatloaf away knowing there are children starving in the world.'

'I put too much oregano in it anyway,' I sighed, looking out the window. 'I'm tired of fighting you. I need a rest.'

'Your grandmother said that to me too. Maybe we should all give each other a rest.'

I took her hand and squeezed it.

'I'm changing, Mama. I'm growing up. I'm finally seeing the light.'

'I'm glad of that, but to tell you quite honestly, you're not that bad a person. Personally I think you're basically a . . . nice person.'

'Don't choke on the words,' I said, rolling my eyes as she leaned over to kiss me.

'I miss not touching you when we're angry with each other.'

'Can I ask you a favour?' I said, facing her.

'Ask away.'

'I've been asked out to the movies on Saturday night by a boy and I really would like to go.'

'Is that what all this buttering up has been about?'

I shook my head, determined that she believe me.

'No way, Mama. If you say no, I'll accept it. I told you. I'm tired of fighting you. You're too tough for me.'

She leaned back in the seat and sighed.

'John Barton?'

'No. Jacob Coote.'

She frowned, pensively.

'Jacob Coote? Isn't he the boy who threw eggs at you once?'

'I know it sounds suss, but he really is nice. He's very deep when he wants to be.'

'Jose, you know how I feel about letting you go out

with boys I don't know. At least I'm familiar with John Barton from debating.'

'Mama, have I ever been interested in anyone foolish?'

'You hang around with Sera. That's enough evidence to consider you foolish,' she said in a dry tone. 'I'll think about it, okay.'

'I appreciate that.'

We got out of the car, grabbing all the groceries. Mrs Sahd, the old lady next door, was on her knees in her garden, still in her dressing-gown although it was four in the afternoon. Her dressing-gown is like a security blanket to her. I'm sure they'll bury her in it.

'Where's my little Josie? I never see her any more,' she said, standing up and walking to the fence.

'It's a very busy year for her, Mrs Sahd. It's very hard to get into university these days if you don't study,' Mama said, kissing her on both cheeks.

'Look at her. I remember when she was this high,' she said, holding her hand as high as her thigh.

Very unlikely that she remembers me that size because she's five feet tall herself.

'Send her over some time, Christina. I'm an old woman. I like the company.'

'Of course, Mrs Sahd. Josie loves the company as well.'

I pinched Mama on her side and she moved away.

'I need to talk to you about those boys, Christina. They are very noisy. The music is much too loud.'

'I'll talk to them, Mrs Sahd. I promise.'

'Rupert is very upset by them too. He came home the other night with nerves, Christina. I had to put a sedative in his cat food. It was because of the noise, Christina.'

'Leave things to me, Mrs Sahd,' Mama said taking her

hand and squeezing it before walking towards our terrace.

'God knows what else she feeds that cat. He looks like he's on steroids,' I whispered as she continued to wave to us.

Mama checked for the mail and walked up the stairs.

'Did Elvis Presley try to get you into bed?' I asked her.

'It's Paul Presilio,' she smiled, unlocking the ground-floor door. 'Not that it's any of your concern, but yes he did.'

I looked at her, horrified, and stopped in my tracks.

'Did you tell him that there is an AIDS epidemic going around? God, what a creep to even try.'

'Jacob Coote will probably try it on you, young lady, so you'd better have the same opinion.'

'I'll tell him that if it's not on, it's not on.'

'You will tell him to keep away from you or your mother will shoot him.'

'Women are being told to carry condoms in their handbags. Someone told me that wearing one is a bit like taking a shower with your clothes on.'

'Who told you?'

'Just someone,' I said airily, rushing up the stairs.

'I don't know if I like you discussing condoms with strange men, Josephine,' she yelled after me.

'Mama, this is the nineties. In the twenty-first century they'll be blowing condoms up on *Romper Room* and playing "punch, punch, punch the ball" with them. Face it, the age of innocence is gone. We abused the act of sex and now God's sitting back and having the laugh of his life.'

'I don't think He works that way, Jose.'

'Well, however He works isn't the issue. The issue is that because of AIDS, sex will now become the most talked about topic in this world, so if you want to start dating, young lady, get used to it,' I teased.

'Yes, Mum,' she mocked.

'And, Mama?'

'Yep.'

'You mightn't regret things you've done in your life, but I sure do regret things I say,' I said as apologetically as I could.

She smiled gently from the bottom of the stairs.

'We just have to learn to meet each other halfway, okay?'

I nodded and descended the stairs. And met her halfway.

12

When I next sat on the couch at my grandmother's place I succumbed to the urge. The urge of asking her to show me her photos. I regretted it the moment I saw the look of glee on her face. Because of the way Nonna makes my mother feel, I hate making that woman happy.

'My first house,' she said, pointing to a shack. 'No matter how much I would clean it, it would always be dirty.'

Don't believe that. My grandmother, like most Europeans, has this obsession about dirt. She cleans her house at least five times a week.

'Sometimes the snakes would come in, Jozzie. Oh, Jozzie, Jozzie, Jozzie, do you know what it is like to have a snake in your house?'

'No, we have heaps of cockroaches though.'

She closed her eyes and put her hands together as if she was praying. 'You do not know how much I hated Australia for the first year. No friends. No people who spoke the same language as me. Your nonno worked cutting the cane in another town and sometimes I was on my own for many nights.'

'Why didn't you go with him?'

'My job was to make a home for us. His was to make the money.'

I turned the page, looking at photos of my grandfather.

He never smiled. He was always standing straight and haughty. He was extremely tall for an Italian and very dark. Nonna was the opposite. She was smiling in the photo and her skin was white and clear. She's right, although very vain. She had been a beautiful girl.

I turned the page and looked at her, pointing to a photo.

'Who's the spunk?'

She looked pensive and reached over to touch it.

The person in the photo was of medium height with golden-brown hair. He was smiling broadly, leaning against a shovel, with no shirt on.

'His name was Marcus Sandford.'

'An Australian?' I screeched. 'You knew an Australian hunk?'

'He was my friend.'

I looked at her curiously.

'Who was he?'

'My first Australian friend,' she sighed. 'I had gone into the town one day. Straight to the post office. Oh, Jozzie, to get a letter from my family was like going to heaven. I would stand there in the middle of the post office and I would laugh at what my sister would tell me about my young brothers and family.

'But this day, Jozzie, this day she wrote to me to tell me that my mama and papa were dead.'

'The mafia?'

'Oh, Jozzie, of course not. It was the influenza. So in the middle of the post office I become hysterical. These poor Australians who are not used to the Italians do not know what to do. We Italians cry out loud, Jozzie. The Australians do not. So nobody moved. There I am on the floor pulling my hair out and suddenly a man picks me up off the floor and carries me out to the back.'

'Oh my God. How romantic.'

It was funny watching her talk about this man. Her face softened and I wondered what he'd really meant to her.

'He spoke to me. I spoke to him. Neither of us understood each other, but he was a comfort to me at the worst time of my life and I will remember him for the rest of my life. Nonno was away at the time so Marcus took me home. He visited me a lot after that. He would bring me stuff from the town when I couldn't go myself.

'Nuting wrong with that, Jozzie.'

'Did I say there was?'

'He would help me with the garden and then he would help me with my English. Oh, but when your nonno came home it stopped, Jozzie. He was a very jealous man. He said it was wrong that this man would come to visit a married woman. He even trampled the garden,' she whispered to me.

I realised then that my grandmother was still a bit scared of Nonno Francesco even though he'd been dead for most of my life.

'It was his garden, he insisted, and only he would tend to it. Anyway, over the next year a few more Italians moved in around the place and I began to have company. Sometimes the company was good. Sometimes bad. But I began to accept the fact that I was never going to go home to Sicily and this country was now my home, so I worked in my garden and I made my house into a home. Sometimes I would have people over and we would speak in Sicilian and I would feel as if I was back home again, Jozzie.' She closed her eyes and smiled.

'I was happy, except people would talk because I

wasn't having babies. Why? they would ask. What is wrong with you, Katia Alibrandi? What are you waiting for? That December, Francesco and I came home after the cane-cutters' Christmas party and sitting on my doorstep was my sister Patrizia, six months pregnant. My little Patrizia with a husband. I was in shock.

'They had managed to get to Australia even though there was a war and they were going to live in Australia for ever. Oh, Jozzie, your Zio Ricardo was so handsome. Just like Roberto. He was such a good husband. Still is. My sister was so lucky.'

'I know. I always wondered what Zio Ricardo would have been like when he was young. I mean he's so strong and so good. Men like him just don't seem to be around these days.'

'Those times,' she sighed. 'They were not the good old days, Jozzie. Not the nineteen-thirties and forties. There was war and there was ignorance. People died in childbirth. If you were sick you could not just go to the doctor and ask him for pills. Sometimes there was no doctor, and if there was, he did not understand what was wrong wit you. Your Zia Patrizia had a terrible pregnancy and sometimes there we were, two young women, alone in the bush.'

She shook her head in distress and turned the page, beginning a story on the Russo-Saleno wedding feud.

I didn't listen to it. I just sat there glad that I live in these times. I get depressed hearing Nonna talk. She remembers a lot in fondness, but just the feeling that nobody seemed to be around most of the time is frightening. Living just outside the city means that there are people constantly surrounding me. I don't think I could ever handle the quiet world she lived in. I don't think I could ever handle the silence of the bush in

North Queenland. Or of the country. Especially the silence of the people.

I hope I never have to live in a country where I can't communicate with my neighbour.

13

The reflection in the mirror was exceptional. I could have been a model for *Hot Pants*. Except that when I finally put my glasses on, reality set in. *Hot Pants* would have to come later.

I poked my head out of the bathroom and watched Mama sew the hem of my uniform, and with a deep breath I walked into the living room.

'Did I tell you about his speech on voting?'

'Uh huh,' she said, without looking up.

'And did I also tell you that Jacob Coote is school captain of Cook?'

''Bout a hundred times.'

'Oh.'

I fixed up the shoulder-pads on my black jumper and teased my hair with my fingers. I decided to leave it out for the night and regretted it instantly because the curls went haywire.

'Did I mention that Jacob was . . . '

'. . . deep and meaningful when he wants to be,' Mama finished off, looking up for the first time.

'I mentioned it, eh?'

'Every day, every minute and every hour. What is it, by the way, that fascinates you people so much with black?' she asked.

'Will you straighten my hair?'

The doorbell rang and Mama raised her eyebrows and smiled.

'The school captain is here.'

I rushed over and knelt by her side.

'Mama, promise me that no matter what, you'll be nice.'

'I've always been nice to your friends, Jose.'

'He's different.'

'The door.'

We looked at it for a second before I stood up and slowly walked over to answer it.

I'm not quite sure why I was disappointed. Maybe because I had spent one whole day trying to look good for him and had spent one whole pay on black Country Road pants. He, instead, wore the oldest jeans I have ever seen and his jumper had holes at the sleeves. We looked at each other and I knew he had done it on purpose.

'Come on in,' I said flatly.

Mama stood up, and I could see her trying to hide her shock at the sight of him.

He also hadn't shaved for days. No trendy designer stubble though. Just this 'hood' look.

Mama and I exchanged glances and then looked back at him.

'This is my mother,' I snapped.

He almost grunted a hello.

Mama looked perplexed and I gave an embarrassed little laugh. 'I'll just go get my jacket.'

I rushed to my bedroom and gave my mother five seconds before the door burst open.

'Josie, he . . . he looks like one of those people who ride motor bikes.'

'Oh, Mama, don't be stupid,' I babbled, turning away so she couldn't see my face.

'I can't let you go out with him.'

I turned back to her pleadingly.

'Oh, Ma, he resented meeting you so much and he's coming across worse than he really is. I mean they don't make you captain if you're a hood even if it is a public school and he's so deep and meaningful when he wants to be.'

'He wears an ear-ring.'

'He doesn't wear black though.'

'His clothes are torn.'

I took her hand and shook my head sadly.

'His mother is dead. Nobody sews for him.'

'Oh, Josie,' she sighed, shaking her head. 'Nonna would have a fit.'

'It's not as bad as it looks.'

'He grunted at me, Josie. I felt as if I was conversing with a pig.'

'I think that's how he shows his nervousness,' I tried.

'The minute that movie ends tonight, I want you home, Josephine. I don't know if I'm going to let you go out with this boy again either.'

'I'm not sure I want to go out with this boy again,' I said, picking up my bag and walking out.

I stalked past Jacob and was down the stairs before he could move. He caught up with me up the road and when he grabbed my hand I turned around and swung at him with my bag.

'You crrrreeeep!'

'What?'

'How dare you?'

'How dare I what?' he yelled.

'Look like you do! You wore a tie to the school dance.'

'And you think I'm gonna wear a tie to the movies?'

'I thought you'd wear decent clothes and it's "going to" not "gonna".'

'Get off my back, woman. I wear what I wanna wear and I speak the way I wanna speak.'

'Oh, you're such a . . . a *pig*,' I spluttered.

He marched to the bike and climbed on, crashing the helmet down on my head as I followed.

'Next thing she's going to tell me how to live my life,' I heard him mutter.

'How dare you treat my mother that way. You didn't even speak to her,' I hissed. 'I told her that I was going out with a human being and you turn up.'

'Oh God,' he yelled. 'That's it, woman. No more, mate. Never again. I must be a prick to ever go through this again.'

'You are a prick, you prick.'

He started the bike and drowned me out, speeding towards the city.

I cursed myself all the way. My first date. My first big favour from my mother and I wasted it on Jacob Coote.

I was freezing to death sitting on that bike. The winter wind was biting into my skin and my face ached from the cold. I envied all around me who were sitting in a car protected from the weather.

Jacob found a parking spot in the back of the Hoyts complex and we didn't mutter a word to each other until we had to cross the road and he demanded to hold my hand.

'So what do you want to see?' he asked gruffly.

'They're showing the Greer Garson version of *Pride and Prejudice* at the Mandolin.'

'No way, mate. I'm not going to see a pansy movie.'

I tried to hold on to my temper as we walked into the complex, but his attitude was making things worse and believe it or not, I began to nag.

I suggested another movie and he gave me a dirty look and shook his head.

'Well, what do you want to see, Bill Collins?' I snapped loudly.

People turned to look at us and he grabbed my hand and pulled me away.

'A normal movie,' he whispered angrily. 'Cops and robbers. Good people winning over bad people. People I can relate to.'

'*Morons From Outer Space* is no longer showing.'

He groaned, shaking his head.

'I gave up a Saturday night for this.'

'Oh, how sad. You could have been going out with someone whose mother you didn't have to grunt at,' I snapped sarcastically.

'You never shut up. You must have the biggest mouth in Sydney,' he said, turning to face me.

'Just because you had to meet my mother, you went and acted like a prick. Why?'

His eyes darkened and I hardly recognised him.

'This is me,' he said pointing to himself. 'This is the way I look when I go to the movies, and pardon my ignorance when it comes to meeting mothers, Josephine. It's just something that I don't need to do on a first date. But then again I have never had to go out with an ethnic girl.'

'Don't you dare call me an ethnic,' I said, furious.

'Well, what the hell are you? The other day you called me an Australian as if it was an insult. Now you're not an ethnic. You people should go back to your own country if you're so confused.'

We looked at each other for a minute before he groaned and shook his head.

'Forget I said that.'

'This *is* my country,' I whispered, before I turned and ran out of the complex back into the freezing weather.

I heard him call out my name once, but I ducked into

one of the arcades and watched him run straight past. When I felt that the road was clear I stepped out and ran in the opposite direction.

A ten-minute date, I thought, as I walked home.

I thought seriously of writing to *The Guinness Book of Records*.

■

While I was walking home thinking my mother would kill me if she ever found out, I realised that a car was slowly following me. If it had been a motor bike it wouldn't have frightened me because I would have known it was Jacob. But it was definitely a car trailing me and quickly I prepared myself for a great dash. I began quickening my step and when it stopped alongside me I could stand it no longer.

'My father's a cop and he'll kill you,' I screeched without looking.

'No, he's a barrister,' I heard Michael Andretti say in a calm voice, 'and he'll kill you if you don't get into this car.'

I looked in, confused, but relieved.

'What are you doing here?'

'Get in the car.'

I stepped in, trying to avoid his look.

'I don't want to talk about it,' I said, in what must have sounded like a prissy voice.

'I certainly don't want to hear about it.'

'Typical. Men don't care about anything but themselves.'

He shook his head disapprovingly and turned into my street.

'Does Christina know you're strolling the streets alone?'

'Yeah, I rang her up and said "Mum, I'm going to

stroll the clean streets of Glebe tonight. Is that okay?" '

'Are you ever at a loss for words?'

'When I have something to say, I say it.'

'I think that if you kept your mouth shut more often you'd learn a lot more.'

He stopped the car and we sat facing the front for a while.

'So what are you doing here?' I asked.

He sighed, lighting up a cigarette.

'I had decided to come and visit you. I thought you'd like to go out for a pizza or something.'

'Why?'

He looked out the window for a while and then faced me.

'Because if I pretend you don't exist you still won't go away. So I thought I'd like to get to know you better, but not in your home. I'd feel uncomfortable and so would Christina if we sat around while our obnoxious creation enjoyed our discomfort.'

'Obnoxious creation?' I said annoyed. 'I've never been obnoxious in my life.'

'So I'm cruising down the road and the object of my thoughts is racing down the street, screaming that her father is a cop. A public servant? Very unflattering.'

'I like a man in uniform.'

He laughed. 'Do you like pizza?'

'What a ridiculous question. I suppose you're going to ask me if I like pasta next?'

He took a deep breath and closed his eyes. 'Okay, would you like pizza?'

'I don't think you deserve my company but I feel sorry for you so I'll say yes.'

'God help me,' he said, half under his breath.

We chose a place on Glebe Point Road that had an open fire-place and was packed with people. The aroma of coffee mingled with pizza was mouth-watering and after the freezing journey on Jacob Coote's bike, I felt comforted with warmth.

It was weird sitting opposite Michael Andretti. I kept on thinking to myself 'He's your father. He's your father' and the reason it was weird was because I really loved the whole atmosphere of it.

I found myself though, looking out the window at all times in search of Jacob Coote.

'Looking for someone?'

'Slap my face if I ever mention the name Jacob Coote again.'

'Okay.'

'Jacob Coote is the most unreasonable pig I have ever met.'

'I wouldn't mind some garlic bread.'

'I don't even know why I went out with him. I think I was desperate.'

'How about a small salad?' he asked.

'Do you know what he said to me? Do you know?' So I told him.

I quite enjoyed talking to Michael Andretti. He was a great listener and didn't try giving unwanted advice. I realised that when we weren't being hostile or sullen with each other we had plenty to say. When we forgot the fact that biologically he was my father, we could be friends. He told me about his move from Adelaide and even confided his fears to me about the move. I told him I was going to be a barrister and he seemed quite rapt.

'I'll get the bill tonight,' I said, taking out my purse when we'd finished eating.

'I think I'll take care of it this time.'

'No way. I've just started working and I haven't bought much yet, so I'll pay for tonight.'

'Where do you work?'

I looked at him, as if daring him to laugh.

'McDonald's.'

He frowned.

'At night?'

I nodded.

'Sure that's safe?'

'I'm earning my own money and I like it that way.'

'I can easily support you. I told your mother that.'

'And she said that if you can't support me emotionally, don't support me at all.'

'You were listening at the door,' he stated, frowning.

'Maybe.'

'How about I issue you with a proposition.'

He called the waitress over and ordered another two cappuccinos.

'You've already drunk one. Do you think I'm made of money or something?'

He laughed aloud for the first time since I had met him and secretly I liked the fact that I could make him laugh.

'Okay, this is my proposition. How about you come and work for me at the chamber? You can do photocopying and help the secretaries,' he suggested.

'But you'd be paying for nothing,' I said. 'You'd pretend that you had work for me.'

'I'm a business man. I don't pay anyone for nothing,' he said. 'If you come to work for me in the afternoon you do exactly that. Work.'

'It sounds great,' I said, beginning to get excited. 'I mean it'd help in regards to me wanting to be a barrister.'

'You won't be doing any legal work, hot shot,' he warned.

'But it'd be great telling people that I will. I mean

the closest anyone has to a Saturday morning job in connection to their ambitions is Poison Ivy. She wants to be a doctor and she works in a chemist. Well, big deal,' I laughed. 'Because all she sells are condoms, tampons and Homy Ped shoes.'

'I think I get the drift,' he said drily. 'I hope you won't be boasting.'

'Of course I will.'

'I've created a monster,' I heard him say to no one in particular.

I left a two-dollar tip and he drove me home. I told him more about Jacob the Creep and John Barton. He seemed to think that John Barton was more my type.

When we got to my place I stepped out of the car and poked my head through the window.

'I'll call you, Michael, okay?'

'I'll call you, Josie.'

I nodded.

'Can I ask you something?' I said, shy all of a sudden.

He nodded this time.

'Did you ever think my mother went through with the pregnancy?'

He looked at me and I saw him shiver for a moment.

'You're such powerful human beings,' he whispered.

'Who?'

'Off-spring.' He sighed and cleared his voice. 'I want to be honest. I would have rathered life to have gone on the way it was going. I feel too old to be a father. I don't want you to be misled about how I feel about you. I'm not sure if I can love you ever, but I want to know you. I want to be part of your life.

'You see it's different to normally having a kid,' he told me. 'You see them as lovable babies and then watch them grow. With you I feel as if I've started reading a book from the middle and have to try and figure out the beginning.'

'But did you think at any time that my mother went through with the pregnancy?' I persisted.

'Would you believe me?'

I looked at his eyes. They were so dark and similiar to mine. His eyebrows seemed so thick and fierce when he frowned or worried. He was a worrier, I realised. That was human.

'I don't think you'd be a liar.'

'We discussed abortion as the number-one option because we were scared shitless. I honestly didn't think she'd go through with the pregnancy. I knew her father. I didn't think that Christina Alibrandi had the guts to stand up to the bastard.'

I nodded, satisfied with the answer.

'But I want to be honest with you. I can't promise you that I would have come back if I'd known she'd gone through with it. I had a lot of problems back then.'

I looked at him pensively and shook my head.

'You would have come back. I know you would have.'

I turned and walked away, and this time when I saw that he was still parked there I gave a wave. He waved back.

■

I told Mama about Jacob and Michael when I walked in.

I was a bit afraid of her reaction on both counts. Would she never let me out again because of Jacob? Would she be hurt that I was seeing my father? Would she be hurt that I would be working for him?

Instead she hugged me and we both clung to each other for a while.

'Were you in love with him?' I asked as we sat on

the carpet in front of the television set.

'As much as a sixteen-year-old can be in love.'

'I'm seventeen years old. I could be in love so deep that it could drive me to suicide.'

'You could also be a great Shakespearian actress, Josie, for all the drama you possess.'

'He's a very impressive man,' I said, watching for Mama's reaction. 'He has good things to say about you too. He can't understand how someone as sweet as you could have a daughter like me.'

'Oh, good. At least he's not feeding your ego.'

'You know that night you went out with Elvis Presley?'

'Paul Presilio,' she corrected.

'Well, I thought you looked fantastic, but I didn't want to say so because I was angry that my meatloaf didn't turn out.'

'Oh, is that the excuse we're going to use for the tantrum?' Mama smiled.

'And I think you could give a lot of women a run for their money.'

'Why don't you go to bed?' she said, kissing me.

I hugged her hard. 'Life could be so great, Mama. I know it could.'

'It's good enough.'

'Thanks for letting me go out tonight.'

'But do you understand why I hesitate, Josephine? You spent half your night alone on the streets. Anything could have happened to you. Do you understand me when I say that nobody looks after you like I do?'

'Yes, I do,' I said honestly. 'I mightn't like it, but I do understand.'

As I lay in bed that night I thought of Jacob Coote. Deep down I really wanted him to ring and apologise. I'm embarrassed to say that I got out of bed three times to check that the phone was on the hook properly. I gave up after midnight and went to sleep thinking about what my mother had said.

I prayed that we'd all be satisfied with 'good enough'.

14

After a few hiccups at MacMichael and Sons I've managed to settle in and things are beginning to run smoothly. I take the bus from school to the Chambers three times a week. It is such a relief not to have to put on the McDonald's uniform and put up with all those psychos. The barristers at MacMichael's are really nice, although not at all on my level. The things they find funny are so unfunny.

I've seen Jacob Coote a couple of times. Once was when he was on the school bus and another time he was at Harley's, a café at Darling Harbour. This girl with a uniform as short as a T-shirt was sitting on his lap.

But at the moment, John Barton is my biggest worry. I was on my way to the Sydney University library on Monday afternoon and bumped into him. He seemed vague and subdued and I wondered if he had decided we couldn't be friends. We took a detour to a coffee shop where he embarked on depressing me out of my head. It was one hundred times worse than debating night. He looked as if he had lost lots of weight, which he really couldn't afford to do in the first place. His eyes couldn't settle in the one place and if I didn't know him better I could have sworn he was on drugs. I don't know whether it was because of Jacob, but I wasn't as attracted to him as I used to be.

'I hate this shit life,' he said to me out of the blue as we sat there.

I looked up, not knowing exactly what to say. I mean life isn't a buzz, but I wouldn't exactly call it shit.

'What happened?'

He shook his head, clamping his mouth together into a thin line.

'My father was home when I got there this afternoon. Went through my mail. He owns my life so of course he's entitled to open my mail,' he spat out bitterly. 'I didn't win the maths competition. I didn't even get in the top five percent. Bloody Sydney Grammar dominated again.'

'Big deal, John. It's not the end of the world.'

He covered his eyes with his hand and then rubbed his forehead.

'It's not the words that come out of his mouth. It's the looks, Josie. The disappointment.'

'I'm sure your father loves you, John.'

'Oh, he does,' he said nodding. 'When I shit all over everyone in academic competitions. When I win a debate. When I win a football game. When I get elected school captain. When I win, win, win,' he gritted. 'And when I lose he hates me. So I have to keep on winning. I have to keep on being the best in the world. Josie, I don't want to do law. It's going to be two billion times worse than this year and it'll go on for five years.'

'Don't get yourself so worked up,' I said, watching him closely.

His face looked blotchy and pale.

'My father will kill me,' he muttered. 'He'll kill me.'

'John, calm down. You're extra intelligent. You can be anything you want to be.'

'But I don't know what I want to be,' he said, grabbing my hands. 'How can I tell my father I don't want to study law if I don't know what else I want to be?'

'You have no idea?'

He looked at me hesitantly, his eyes almost glazed. 'I don't think I want to live this life any more, Josie.'

At first I misunderstood. I wondered what other life there was to live and it wasn't until I was biting into my apple strudel and watching those vacant eyes of his that I realised he meant no other life.

'This life is shit. All we care about is making money and being big. Look at all the injustice and terrorism and prejudice, Josie.'

And for a minute, no, just a second really, I wondered if he was right. I wondered if it was all one big useless existence. In that tiny second I wondered if I wanted to live this life any more. If I wanted to have a major heart attack every time I heard an American voice crackling over our news. Americans take their accents so much for granted. Every time I hear it on the radio I think they've managed to involve us all in another horrible conflict. I wondered if I wanted to raise my children with that fear in their hearts. I figured that heaven must be a great place to go to get away from the madness, but I'm not ready for heaven yet and I don't think heaven is ready for me. The terrible thing about it is I find the horrible conflicts and injustices comforting compared to this place where we're supposed to go to one day where everything is perfect. So my second was up and I went back to liking this useless existence.

'Father Stephen said that peace is a state of mind. We will never have world peace, John, so we have to be peaceful within ourselves and that will make us happy.'

'Father Stephen? What the hell does he know? There is no God, Josie.'

'You don't believe in God?'

He looked at me incredulously. 'God, you're naive.'

'You just said "God".'

'It's become a figure of speech.'

I'd never spoken to an atheist before, so I didn't know what to say.

I made jokes about things and shouted him another cappuccino and hoped that the next time he saw me he would say 'April Fool, Josie' although it was the middle of June. Sitting opposite him made me desperately want to be with someone as uncomplicated as Jacob who enjoyed his simple life.

I wished I could walk out of the coffee shop and just see Jacob. I could see now that it was my fault as much as his that our movie night hadn't turned out. I'd had too many expectations. I'd wanted him to be what I wanted and not what he was. My thoughts turned back to John and I reached over to touch his shoulder.

'We've been asked to write down the way we feel at the moment,' I explained to him. 'It's because everyone is really stressed out about the HSC. We can do it in any style we want. Like a poem or a letter. We have to hand it to someone we trust and after the HSC we ask that person to read it. They're to ask us if we still feel the same way.'

'How do you feel at the moment?' he asked me.

I shrugged. 'There have been a few changes in my life this year, including a change in the way I feel about people and things. But I need to write them down. It'll be like some kind of therapy. Can I give it to you? I know you'll understand the way I feel.'

He took a breath and nodded.

'Can I do the same? Like give you my feelings on paper?'

I smiled at him and nodded.

We spent the rest of the afternoon writing down our thoughts. We folded the papers and sealed them with sticky tape.

When he passed over his sealed paper his hand was trembling. When I handed mine over I instantly wanted to take it back. I had just handed over the deepest of my feelings. Feelings that I couldn't even explain to my best friends or to my mother. It was as if I had let him into my soul and thinking about it now, nobody should be allowed into your soul.

When I got home I placed his sheet in my jewel-case. Maybe because my jewel-case contained my most worthy items and the soul of John Barton seemed priceless.

I felt guilty in a way. Because I go on so much about my problems but compared to John and all the other lonely people out there, I'm the luckiest person in the world.

■

We had confession on Friday. We have it once a term. It's the same thing every time. I sit there mumbling to myself because I usually forget the 'Bless me Father for I have sinned' bit. Once I get over that I go through my sins. The same ones every time.

I was disrespectful to my mother and grandmother.

I've been lazy.

I've been selfish.

Once, last year, I started going through my sins and Father Stephen said, 'Oh, it's you, Josie.'

Can you believe it? He recognised me by my sins. I'm so boring that I can't even change my sins from term to term.

I'm a bit in love with Father Stephen. He's not young or anything. He's about forty. But there is just something about him. So much heart and soul.

Once he made me say a whole decade of the rosary for penance because I told him that I didn't believe in God and that the crucifixion was a big publicity stunt by Jimmy Swaggart's ancestors to raise money. (For a few months in Year 9, I professed that I didn't believe in God because sometimes not having a God in your life means you don't have to feel guilty or scared about so many things.)

Father Stephen is the most learned and advanced of all men in the world. The man surfs at our school picnics and arranged for the Cockroaches to come and perform at our school, free of charge.

He was the first person in our area to arrange for AIDS talks. He said he didn't want young people dying of ignorance. So confession when he is around is always packed.

Sera is always in there the longest. I don't know what she says to him exactly, but I can't imagine her telling a priest that she's extremely sexually active. At times she drives me crazy because she loves to bait. Like on Friday outside confession.

I mean she knows I'm a virgin. Lee, Anna and I are, but still she continually loves to make digs. Like she asked me on Friday what type of contraception I use.

'Underwear,' I said. 'Keeping it on prevents pregnancy.'

She laughed. Trilled more like it, but then in her usual Sera way, she stopped.

'Sorry, Josie,' she said in a hushed whisper. 'You must be so worried that what happened to your mother will happen to you. Wouldn't that be terrible? People would have a field day.'

I just ignored her. I'm getting good that way. Things that worried me a few months ago no longer worry me as much. I can't say that I'm completely oblivious. The gossiping of the Italian community might not matter to some, but I belong to that community.

Sometimes I feel that no matter how smart or how beautiful I could be they would still remember me for the wrong things.

That's why I want be rich and influential. I want to flaunt my status in front of those people and say 'See, look who I can become'.

Mama says that satisfaction isn't what I should search for. Respect is. Respect?

I detest that word. Probably because in this world you have to respect the wrong people for the wrong reasons.

15

Because we were allowed out early on Wednesday afternoon, we decided to go down to Harley's at Darling Harbour to make great career decisions over a cappuccino.

I think if I'm ever asked to recall what Year 12 was all about, I'll remember it as one big cappuccino experience.

Harley's is our hang-out. Between four o'clock in the afternoon and six in the evening the place is packed with students from schools all around the inner-city area. It works out well for the owners because they don't get many business people coming in during those times who would be scared off by loud teenagers squashed together just to be seen. It's a fifties-style place with a juke-box and pleasing food like hamburgers and French fries. On the wall there's fifties memorabilia like posters of James Dean and Natalie Wood in scenes from *Rebel Without a Cause*. The music is modern though and it never stops. Working with Michael means that I don't go as much as I would want to, but once a week is enough to catch up on the gossip.

'I'm going to be a fashion designer,' Sera suggested after we sat in a booth which had just been vacated.

'I know so many people doing fashion designing,' Anna said, flicking the page. 'You end up working as a sales assistant in Katies or Sussan's.'

'Make-up artist?'

'Sera, admit it, you are not artistic,' I told her bluntly.

'Are you saying my make-up doesn't look good?'

'I knew this would happen,' Lee said, slamming the book shut.

'If I wasn't thinking of doing law, I'd be a translator for the Italian consulate in some mysterious country,' I told them, dreaming of how exciting it would be. 'But I know that the proper Italians would pick out my Sicilian accent. The northerners are snobs just because they're blonde.'

'I'm blonde and my parents aren't from the north,' Sera said, using my glasses again for a mirror.

Lee, Anna and I exchanged glances.

'Should I tell her, girls?' I asked, feigning pity.

'Go ahead, Josie,' Lee said, adopting a sad voice.

I took hold of Sera's hand gently.

'Sera, my poor sweet disillusioned Sera. You were not born with that colour hair.'

'No?' Anna said, horrified, before we all burst out laughing.

Sera grabbed the careers book from Lee's hands and flicked through it again.

'How about teaching?'

'How about the public service? You'd be happy there, Sera.'

Sera looked at me suspiciously, wondering if I was teasing her.

'I'm going to be doing teaching,' Anna said definitely. 'The Catholic Campus at Strathfield.'

'I can see you as a teacher,' Lee agreed.

'No way,' I laughed. 'Anna will always be a McDonald's worker to me.'

Anna laughed and then bent her head, urging us to close in.

'Guess what?'

'What?'

'I think Anton Valavic likes me.'

Sera almost fell off her seat laughing and Anna looked wounded.

'Sera, grow up,' Lee said, lighting up a cigarette. 'Go on, Anna.'

'Let me go on,' Sera said, wiping the tears on her face. 'I've seen Anton Valavic. He's a man. I mean have you ever seen the way the guy fills out his school pants? Could you imagine our little Anna appealing to him?'

'I think he's a softy,' I told them. 'Well, deep down anyway, and Jacob Coote told me at the dance that Anton liked you, Anna.'

'Well,' Anna said in a hushed tone, looking around to see if anyone was listening. 'Every night when I finish at McDonald's he's out there, sitting on his bike. When I drive away, he rides home in his direction. Every night.'

Her large blue eyes looked misty and her cheeks were burning red with embarrassment.

'Are you sure he just doesn't like Big Macs?'

She shook her head.

'He never ever comes inside.'

'He'll break your heart,' Lee said, passing her cigarette to Sera.

'Speak of the devil. Here he comes with Josie's boyfriend,' Sera said slyly. 'Why don't we just ask him?'

'Sera,' Anna hissed, putting her head on the table.

We all knew that Sera only needed a dare issued and she would go ahead and embarrass anyone.

'Sera, if you say a word, you will regret it till your dying days,' I told her.

'Are you threatening me, Josie? You of all people can never say anything to embarrass me. People talk about you enough.'

The booth behind us was vacant and Jacob Coote, Anton Valavic and four others squashed in, much to the despair of Anna and I.

One of the girls had sandwiched Anna's plait between her back and the booth and Anna tried in vain to yank it out.

'Do you mind?' Lee said loudly to them.

The others turned around to look at us with disinterest.

'Oh look, it's Saint Martyr's,' one of the girls snickered.

I met Jacob's eye for a minute and looked away.

Anna and Sera still had their backs to them and one of the boys began to swing Anna's plait back and forth. He pulled out the silk scarf she had tied around the plait and wound it around his fingers.

'Just grow up and give it back to her,' I snapped.

'Give it back,' Anton Valavic said quietly.

The boy threw the scarf over to Jacob where it fell on the table just as one of the girls knocked over a bottle of tomato sauce. Anna stood up sighing, and reached for it, folding it up and placing it in her satchel. 'My grandmother sent this to me from Croatia. It's pure silk.'

I packed up my books and threw them into my bag, nudging Lee.

'Let's get out of here.'

We paid for our coffee and squeezed through the crowd that had just come in from Glebe High.

'He really looks like he likes you, Anna,' Sera said, sarcastically.

'Shut up, Sera,' both Lee and I said at the same time.

We browsed around for a while looking at all the stalls with their trinkets and T-shirts and spent half an hour in Sportsgirl and Portman's trying on clothes we knew we couldn't afford to buy. The crowds got to us after a while.

Lee and I said goodbye to Anna and Sera and walked outside along the pier where the sun had appeared out of the blue. We sat looking out at the water, watching the activity on the other side where the city centre lay.

'What am I going to do with my life?' she asked me in dismay. 'You've known since you were five. I change my mind every week.'

'I thought you'd decided on advertising?'

'That was last week. I spent three days sick at home, remember. I watched TV all day long and was insulted by the advertisements I saw. I don't want to be into bullshit. Anyway, to get a foot in the door you have to be glamorous. I'm not into glamour.'

'I think that glamour in advertising is a myth. They make it look glamorous on television, but I doubt it is.'

'My father started out in advertising you know. A thousand years ago when he used to be sober.'

I get embarrassed when Lee speaks about her father's drinking problem. It's a subject she hardly ever brings up and if something bad happens we don't find out about it until months later. Lee's father is one of those charismatic men and his five children absolutely adore him. But when he drinks he's abusive. Not physically, though, but verbally. Lee once told me that she'd rather have her bones broken by sticks and stones and that words did hurt. She spends a lot of time living with her brother's family when things get too much at home.

'I feel sorry for my parents,' she went on. 'They're

forty and their life is shit. She won't leave him and he won't do anything about his problem. They tend to think that one day the problem will go away without them having to work on it. I'll probably be exactly the same.'

'Anyone who takes your attitude deserves a bad life, Lee. We're masters of our own destiny.'

'That's rubbish. If your father's a dustman, you're going to be a dustman and if your father's filthy rich, you're going to be filthy rich because he'll introduce you to his rich friend's son. People breed with their own kind. Rest assured that John Barton will marry one of the Poison Ivys of the world, just like his brothers have married daughters of the well-known. The rich marry the rich, Josie, and the poor marry the poor. The dags marry the dags and the wogs marry the wogs. The western suburbs marry the western suburbs and the north shore marry the north shore. Sometimes they cross-breed, though, and marry into the eastern suburbs.'

She sighed sadly, shivering from the cold breeze that was coming from the water. 'And we all end up where we started.'

'That's not true. My future has nothing to do with what my family did.'

'Josie, whether you want to admit it or not, you are going to be a barrister because of your father. Without being there he's still managed to be the greatest influence of your life.'

The sun went completely and we cuddled up to each other for warmth.

'This is depressing me.'

'You? I'm the one who doesn't know what she's going to do with her life,' she wailed.

We stood up and began walking towards the stairs that led to the main road.

'How about being a cop?' I suggested.

She gave me a sour look. 'Your cousin is going to be one. He probably thinks I'd want to be close to him.'

We both laughed, trying to keep the hair out of our faces and having to walk backwards for a few seconds to achieve it.

'You know what? I'd like to join the circus. I've wanted to do that ever since I read *Mr Galliano's Circus* by Enid Blyton,' she stated.

'How about a journalist?'

'They twist words and print rubbish.'

'An air-hostess?'

'They clean dunnies on planes.'

'A teacher?'

'Hate kids.'

'So what would you be doing in a circus?'

'I'd be a fortune-teller,' she said, wrapping her tie around her head. 'I would tell the yuppies that the stock market was going to fall and watch them go berserk.'

'Tell me my fortune, Madame Lee,' I said theatrically.

She grabbed my hand and looked at my palm.

'You, my dear Josephine, will travel the world in pursuit of happiness and find it.'

'Where? In Rome? Paris? New York?'

'Redfern. He will make you happy and give you ten bambinos. You will breed with this man and the world will follow your example of cross-breeding. They will call it the 'Alibrandi' method and you will become famous.'

'Jacob Coote? Get out of here.'

'He was staring you out like crazy in there. For God's sake, Jose, I'm envious. He is hot. He is without pretention. He's the only person I know who will not put up with your melodrama.'

'Melodrama? Thanks a lot.'

'Jose, believe me,' she said when we stopped at the top of the stairs that led on to the road. 'Your problems are out there, I believe that. But they're small. They only grow out of proportion when they climb inside your head. They grow because of insignificant people like Carly and Poison Ivy and Sera who feed on them because they know how you feel.'

I looked at her and nodded with a smile and we gave each other a small, embarrassed hug.

After we went our separate ways I sat at the bus-stop talking to my cousin Robert's best friend who goes to St Anthony's. His bus came soon after and before I knew what was happening, Jacob Coote was sitting next to me.

'Who was that?' he whispered angrily.

'Jacob, get lost. That really upset Anna. You don't know how sensitive she is.'

'I'm sorry,' he said grabbing my hand. 'Listen, we'll start over again, okay.'

I looked at his clear green eyes which always seemed so warm and sincere no matter how bad he looked at times. Eyes, my mother told me, never lie.

'Did you end up watching the movie that night?' I asked sulkily.

'No, I went and picked up a girl and screwed her brains out.'

I looked at him, unamused, knowing he was lying.

'That's what you want to hear, isn't it?' he asked.

'No, not really.'

'I went home,' he said gently. 'Satisfied?'

I looked around at anything but him and he leaned forward and kissed me slowly on the mouth.

'Another chance,' he said. 'We were both hot-headed and I said things I didn't mean. I'll never say them again. Cross my heart and hope to die.'

'And never lie again?'

He kissed me again and I looked around, embarrassed.

'People will see,' I said, stepping away. 'We're at a bus-stop.'

He grabbed my hand and squeezed it, looking pleased with himself.

'You'll have to come over again and redeem yourself with my mother,' I told him honestly. 'She was very unimpressed.'

He shrugged. 'I've lived through it once.'

I hugged him quickly, noticing that the bus was approaching.

'I'll meet you at Harley's at four-thirty tomorrow.'

'I work.'

'Hell,' he cursed. 'How about after work?'

'Can't.'

'Wanna wag?'

I looked around, agitated. I didn't want to do things behind my mother's back but there was no other time to see him.

'Poison Ivy wouldn't wag.'

'You're not Poison Ivy. You're no saint, Josephine, so don't try acting like one.'

I covered my face and shook my head. 'Okay,' I said. 'Eight-thirty, Friday morning at Circular Quay.'

He looked excited and I was pleased. Captain of Cook High, leader among the boys of the school community and voted sexiest male in the rebel St Martha's poll, and he was excited because I was going out with him.

He kissed me quickly this time and looked up when the bus stopped.

'I'll be waiting.'

I stepped on the bus, waiting for the person in front of me to pay.

'I'll take you to go and see that prejudice movie,' he yelled.

'*Pride and Prejudice*,' I called out. 'It's very romantic.'

I sat on the bus grinning from ear to ear, and wondered if I'd have something interesting to confess at confession next quarter.

16

I wagged school on Friday and went to Manly with Jacob Coote.

When I think of it now, wagging in a St Martha's school uniform was pretty stupid, but I was so caught up with seeing him that I didn't care. He was waiting for me by the quay and I felt as if I was going to be sick when I saw him. I mean he's the first guy who's ever passed the test, because usually when I like a guy I get instantly turned off when he likes me back.

But when he winked at me, my heart melted.

'I didn't think you'd show,' he said, lighting a cigarette and putting an arm around my shoulders.

'I didn't think you would either.'

He paid for my ferry ticket and I allowed him to because I didn't want to get into an argument about me paying for myself just yet.

It was the most glorious day. Sometimes there are these beautiful days in the middle of winter and Friday was one of them. The sun caressed our faces. People were walking around looking happy and buskers were singing and dancing along the pier.

It was the most beautiful day of my life.

To give you a run-down on Jacob is very hard. Sometimes he speaks really stupidly and doesn't know what I'm talking about, and other times he speaks really well, and I don't understand what he's talking about.

Sometimes he's a tough guy and I can imagine him bashing someone's head in and other times he's this real nice sensitive guy who smiles at babies and helps old women across the street. He smokes dope, drinks and I think he sleeps with a lot of girls, but on the other hand he really loves his family and has respect for people.

He looks like a grot sometimes because of his hair and ear-ring and wild look, but when he smiles it's warm and sincere. Never ever fake.

For lunch we sat on the beach and ate fish and chips off grease-proof paper.

'Mum used to bring me down to the beach when I was a kid,' he said, leaning back on the sand with his hands behind his head.

'We used to go to the beach every Boxing Day with my grandmother's relatives,' I told him, laughing at the memory. 'Ever seen those big Italian families at a beach picnic? It's not your typical sausage on the barbecue. It's the spaghetti leftovers from the day before, schnitzel, eggplant and all these other fancy things. I used to envy the Aussie kids who had a piece of meat between their bread.'

'And the Aussie kids with the piece of meat between their bread probably envied you.'

'Of course. Grass on the other side, etcetera,' I agreed.

I lay back on the sand next to him, silence reigning for a while.

'Do you miss your mum a lot?'

'Yep,' he said, closing his eyes. 'I mean it's been a while, but sometimes I think of her. I think my sister Rebecca misses her the most because she's a girl and they used to talk all the time.'

'How old is Rebecca?'

'Twenty-four, I think. She's married to Darren, who's just bought the garage he's been working in for the last couple of years and they've just had a baby. She used to work at the university library and had a complete black wardrobe. My father hated it.'

I laughed, thinking of my mother. 'So it's just your dad and you at home?'

'Most of the time. Dad's girlfriend Eileen stays over a lot and looks after us because we're hopeless with the food and cleaning and all.'

'Are they engaged?'

'God no. Why should they be?'

I looked at him and shrugged.

'I suppose it's the different cultures. I mean Italians don't live with a guy unless they're rebel Italians in the first place.'

'Was your mother a rebel Italian?'

'My mother was a naive Italian. She didn't have me just to make a statement. She had me because . . .' I shrugged. 'I don't even know, but in those days you didn't do things like she did.'

'How about if she was married and her husband died, would she live with a guy or marry him?' he asked, propping himself up on his elbow.

'Want to know the truth?' I murmured. 'Most Italians who're older, just say in their forties or fifties, they don't remarry, unless they're men of course. Men can't do without.'

'Without what?'

'Without everything. But women, God no. People would talk. They'd say that she didn't wait long enough, or she's making a fool of herself. An Italian woman has to wear black for ages. It's not a written law or anything, but if she doesn't, people will talk. If she gets involved with a man within a year people say that she's a sex-maniac. It's all rather political, mourning is. There are rules.'

'Bloody hell, you're all weird. What would you do?'

'Me? I'd like to be a rebel Italian. I'd like to shock everyone and tell them to stick their rules and regulations. If anyone ever died, I'd wear bright colours to the funeral and laugh the loudest. But I can't.'

'Why not?'

I looked at him and wondered if he understood.

'Because I have no father. Because if I did all those things hypocrites would shake their heads smugly and say "See, I told you she couldn't amount to anything." They're waiting for me to make an error so they can compare me and my mother.'

'But what's the big deal? Everyone has babies without being married these days. Everyone lives together and gets remarried,' he said, turning on his side.

I shook my head. 'I can't explain it to you. I can't even explain it to myself. We live in the same country, but we're different. What's taboo for Italians isn't taboo for Australians. People just talk and if it doesn't hurt you it hurts your mother or your grandmother or someone you care about.'

'I'd hate them all. I'd hate to be Italian.'

'No,' I smiled, looking at him. 'You can't hate what you're part of. What you are. I resent it most of the time, curse it always, but it'll be part of me till the day I die. I used to wish when I was young that my mother had made a mistake and that my father wasn't the son of an Italian, but an Australian. So I could be part of the "in crowd" you know. So if you said "Let's go away for the weekend" I could say "Hey, sure thing". But there is this spot inside of me that will always be Italian. I can't explain it in any other way.'

'And your dad?'

'I met him for the first time a couple of months ago. I'm working with him at the moment.'

'No joke?' he asked incredulously.

I shook my head.

'He's a barrister and although I didn't want to, I like him a lot. He's honest and not a hypocrite and I sometimes want to hate him for what he did to my mother, but it'd be stupid to hate someone for something they did eighteen years ago. I mean you could change heaps, couldn't you?'

He leaned over and kissed me quickly.

'What was that for?' I asked, embarrassed, but laughing.

'I like the way you talk. I like the way you think. So much passion behind those bifocalled eyes. So much to say.'

I shrugged.

'A lot makes me angry. Maybe angrier than most because of the so-called "sin" surrounding my birth. So much pointing and talking.'

'We used to make fun of you, you know?'

'Oh, great. Confession time,' I groaned.

'This was years back when we had community week and you had to get up there and say what your school was doing,' he said, pulling me down to lie with him. 'I know now that beauty is skin deep and all that shit.'

I looked at him incredulously.

'Meaning I'm still ugly but you're getting accustomed to my face?'

'I've grown accustomed to you,' he said, looking down at my body. 'You're just not what I'm used to.'

'Well, I'm so sorry, Jacob,' I said in a mock submissive tone. 'I'll try hard. I promise to be the type you go out with. Please give me another chance.'

'And you've got the biggest mouth I've ever met.'

'Lovely. Why am I lying on the beach with a boy who's insulting me?'

'Because you're attracted to me sexually.'

'Yeah, sure.'

He leaned forward and kissed me.

When I think of it, it was my first passionate kiss. Paul Sambero kissed me in Year 8, with no tongue contact whatsoever, but Jacob's tongue went straight in before I could think of anything else and I was so worried because I didn't know what to do.

Jacob, when kissing me, has a habit of putting his hands all over my face and he even pushed up my glasses so I was half blind, but who needs eyes when kissing? I loved it. No dramatics like in the *Mills and Boon* books, but different. Intimate, because part of him was inside part of me. Tasting someone's breath is so spiritual.

Fifteen minutes later I was an expert. That's all you need. I think I was even getting the upper hand which is very simple with a guy. Anything seems to turn them on.

It was difficult to get any further than that because we were on a public beach and I was scared we'd be seen by someone I knew, so we took the ferry back and as I sat with my head against him and listened to his heart beat, I felt that I would never be closer to another human being again.

I felt so in touch with him. I had never felt like that before. Jacob Coote knew who I was. I didn't have to impress him with clever conversation or anything. Maybe I just had to educate him a bit, just like he had to educate me.

We kissed again on Circular Quay and he said he'd call me. I waved and walked to the Chambers, wanting to tell Michael all about it, but I knew I couldn't.

I'm in love.

I don't want to be in love with Jacob Coote. I want to be in love with John Barton and have people look upon me with envy, but John doesn't make me feel like this. I'm beginning to realise that things don't turn out the way you want them to.

And sometimes, when they don't, they can turn out just a little bit better.

17

Really getting to know Michael Andretti took place during the June holidays when I went to Adelaide with him.

We had kind of established a relationship during my afternoon stints at work with him, but most of the time he made me photocopy and make him coffee. If they're handing out degrees for photocopying, I'm sure I'll get honours.

I'm still shocked by how fast things are going between us. Six months ago I hadn't met my father and I didn't want to. These days I see him three times a week and the days I don't see him he rings me. Somehow we've developed a great relationship. We're still stilted and a bit embarrassed around each other but there is a great respect there. I never really thought I would respect my father.

'If you're so rich, why are we driving to Adelaide and not going first class on Ansett?' I asked him after we'd driven through our one-hundreth small town which seemed to be populated by old men and middle-aged women.

'Because I thought that driving would be nicer and I don't fly first-class Ansett. I fly business-class Australian.'

'I hate long-distance travel.'

'The scenery is beautiful, Josephine. Appreciate.'

I gave him a side-long look.

'Beautiful? Michael, everything is brown and the scenery has looked the same for the last five hours. I'm bored and I can't believe you haven't got a tape deck.'

'A lot of teenagers don't get the opportunity to meet the people you have since we left Sydney. Think yourself lucky that your horizons are expanding.'

'They're boring. They tell boring stories. There are no kids around and that last pub served us spaghetti out of the can warmed up. I'm going to puke and I have a headache,' I complained.

'You should get sun-shades for your glasses. Like these ones I'm wearing,' he said, glancing over to me.

'You look like a CIA agent with them on.'

'CIA agents don't go around looking after seventeen-year-old pests who think they're smart enough to rule the world,' he said drily.

'Well, they spent eight years looking after a seventy-year-old geriatric who thought he was smart enough to rule the world.'

'And you could do a better job, I suppose?'

'Naturally.'

I stuffed four Lifesavers in my mouth, trying to avoid car-sickness, and sat back in sufferance.

'So how was Jake when you rang him?'

'Jacob,' I corrected. 'He's fine.'

Michael met him when he came to pick me up from the Chambers. I'm not sure what he thinks of Jacob, but he keeps on asking me what Mama thinks of him and interrogates me frequently on what kind of person Jacob is. Mama's first impression of Jacob has changed. He came over for dinner the other day and washed the plates. The way to my mother's heart is through housework, so Jacob's a hit.

'He told me to call him Jake the other day when he rang for you at the office. We had quite a friendly chat after I told him he isn't to disturb you at work again.'

'Oh, did you? What did you talk about?'

'Cars. If you know anything about the engine of a car Jake will like you.'

'Wrong. I don't know anything about the engine of a car and he likes me.'

'Ah, but you're smart and physically attractive. Of course he likes you.'

I laughed aloud, turning to him and grinning.

'Physically attractive?'

'Good-looking definitely. Like your mother at her age. Men have to beware.'

'Wow. Do I remind you of her back then?'

'She wasn't as rude as you and better looking, but she had the same disdainful air about her. Wouldn't look at me for weeks after I first tried to kiss her.'

'I wouldn't look at you either. You're not that great looking.'

'Oh, thanks a lot,' he said, looking wounded. 'If you'd like to know, you look more like me than people give you credit. You managed to look a bit like everyone.'

'Did you like her a lot?' I asked quietly.

He shrugged. 'I liked all girls back then and they all liked me,' he added with a mocking evil chuckle.

It was funny seeing this part of him. He was usually so straight and practical.

'Has she told you the story?'

'Not really. A few bits and pieces years ago.'

'Well,' he sighed. 'She lived next door to me ever since I could remember. Naturally she hated my guts and used to bash me up. Broke my nose once. Made my lip bleed. I think she was also the one who knocked out two of my teeth.'

'My sweet fragile mother? Surely you jest?'

'The very same. Of course this was when she was a foot taller than me and I led a terrorist gang in the street. Then one day I grew taller and she decided to become a lady and all the guys in the street fell in love with her. We called her Prissy Chrissy. We thought she was a snob, but she was only shy. Deep down, of course, I knew she secretly loved me.'

'Of course,' I mocked.

'She did,' he argued. 'We were fourteen and infatuated. Probably more mature than you are now.'

'Fourteen,' I scoffed.

'Uh-huh. Then, when we were sixteen I heard her crying in her garden shed while I was fixing my car on the other side of the fence. I asked her to come over and we sat in my garage and became best friends. She told me all her problems and I told her all mine.'

'What were her problems?' I asked.

'She was forever in trouble with your grandparents. God knows why, because she was such a perfect daughter. All I know is that she lived in the same house with a man who didn't talk to her and she couldn't understand why.'

'And your problems?'

'Maria Lucianni's mother. I danced with the girl at a wedding and her mother saw wedding bells. She'd come and visit my mother all the time bringing over stuff from Maria's glory box. If I'd married Maria, Josie, I would be sleeping on purple satin sheets.'

'Imagine waking up to them with a hangover,' I said, feeling green at the thought. 'So you became friends?' I added, wanting to get back to the subject of my mother.

'The very best. She forgot she was shy and I remembered that I had a crush on her and we became pals. Over the next few months it kind of changed. We became closer . . . and then we went into something we shouldn't have.'

He took his eyes off the road and looked at me gently.

'We can look at it now, Josie, and say that you were a result of it, so it had to be worth it, and we can never regret you as long as both of us live, but it was a thing that we couldn't handle. Kids shouldn't play grown-up games. I don't mean having the baby bit either, because I wasn't around for that so I don't know how hard it was. I mean the sex bit. It was a whole new ball game for me, because I was involved emotionally and not just physically. What we did made her feel so ashamed and me so inadequate. I wasn't making her feel good as far as I was concerned, so I hated her. When I think of it now, very few men know how to make teenage girls feel good emotionally as well as physically. They always lack something. It comes with practice.'

'Not what I've heard. Boys are at their sexual peak at seventeen. Women at thirty,' I said informatively. 'I've got thirteen years to practise. You're definitely over the hill.'

'Brat.'

I dug into my bag and took out some chocolate. When I feel car-sick I eat, but I knew that sooner or later I would feel like throwing up from all the food I was consuming.

I looked out the window again and was met with the same scene and same feeling. Tree stumps. Bush. A road with two lanes. A radio that didn't work because we were between transmissions. Heat that didn't seem normal in the middle of winter. Boredom.

'Do you have a girlfriend?'

'Yes, I do.'

'Hmm,' I said, the boredom vanishing. 'Are we going to visit her?'

'No, *we* are not going to visit her. *I* may visit her.'

'Hmm. What does she do for a living?'

'She's an accountant.'

'Hmm. What a pity. I would have liked to meet her. We could be great friends.'

He looked at me distrustingly. 'You sound really sincere,' he said sarcastically.

'She'd have a nervous breakdown being my stepmother.'

'I'm sure you'd try your hardest.'

'My mother is going out with a doctor.'

'How interesting,' he said in a bored tone.

'An Italian one.'

He looked at me for a second and somehow I was kind of pleased with his reaction.

'Great-looking guy. I adore him.'

Okay, slight exaggeration. She's gone out with him once and I threw the meatloaf down the sink when I found out, but my mother has had men after her for years.

'I like you better. You're "good people" as Zio Ricardo would say.'

He looked over at me and smiled so beautifully that I began to fall in love with the idea of this man being my father.

'If I had to choose a daughter, I would have chosen you.'

I was touched because I knew, especially after our first few meetings, that I was a bit hard for him to take.

'I have that effect on people,' I said in mock modesty.

He laughed and reached over to touch my face.

'You're a good girl, Josephine.'

'No. I'm a nice girl. There's a difference between "good" girls and "nice" girls.'

'Ambiguous meanings?'

'Yep.'

I offered him some of the chocolate and he shook his head.

'You're making me sick. Don't eat any more, Josie.'

'If I eat, I don't have to concentrate on this shit scenery.'

'Sit back and get some sleep.'

'Oh, great. So if we have an accident and I'm asleep my resistance towards fighting death will be down and I'll wake up in a morgue.'

'I won't say the obvious,' he said, shaking his head.

'Jacob told me that. Says that I should never read in the car either.'

'We'll be in Broken Hill soon, so get your clothes out if you want to shower.'

'How could people live out here? I never could.'

'You might have to one day.'

'But I won't.'

'Maybe you'll marry someone from out here.'

'So,' I shrugged, 'he can come and live in Sydney.'

'You'll want to compromise.'

'No, I won't,' I said frankly. 'I'll never do anything I don't want to do.'

He growled, opening the sun roof.

'One day you'll understand, Josie.'

'You sound like Mama,' I said, standing up through the sun roof.

'Get down,' he shouted.

'I love a Sunburnt Country . . .' I recited.

'I detest that poem, Jose.'

'A land of sweeping plains . . .'

I spent the rest of the hour reciting poetry to him,

just to see how much he could take and discovered just how much of Michael Andretti I had inherited.

■

We arrived in Adelaide three days after we left Sydney. I loved it on sight. The houses were absolutely gorgeous with the most enormous front yards. Michael's flat was in a suburb near the beach called Glenelg. It was on the third floor so we could see the water and no matter how cold it was at night it was just fantastic sitting on the balcony drinking Milo and just looking out.

I must confess, though, that I did have pre-conceived ideas of what my holiday would be like. I imagined how my paternal grandparents would react. Maybe they'd hug me and cry and say that I looked exactly like Michael. But they didn't. Michael had told them about me only a month ago so it all seemed too unbelievable for them.

But I adored being with Michael. Finding out what he was like was great. I mean who really gets to know their parents as strangers first?

He's more of a fool when he's relaxed. Tells the corniest jokes and hates all modern music, except Billy Joel. He doesn't believe in commercial TV (*Four Corners* is his favourite program). He also doesn't know how to cook so we lived on takeaway for two weeks.

It was weird living in the same flat as a man too, because I've never been under the same roof with one. I mean I'm not used to someone leaving the toilet seat up in the middle of the night, or seeing men's undies, or whatever they're called, hanging on the clothes-line. Kind of weird. I just noticed the other day that you can buy the ones with Y-fronts, and others that are just normal.

But the best thing about living with him was that he

snored. Remember how I said that night-time scares me a lot because I feel as if everyone could be dead? Well, just being able to hear Michael snoring made the night-time sound so alive. Sometimes I'd just lie in bed grinning. I'm not sure why. Maybe because I really felt as if I had a father. I didn't realise how much it would mean to me.

As for his family, well, Paulina, his sister, took me shopping one day and I ate at her place that night. She has three children who were all over me like a rash. It felt great to have first cousins. I think, by the end, my grandparents half-heartedly accepted me. Paulina took me over one day and the kids brought out some photo albums.

My grandfather pointed everyone out. He was pretty rapt that I spoke Italian and told me I should keep on with it and at one stage my grandmother pointed my mother out in a photo of all of them down at Cronulla beach in the sixties.

Mama was tall and skinny and Michael was short and looked like a devil.

So by the end of my stay we had formed some kind of relationship, although my grandmother still tended to speak to me via Paulina as if I didn't understand. Maybe I do understand how they felt. Just a tiny bit. All in all I missed my mother heaps and was glad to be back with her.

She lets me go out with Jacob now, on weekends, but I have to be home by eleven-thirty. How embarrassing. On Saturday night he told me never to go anywhere again because he'd missed me.

We've only been together for a short time, but I feel as if I've known him for years. The same with Michael. I feel as if I've known him for years too. It kind of makes me glad that God didn't take me up on my 'I'd rather die than meet my father' statements.

18

This year is going by so fast. It's already more than halfway through and I still feel unsettled. I always thought that I'd start university with a fresh mind and no problems. I thought it would be the beginning of a new life. But it's six months away from university and things are just more confusing because of Jacob, and I still have hang-ups.

I've come to terms with the fact that Poison Ivy, one of my greatest hang-ups, and I are never going to be bosom buddies and Friday really put the lid on things.

Both of us were reading the same paper while we were waiting for Sister Louise in her office. One of the stories was re-hashing the funeral of an Italian businessman who was supposedly murdered.

'You new Australians wear black a lot, don't you?' she asked, looking at the picture.

'New Australians?' I asked incredulously. 'Me? A new Australian?'

'Yes.'

She had the audacity to look surprised at my outburst.

'How dare you call me a new Australian.'

'You're Italian, aren't you?'

'I'm of Italian descent, thank you,' I snapped. 'And I'm also two months older than you, if my records are right, so if anyone is a new Australian you are because you're two months newer than me.'

She rolled her eyes and shook her head. 'You know what I mean. You're an ethnic.'

'I'm not an ethnic,' I spat out furiously. 'I'm an Australian and my grandparents were Italian. They're called Europeans, not ethnics. Ethnic is a word that you people use to put us all in a category. And if you'd really like to know, Ivy, the difference between my ancestors and yours is that mine came out one hundred years after yours and mine didn't have chains on their feet. They were free and yours weren't.'

'Your ancestors were on the German side in World War Two,' she yelled. 'They probably killed my grandfather and John's grandfather. They were friends during the war.'

'My grandfather and uncle were in a labour camp in Adelaide so I doubt very much that they killed your grandfather or John's.'

'Well, one of your other thousand uncles could have. My grandmother had to bring up ten kids all by herself.'

'All Italian families don't have one thousand members, and my grandmother had to fend for herself in a country where she didn't know the language and the people were ignorant.'

'She should have learnt the language then.'

'Well, maybe she didn't have a chance and your grandmother should have said no to your grandfather more often so then she wouldn't have been stuck with ten children. Anyway, I'm sure she would have had *John's* grandmother to help her.'

'I'm sure John would be very unamused about you being glib about his grandfather's death.'

'I don't think John gives a damn, Ivy. I don't think he gives a damn about anything.'

'Oh, you think you know him so well, Josie? What are you hoping to achieve by assuming you know him so well?'

'You may have known him all your life, Ivy, but I think that I know how he feels a bit more than you do.'

'Don't presume that you know anything about my relationship with John. It's deeper than you think.'

Sister interrupted us at that point and gave us a funny look because we were both sulking. But I'm past the caring stage with Sister Louise. She doesn't like me, so big deal. But I thought it was just like Poison Ivy to consider me a new Australian. I wonder if Jacob thinks of me as one. Or his family.

I think if it comes down to the bottom line, no matter how smart I am or how much I achieve, I am always going to be a little ethnic from Glebe as far as these people are concerned.

Do you know how frustrating it is? Why can't these people understand that this is my country as well? Why do I feel like cursing this country as much as I adore it? When will I find the answers and are there ever going to be answers or change?

It was a great relief seeing Jacob that afternoon when he picked me up from work at the Chambers. I needed to be reassured by his presence, to know that he accepted me. He bent down and kissed me in the lift, but stopped when the doors opened.

'Close your eyes,' he said, as he dragged me outside.

'What are you doing? Everyone will see us.'

'I got a surprise for you.'

'I've got a surprise for you,' I corrected.

'You mean you've got a surprise for me too?' he asked astonished.

'No,' I said, shaking my head. 'It's "I've" not "I".'

'Whatever,' he said, with an irritated wave of his hand. 'I've got a surprise for you.'

'What is it?'

'If I tell you, it's not a surprise, dummy, so guess.'

'Give me a clue.'

'It's roomy,' he said, kissing me. 'It's got windows,' he added, hugging me hard. 'And it hasn't got bucket seats,' he yelled, lifting me up and swinging me around.

'A car,' I screamed, oblivious of those around me.

We ran down the steps of the court house to where an old, metallic-blue Holden was parked.

'Someone dumped it at Darren's garage a couple of weeks back so we put in a new engine, played around with it for a while and gave it a paint job.'

'No more motor bike?' I asked, looking at the interior.

'I'm still keeping it, but you never have to ride on it again,' he said proudly. 'So what do you think, Lady Josephine?' He bowed.

I curtsied and laughed. 'My lord Jacob, I am indeed overwhelmed,' I said, fainting dramatically into his arms.

Michael came rushing down the stairs like a mad man. 'What happened to her?' he asked, grabbing me from Jacob.

'It's a joke, Michael.'

Both Jacob and I laughed hysterically.

'Bloody kids. What's so funny?' he said.

'Jacob's got a car, Michael. Isn't it fantastic? He did it all himself.'

'A Holden. I have a passion for Holdens,' he said, looking at me wickedly. 'Conceived my one and only child in one.'

He walked away, leaving me spluttering.

'How grotesque,' I groaned. 'How could he discuss that in the open?'

'I think it's wildly erotic actually,' Jacob said, looking at Michael as he walked away. 'Your mother and him in a Holden making the great Josephine Alibrandi. For all you know, it could be this Holden.'

'It could've been a Merc. Do you think my life would have been different if I'd been conceived in a Merc?'

He laughed and unlocked the door, letting me in.

'You should have seen it, Jose,' he said, like an excited boy. 'It was a pile of crap and I put it together.'

'Well, whoever said you couldn't? I myself have always thought you to be a genius.'

'Yeah?' he asked, blushing.

'Yeah.'

He kissed me gently on the mouth before he started the ignition.

'I'm good with my hands, Josie,' he said, looking at them. 'I might not be a great university scholar, but I'm good with my hands. You're different. You're good with your head.'

'Well, with my head and your hands we could be famous,' I said, taking hold of his hands and kissing them. 'We could go into partnership.'

'What would a fancy barrister want with a mechanic in business?' he asked solemnly.

'Tons of things,' I said excited. 'We could form a company. I'd be the theory part of the business and you'd be the practical.'

'Yeah, we could be the first husband and wife . . .'

He stopped suddenly, realising what he had just said.

'Forget I said that,' he muttered, taking out a cigarette.

I folded my arms and sent him a quick look. 'I think you'd be a lovely husband.'

He sneaked a look over to me and shrugged. 'Bet you'd be good with kids and all.'

We laughed and hugged each other before he let go and began to drive.

'Know what?'

'What?' he asked.

'I'm glad it hasn't got bucket seats.'

'I would never have fixed it up for us if it did.'

I moved across the bench seat and squeezed in closer to him and hugged his arm and at that moment, that very second, I pictured myself with Jacob Coote for the rest of my life.

19

Tomato day.

Oh God, if anyone ever found out about it I'd die. There we sat, last Saturday, in my grandmother's backyard cutting the bad bits off over-ripe tomatoes and squeezing them.

After doing ten crates of those, we boiled them, squashed them, then boiled them again. That in turn made spaghetti sauce. We bottled it in beer bottles and stored it in Nonna's cellar.

I can't understand why we can't go to Franklin's and buy Leggo's or Paul Newman's special sauce. Nonna had heart failure at this suggestion and looked at Mama.

'Where is the culture?' she asked in dismay. 'She's going to grow up, marry an Australian and her children will eat fish and chips.'

Robert and I call this annual event 'Wog Day' or 'National Wog Day'. We sat around wondering how many other poor unfortunates our age were doing the same, but we were sure we'd never find out because nobody would admit to it.

His grandmother and mother and father and brothers and sisters came over as well and we all sat around like Sicilian peasants. My Zio Ricardo had a hanky on his head with each of the four sides tied in a knot. By the end of the day all the little kids had the same type of head-piece.

'We have been doing this for over forty years, Guiseppina,' my Zia Patrizia told me, wiping her hands on a polka-dot apron (the same apron as every other woman in the yard because my second cousin Rita had once bought ten metres of material on sale).

Nonna and Zia Patrizia were sitting side by side, beaming at me. They look very similar except Zia Patrizia isn't as vain as Nonna and has done nothing about her greying hair. I looked over to where Mama was with Zio Ricardo wishing she would look my way. I wanted her to save me from Zia Patrizia and Nonna Katia. From their reminiscing and gossip.

'Remember the year Marcus Sandford helped us, Katia? An Australiano squeezing tomatoes wit us.'

'Marcus Sandford?' I asked, looking at Nonna. 'He came back on the scene?'

'Who's Marcus Sandford?' Robert asked, wiping his hands on my T-shirt.

'He was an Australian policeman who helped Katia and me when Nonno Ricardo and your Zio Francesco were in camp.'

'What camp?' Robert asked.

'During the war Zio Ricardo was working with Nonno Francesco in the sugar fields so I had to look after Patrizia because she was pregnant again,' Nonna explained to us.

'One day,' Zia Patrizia interrupted, 'they came with the truck. They started from the north of Queensland and drove down. They took every Italian man. Even the boys. It was because of that bastardo Mussolini.'

'Aliens, they called us,' Nonna Katia said. 'They caught Francesco in the first truckload, but it took them days to find Zio Ricardo.'

'Ah, *Madonna mia*,' Zia Patrizia said, waving the knife in her hand around. 'We cried and cried. What were we going to do, we asked ourselves? Where is Ricardo? Is he dead?'

She was fanning herself and Robert patted her hand.

'It's okay, Nonna, you know he's not dead. Don't get worked up.'

We exchanged looks, grinning at their theatrics.

'An Australian family down the road was hiding him,' Nonna tried to get in before Zia Patrizia. 'Zio Ricardo was one of the very few Italians who went out and mingled wit the Australians. He learned the language and demanded that everyone spoke it. Nonno Francesco refused to and wouldn't let me learn, but Zio Ricardo was strong and taught Patrizia, so she taught me during the day.'

'Did they ever find him?' Robert asked.

'Ah, *Dio mio*,' Zia Patrizia prayed.

Robert and I rolled our eyes again.

'He snuck around during the night to be wit us, but one day those people next door, Turner . . . Thompson, whatever their stupid name was, they told on him. If I saw them today I would spit on their faces.'

They both swore in Italian, agreeing with each other.

'There we were, Giuseppina, two defenceless women on our own. Me, wit one little boy and a baby on the way. Katia wit her garden ruined because nobody could look after it. We had no money. Snakes came into our house, Roberto, snakes!'

'So one day I said, enough is enough,' Nonna butted in whipping her hands in the air dramatically. 'I went to speak to the army.'

'We all were hysterical,' Zia Patrizia said. ' "No, Katia" we pleaded. The other Italian women went crazy. We thought that the army was going to come around and take us or our children next, but Katia said "enough".'

'I thought that maybe if I spoke to someone they would feel sorry for us and send us back one man. Maybe all our husbands.'

'But they didn't,' Zia Patrizia hissed. 'So she is walking out and this big tall Australiano stops her. "Katia?" he says. We all look at her. How could Katia know this man?'

'It was Marcus Sandford,' Nonna giggled to me. 'He was in the army. It had been two years since I had seen him. He was pleased to see me. Pleased that my English was better and when he heard about our problems he did all he could to have one of the men released. But it was impossible. All he could do was reassure us that they were treated well. But we didn't want reassurance. We needed an extra pair of hands.

'So Marcus Sandford became our extra pair of hands. He squeezed the tomatoes wit us, he helped us grow our spinach, he fixed the garden, everyting.

'But the other women,' Nonna Katia groaned. 'Remember, Patrizia, Signora Grenaldo? Talk talk talk. "What is a man doing in Katia Alibrandi's house?" she would ask. Stickybeak.'

'But we did not care. It was all innocent,' Zia Patrizia defended. 'He helped us. He loved my little Roberto and he even helped deliver your Zio Salvatore, Roberto.'

'Is little Roberto the one who died?' I asked.

They both made the sign of the cross and kissed their fingers.

'Oh, my *gioia* Robertino. I still cry for him, Katia. I still cry.'

'One day when we couldn't find him, everybody started looking. Italian, Australian, Spanish . . . everyone,' Nonna Katia said. 'For one whole day we looked for little Robertino. Marcus? He never stopped.

'Even the Australian women came around with tea and sandwiches while we prayed and cried. Later that night while we sat on the verandah watching the search-lights through the trees, Marcus walked through holding someting in his arms. He was crying. I was crying. Patrizia was crying. We walked towards him looking at what he had in his arms.'

'It was my little Robertino. He had drown in the creek,' Zia Patrizia said quietly.

'He put Robertino in my arms, still crying.'

'And I yelled and yelled,' Nonna Katia said, looking at Zia Patrizia. 'Screamed wit such anger. I blamed Marcus Sandford. I blamed this country. If the men hadn't been away we would have been able to see what Roberto was doing, but we were too busy being the men of the house because the Australians had our men in their camps.'

'Everyone in the town came to the funeral. Remember, Katia? But we never saw Marcus Sandford again.'

I looked at Nonna Katia but she turned away. Somehow I doubted that she never saw him again.

'Enough of old stories. How about you, Giuseppina? Do you have a boyfriend?' Zia Patrizia asked me.

'I've got one hundred boyfriends, Zia,' I said, kissing her, picking up the tub full of tomatoes and taking them to where Mama and Zio Ricardo were.

Like all tomato days we had spaghetti that night. Made by our own hands. A tradition that we'll never let go. A tradition that I probably will never let go of either, simply because like religion, culture is nailed into you so deep you can't escape it. No matter how far you run.

20

On the 29th of July, we celebrated St Martha's day by having our annual walk-a-thon. It's one of those events I hate with intensity.

The excitement of seeing the nuns in Reeboks left me in Year 8 and the only thing we enjoy about it these days is being able to wear what we like.

I did the usual rounds with my family on Sunday and managed to collect one hundred dollars for Amnesty International, then on Monday morning we sat in the auditorium listening to Sister Louise give out the same instructions, crack the same jokes and make the same threats as she did the year before.

I think it was the effect of trying to organise five hundred students that allowed me to be hijacked by Sera with only a whimper.

'Trey Hancock is in Sydney,' she said as the last students set off. 'He's staying at the Sebel Town House.'

Trey Hancock is the lead singer of a band called The Hypnotists. He's from the States and is the most gorgeous guy in the world.

'Why is she telling us this?' I asked Lee.

'Oh for God's sake, Josie. Do you want to spend the rest of the day looking after those idiots?'

'Where did you hear that Trey Hancock was in Sydney?' Anna asked.

'Molly Meldrum hinted it in *TV Week* and my cousin works at the Sebel and said she saw him.'

'And the word was made scripture,' I said sarcastically.

'Well, I'm going,' Sera said, pulling up her black tights in the middle of the road.

'Sister will chuck.'

'Sister, Sister, Sister,' she mimicked. 'God, Josie, live dangerously. You'd think she appointed you God or something.'

Lee shrugged and looked down the road where the others were disappearing.

'I suppose it'd be better than being the tail end of a walk-a-thon,' she said.

'I know it would be better, Lee, but I can't. I have to supervise.'

'Who's going to be checking up on you, Jose?' Anna said. 'Could you imagine if we saw Trey Hancock? Could you imagine if we spoke to him?'

'I've got a camera,' Sera said, taking it out. 'Could you imagine if we got a photo of him?'

'Who's going to guide those who get lost or are too slow,' I continued to argue. 'I have to stay behind all the students.'

'Oh, great job, Jose. You should be proud of it,' Sera said sarcastically. 'That means this walk-a-thon will take us about two hours more than everyone else.'

'It is a bit of a shit job, Josie,' Anna said. 'Ivy's leading it.'

A bus came towards us and before I knew what was happening the four of us jumped on it, giggling all the way to the back.

'If I see him, I'm going to jump all over him,' Sera said, taking out her make-up bag.

'*Duck*,' Lee said, pulling me down. Still laughing

hysterically we crouched on the floor of the bus, allowing Lee to peek out and tell us when the coast was clear.

The bus came to a stop and we looked at each other with dread, but still laughing.

'It's a crossing and half the school is crossing it,' Lee whispered, bursting into laughter.

'Oh my God, oh my God, oh my God,' Anna said, closing her eyes and trying to squeeze under the seat.

We sighed with relief when the bus took off again and sat back to enjoy the ride.

I'm not quite sure where we supposed we'd see Trey Hancock. Maybe in the foyer where he would introduce himself to us and take us to his room to discuss world peace.

We arrived at the Sebel Town House and not wanting to be seen, we took advantage of an open lift, rushing into it and hitting any number so the doors would close.

The Sebel Town House accommodates a lot of movie and rock stars, so a group of teenagers walking around the place makes the hotel staff suspicious. We spent half an hour walking up and down corridors and I figured that if Sera's cousin worked there, she could at least have given us some hint as to where they were.

'C'est la vie,' Sera said on our way down in the lift, dancing around. She was teaching Anna to 'vogue', a way of dancing with your hands which Madonna had made famous.

I began to feel uneasy then. What if there was a roll call at one of the stops? What if the police were looking for four missing girls? What if my mother received a call from the school saying I was missing?

'How about we hang out in the bar? There's always supposed to be someone famous in this hotel bar,' Sera said, taking out her camera.

'Sera, in our jeans and anoraks we do not look over eighteen.'

'It's worth a try. Live dangerous, Jose.'

Anna grinned and Lee punched me playfully on the arm.

'It's better than being at a stupid walk-a-thon,' she said.

I agreed. It was better than being the tail end of a walk-a-thon. Did anyone appreciate that I had to lag behind because some people were slow? No. Then I didn't care either. When the doors opened we were blinded by lights and photographers. There were news cameras and people all over the place.

'Maybe they're here after all,' Anna said, excited.

I looked across the foyer and shook my head, trying to hide from the cameras.

'The Premier is here, dickheads. I suppose you think he's here to give Trey Hancock the key to the city?'

'Must be a press conference for something or other,' Lee said. 'We might see someone famous after all.'

Anna was smiling at the excitement around her and I wanted to slap her face.

'Guys, let's get out of here.'

'Let's get the Trey Hancock rock video and go back to my place. We'll order pizza,' Lee said.

The feeling of dread didn't leave me. No matter how much I told myself that there was no problem with what I had done and that nobody would find out, I couldn't enjoy the video. The others seemed to be relaxed and enjoying it all, but no matter how much pizza and how many Cheezels I consumed, I couldn't begin to relax.

I always wondered what I'd look like on television. My curiosity was sated that night. While the Premier shook hands with a delegate from China, the four of us became two-minute mega-stars. Sera was seen voguing around the foyer and Anna, dumb stupid Anna, even waved at the camera while the Premier gave his speech.

I prayed that nobody else would see us. I dedicated a whole decade of the rosary that the divine intervention of the Virgin Mary would break the television at the convent and in the home of every teacher.

But sure enough, while sitting in home room on Tuesday morning, four names were called out and I don't think I have to tell you whose names they were. Sister handed us back our sponsor sheets with such anger that I felt each sheet fan my face with the force of an air-conditioner.

She looked cold and mean and I wanted to remind her that she was a Christian, but I've learnt from the past that you don't try to teach Christianity to nuns and priests as they seem to think they have the market cornered.

'I want you to return any money you have collected and I want the signature of every person who sponsored you on this sheet after you explain to them what you did yesterday.'

'But, Sister, it's all for Amnesty International.'

'How dare you!' she snapped. 'Those students trusted you. I trusted you. Here I am thinking that all the girls are on a walk-a-thon. We promise your parents that we'll look after you and they trust us. Yet there you are on television with Sera making vulgar thrusting movements and God knows what with her hands around her face.'

'I was voguing, Sister.'

Sister Louise looked at us all with such disgust that I felt sick to the stomach. I think at that moment I would rather have been dead than disgusting.

'You'll come here every afternoon until four-thirty.

I'll have notes prepared for your parents. You will also be banned from any further school excursions for the rest of the term. You're all a disgrace. Get back to class.'

We looked at each other and turned to leave, but my disgrace had not yet stopped.

'Stay, Josephine.'

Lee pinched me as she walked out and I caught Anna's look of sympathy. When Sister wasn't looking, Sera vogued out of the room, and as serious as it all was, I wanted to laugh. We were alone for about three minutes before she looked up.

'Why do you do this to me?'

'I'm sorry, Sister.'

'You are not sorry, so don't insult my intelligence. Don't say things to me because you know they are what I want to hear.'

'I don't know what came over me, Sister. I know it was wrong.'

'I said not to insult my intelligence,' she gritted.

I opened my mouth to say something but stopped. I figured anything that came out of my mouth would insult her intelligence.

'I know what came over you. You decided to become a sheep for the day, Josephine. You weren't a leader. You were a follower. You'll never amount to anything if you can be so easily influenced.'

'I wasn't a sheep, Sister,' I said angrily.

'It was Sera's idea, wasn't it?'

She looked at me with such contempt that I wondered if anybody in this world would ever intimidate me as much as this woman did.

'No,' I lied.

'You are a prefect. Do you know what that means?'

'Yes.'

'What does it mean? Let me guess. It means you wear a badge and you feel important, right?'

'No,' I said irritated. 'It means I . . . I have responsibilities.'

'To whom?'

I looked down and then back to her.

'To the students.'

'Oh, you're responsible for the students are you? Like yesterday? How responsible were you yesterday, Josephine? I want you to tell me how responsible you were. There were twelve-year-old girls in that last lot, Josephine. Darlinghurst is a dangerous area. You were there to make sure nothing could happen to them. You were responsible.'

I swallowed and shrugged.

'I wasn't responsible yesterday.'

'Do you know what responsibility is, Josephine? If you don't, try following Ivy Lloyd around one day. That is responsibility.'

My blood boiled at the mention of Ivy's name.

'I'm just as responsible as Ivy, Sister. Yesterday was a one-off.'

'Ivy doesn't have "one-offs". She's responsible from the moment she walks into this school till the moment she walks out.'

Good for Ivy, I wanted to say.

'I made a decision late last year which I've regretted during this year, Josie, but now I know it was the right one,' she said. 'You were voted school captain but I gave the job to Ivy because I knew she'd do a better job.'

'What?' I shouted. 'Why?'

'Need you ask me that after yesterday?'

'I wouldn't have done what I did yesterday if I was school captain,' I said.

'Yes you would, Josephine, and that's what I was afraid

of. You and your friends are trendsetters. The girls look up to you. They copy what you do. They'll probably slap you on the back to congratulate you when you get back into class. I couldn't afford to have my school captain set such a bad example.'

'You're wrong. We're not trendsetters and they don't look up to us. They think they're more superior than us.'

'Believe that, if that's what you want to believe, but I can't have you being a leader, Josie. I'm thinking seriously of choosing another vice captain.'

'You can't do that,' I said standing up. 'It's the only thing I have going for me in this school.'

I was embarrassed because I was crying, but I didn't realise until then how much it meant to me to be a prefect.

'Things would have been so different for me if I was school captain,' I told her. 'I would have felt different. What did I do for you to take that away from me?'

'A lot, Josephine. There was that time you walked like an Egyptian up to communion in front of the bishop.'

A Sera dare.

'And the time you stood up at the Catholic Association's seminar and said the church stank with its rules on the IVF issue.'

'I said it sucked.'

'Yes, and you said it in front of the bishop.'

'I have the right to an opinion.'

'Yes, you do, but you're not the first person who ever had one, Josephine. You seem to think you are. You have to learn that sometimes you have to keep your mouth shut, because what you do reflects on this school and on me and others. They don't make you principal of a school because you're middle-aged and wear a habit.

You have to stop believing that your actions are always right and you have to remember that you aren't a leader because you're given a title. You're a leader because of what is inside of you. Because of how you feel about yourself. Having a badge saying you're school captain shouldn't have stopped you doing what you did yesterday. You should be able to do that on your own. Now go back to class and think about that.'

I walked out, crying all the way down the corridor and it wasn't until I got to the end that I stopped.

Trendsetters. Examples. School captain. Leaders. The words kept on running through my head and I began to see that maybe Sister wasn't lying.

Everyone loved Anna and everyone wanted to be Lee's friend and although Sera got on everyone's nerves she still managed to make people do the most incredible things and nobody ever called her a wog because she didn't give a damn.

And me? I was voted school captain. Socially we weren't as shitty as we thought we were. So I turned around and walked back into her room without knocking.

'I'm really sorry, Sister. Don't call me a liar because I do mean it.'

She looked up, no forgiveness evident in her eyes. 'I'm not here to make you feel good, Josie.'

'You're supposed to forgive me. You're a nun.'

'Priests have the authority to forgive, Josephine. Nuns don't.'

'So I go around with this sin on my soul for the rest of my life?'

'No, only until I think you mean it. Until I can trust you again. You have great potential, Josephine, but so do many others. It's up to you to use that potential.'

'I'm not a sheep,' I whispered.

'You were yesterday, Josephine.'

When I walked back into the classroom I did get pats on the back.

'Better than going on the dumb walk-a-thon,' everyone said.

'What I did was wrong,' I told them quietly.

'What's the big deal?' someone asked. 'Don't let her make you feel guilty.'

'One of the Year 7 kids could have been grabbed by a mad man. I was responsible for them. That's what the big deal was. I was wrong in what I did yesterday.'

I was wrong, I thought to myself. I honestly believed it. Not because Sister Louise told me or because she made me believe I was. I knew deep down that I was wrong and I think that my emancipation began at that moment.

21

John Barton rang me on Monday night. I didn't experience the same rush of excitement I would have felt a few months ago, but I was glad he called after all. He wanted to know whether I wanted to see *Macbeth* with him so we decided to go on Tuesday night because it was half price.

I was a bit worried that he would be depressed again, but when I saw his smiling face in front of the theatre I knew things were back to normal.

'You really scared me last time, you know,' I told him.

'I scare myself sometimes. Never listen to me when I'm depressed. It was the exams and all.'

'Isn't it freezing? I'm really getting sick of winter now,' I told him as we rushed into the movie theatre.

He smiled at me and shrugged.

'I'm really sorry about how I acted.'

'Don't worry. I go through failure periods as well. When that happens I think of all the things I can do that other people can't.'

'Like what?'

I thought for a moment and shrugged.

'Okay, I'll be the first Alibrandi to be eligible for university. I'll also be the first Alibrandi woman to have a say in how her life will turn out.'

He nodded as well.

'I've got one. I'm the only Barton who can play "Blowin in the Wind" on the recorder as well as "Peace Train".'

We laughed for a while and then discussed some movies which we had seen previously and I found that it was that which I liked about John Barton. We had the same interests. He knew what I was talking about when I mentioned books and movies and certain subjects. That was one area where I wasn't compatible with Jacob. We hated each other's taste in movies and he wasn't much of a literary fan.

'Ben Peters dropped out, you know. He couldn't cope. Imagine dropping out a few months before the HSC.'

'I can't believe it,' I said amazed. 'I'm surprised his parents let him.'

'I think he had some kind of nervous breakdown.'

'How sad,' I said, thinking of the boy. 'He was such a good student. Doesn't it scare you? Like not getting great marks in your HSC. The system changing and everything is a real worry. So many people aren't getting into the subjects they want and the aggregates are getting higher.'

John took off his coat and looked the other way.

'Let's not talk about careers and school marks. It's all I hear about at school and home.'

I thought he was going to go all strange on me again.

'Popcorn and a drink?'

'Twisties, thanks,' I said, looking around the complex.

My heart stopped for one single second when I found myself facing Jacob on the other side of the room. His arms were folded and he was looking at me furiously. I gave a small wave and walked hesitantly towards him.

'Hi, Jacob,' I said in a small voice.

'What are you doing here with him?' he asked.

'We're going to see a movie.'

'Oh, really. I would never have guessed that,' he said sarcastically. 'You know what I mean, Josie. What are you doing with *him*?'

'Jacob, he's a friend of mine, for God's sake. Because I'm going out with you doesn't mean I'm not allowed to go out with friends.'

'He's a guy for one. He's also someone you like and you could have told me you were going out with him. Why didn't you?'

Anton and a few of his friends walked up to say hello and then John joined us, and I desperately wanted to dig a hole and bury myself.

'John, you remember Jacob, don't you?'

'Yes, of course,' he said extending a hand politely.

'I thought you were going out with her,' one of Jacob's loud, uncouth friends said.

'Yeah, so did I,' he said looking at me.

Anton pulled the others away, leaving just Jacob, John and myself.

'John, can you just excuse us?' I asked.

'Don't worry John, I've got nothing to say,' Jacob said roughly.

'We're friends, Jacob. There's nothing to worry about,' John explained.

I looked at them both and sighed, not knowing what to do.

'Jacob, we'll talk about this after, okay?'

'I don't want to talk about anything after. What is this, Josie? What have you been doing for the last couple of months? Stringing me along?' he snapped.

'I think you should cool down a bit, Jacob,' John said practically.

'You don't really want to hear what I think you should do, John,' Jacob said.

'Well, I don't like the way you're talking to her. We decided to see this movie, way before you were on the scene,' John snapped, taking my hand.

Jacob pushed him back roughly. John, in turn, pushed him back gently. I don't know who got on my nerves more.

'Come on, Josie. You can't reason with him,' John said. 'He's probably drunk.'

Jacob grabbed him by the shirt and John pushed back viciously and I pulled him away as quickly as I could.

'John, I'll meet you by the door,' I said firmly.

They exchanged filthy looks and I had to tell John to go again before he walked away reluctantly.

'I can't believe you're taking it this way,' I said.

'Do you know how embarrassed I was, Josie? My friends have to listen to me go on about you every day and I come here and what do I see? My girlfriend with that wanker.'

'He is not a wanker,' I snapped. 'He's my friend.'

'See that girl over there,' he said, swinging me around and pointing to a tall red-haired girl wearing a black mini-skirt and looking like someone who could easily pass as a model.

'What about her?'

'Her name is Arianne and she goes to school with me and she's a friend. Now how would you react if just Arianne and me went to the movies?'

I looked at her and wanted to lie and say it wouldn't worry me. But I shrugged instead. 'I'd be angry,' I said quietly.

'You'd think I was fucking around behind your back, wouldn't you?'

I nodded. 'I didn't think you'd want to see the movie I'm seeing, Jacob, and John did. We arranged it ages ago. Before you.'

'What movie?'

'*Macbeth*.'

'Well, for your information, Miss Intellectual, we're studying *Macbeth* at school and that's what I'm going to see tonight, so never ever presume what I like and what I don't like.'

'Jacob . . .'

'Don't say anything, Josie. You talk too much.'

He walked away and I desperately wanted to cry, but then I remembered John standing by the door and walked towards him.

'Sorry about that.'

'I don't know what you see in him, Josie,' John whispered angrily. 'He's not your type.'

'If we all went out with people our type we'd be bored out of our brains.'

'Yeah, but just think one day of you being a barrister and he being a whatever he wants to be.'

'Mechanic,' I said quietly.

'How many barristers do you know married to mechanics?'

'I don't know many barristers.'

'Well, I do, Josie,' he said, taking my hand and giving the tickets to the guy at the door.

I don't remember how good a movie *Macbeth* was. I hardly heard a word of it. All I could think of was where Jacob was sitting. Wondering if it was over between us and I didn't want it to be.

All I could think of was all the mistakes I seemed to be making lately. I was angry with John as well. Not that it was his fault or anything but I felt that he was warning me away from Jacob, not because he liked me, but because he felt that future professionals shouldn't mix with future tradesmen. I began to realise that it didn't matter what others thought about what was right and wrong. It only mattered how you felt and personally I could be with anyone of any profession if their personality was like Jacob's.

When it was over we walked out and I tried to be enthusiastic when John began to rave, but I think he caught on because he seemed to be looking at me sympathetically.

'Don't worry. It's not the end of the world.'

I nodded and he kissed me on the cheek.

'We'll do this again, okay?'

'Of course,' I lied, knowing that I would never do this again if Jacob spoke to me.

'You're a good friend, Josephine. I feel good when I'm with you.'

'And I feel great when I'm with you, John. Don't ever change.'

We hugged each other and he walked out while I desperately looked around for Jacob. He eyed me as he was walking out and I waved, but he just walked past.

I waited until he parted with his friends and approached him, but I knew I would get nowhere by the look on his face.

'I'm sorry,' I said.

'Forget it.'

'Why is it that every time I apologise to someone these days they won't accept it?' I asked in frustration.

'Because you probably come across as insincere. You probably think that an "I'm sorry" is going to make you feel better,' he said angrily.

'I didn't realise.'

'You never do,' he said in a tired tone. 'You go about whinging and wailing about the way people treat you, but you never think about the way you treat people. I was hurt. But you wouldn't understand that, would you? You don't think that people like me get hurt.'

'Jacob, please . . .'

'Go home, Josie. Just go home,' he said walking away.

So I sat at the bus-stop because I didn't have enough taxi money and cried.

The lady next to me gave me a sticker that said 'Jesus Loves You' on it and I cried and told her that he didn't. I felt that my life was coming apart and it was nobody's fault but mine and just as I ran out of my last tissue and was using it, folded over and over again, I felt someone press a clean white hanky in my hand.

'It's been washed since last time.'

I sobbed into it and felt him put his arm around my shoulder.

'You drive me crazy, do you know that?' he sighed.

'I would never hurt you deliberately,' I sniffed.

He pulled me up and took me to where he had parked the motor cycle and sat me down, putting the helmet on my head and fastening it.

'Educate me. Is it the modern thing for a girl to go out with another guy while she's going out with me?'

'He is my friend, Jacob. That's the honest truth. I would never let him kiss me while I'm with you. But I've known and liked him for so long that when he asked me out I felt as if I had to for my sake. Haven't you ever liked a girl for so long? Someone who's the answer to the dreams you've dreamt for ages? Well, that's how I feel about John.'

'But what's his attraction?'

'He's smart and he talks . . . I can't even explain it. He speaks with such passion about things. You probably think that's for pansies, but John is a good person. He believes in what the next person is saying and he gives them a chance.'

'I think that you like being with people like him so if they accept you, you can be one of the beautiful people. The elite of the community. Why can't you be just you?'

'I am me. But I'm human. Not a stone. I can be influenced by different things. Is that a crime? You're so . . . I don't know. You don't have any hang-ups or anything. You've found your niche in life and you're happy there and you presume everybody who's looking for something else is a try-hard or a pansy or pretentious. Be thankful that you've found your place, but be patient with me for still looking for mine.'

He sighed and got onto the bike. I got on behind him and when I wrapped my arms around his waist he picked one up and kissed it.

'We have so much to teach each other, Josie.'

'But isn't it a step that we're willing to learn? Wouldn't it be terrible if either of us wouldn't budge?'

He nodded and turned around.

'Will you do me a big favour?'

'Yes.'

'Will you go to see *Macbeth* with me on Saturday night? I didn't hear one word of it tonight.'

I laughed and nodded.

'Nor did I.'

I closed my eyes, leaning my head across his back, feeling more for him every moment that went by.

22

Mama and I decided on a splurge the first Sunday in September. A day when we do just that. Splurge. Break the budget. Stuff ourselves. And celebrate the start of Spring.

We decided on one of the harbourside restaurants and although the weather outside was cool, it wasn't wet enough to ruin the view.

I like the harbour on a cool day. The waters look as if they have character, as if they are going through their own turmoil. It looks almost human, unlike its perfection on a summer's day.

'This has to be the most beautiful city in the world,' I said looking around.

'Says the expert after she's just seen her only other city,' Mama said drily.

'I liked Adelaide,' I defended. 'It has lots of character and the most beautiful houses, Mama. We could be living in decadence compared to the crazy prices they have here. Michael says that the rent here is killing him, but it's no use buying something because he'll be going back to Adelaide next year.'

'Really.'

'He's not talking to me at the moment, by the way. Ever since I had to get him to sign the walk-a-thon sheet he's gone on and on about it. He reckons he's disgusted with me. If I have one more person disgusted with me, I'll slit my wrists.'

'Remind him about the incident with him wagging school to see the Rolling Stones one day,' she laughed.

'Just wait till I see him.'

'I'm so happy that you're getting to know him, Josie. I was scared you'd both reject each other and that would have been so sad,' she said, handing me the menu.

I shrugged.

'He's ultra-cool, you know. Not cool as though he drives a sports car and dresses trendy, but he's a cool guy. He's up front. No bull.'

'Take things slowly, and they'll work out.'

'I'm surprised, you know,' I told her. 'I thought you'd be possessive and jealous and wouldn't let me near him and all that jazz. I would have respected your wishes if that had been the case.'

'You would not,' Mama laughed. 'Anyway, he poses no threat to me when it comes to you. You're old enough to make your own decisions although if you come to me next year and tell me that you want to go live in Adelaide I'll shoot you through the eyes.'

'Shucks. Cross that one off my list,' I said with a laugh.

The waiter came along and we ordered lunch, laughing along with him as he tried his Italian out on us.

'I wish we could do this every week,' Mama said with a sigh. 'I would have liked to have given you more out of life, Josie.'

'Mama, you sound as if one of us is dying, for God's sake. I grumble about my life because I'm selfish, not because you couldn't provide. For a one-parent family we are pretty perfect.'

'Perfect?'

We both laughed.

'Well, you are anyway. Michael told me a bit about when you guys were young. He said you were sexy.'

'That's because he was a sex-crazed young man when I knew him. He was very smug. Girls were crazy about him and mothers adored him and wanted him for their daughters. He seemed to breeze through life with no problems.' She looked sad and pensive and I wondered really if she had ever got over him. 'Except I was a problem. You and I. He should have had the guts to deal with it. I was sixteen years old, Josie, and I was so scared when he left me to face my father. My father was the most terrifying thing in my life.'

'Why did Nonno treat you like he did?'

She shrugged.

'I don't think he really loved me and I always wondered why. I don't think he loved Nonna either, but she was such a good wife to him. She never took anyone's side but his. It was as if she owed him something, but I can't understand what. She was beautiful. It wasn't as if she was ugly and nobody else would marry her.'

'You never talk much about him.'

She gave me quick smile.

'I used to pray at night that Zia Patrizia and Zio Ricardo were my parents, but then I'd feel as if I was betraying my mother. No matter what, I know she loves me in her own way. The trouble is that she feels guilty about it.'

'I'd love to marry someone like Zio Ricardo. He sounded so romantic when he was young. Nonna's told me stories about them all.'

'He couldn't take me in when I was pregnant with you. My father wouldn't have let my mother see her sister again if he did. But he let Robert's mother take me in, saying that he couldn't govern who his daughter let into her house.' She looked pensive. 'My father practically spat at me. Called me every name under the sun. A tramp, a slut. He hit me across the face and even hit my mother. Worse still, he never saw you, Josie. Never saw his own granddaughter. Tell me, what comes first? What other people think of your family, or love?'

'You went through so much for me, Mama, and I never seem to appreciate it, but I promise that I'm changing.'

'Oh, Josie,' she sighed. 'I'm not telling you this to make you feel guilty. You are the most important person in my life. You are the only person who really loved me properly. Everyone else I've ever loved has hurt me. Michael Andretti broke my trust. My mother has always held back and my father never loved me in the first place. But you have never left my side and the disrespect you've shown me has been the disrespect any child shows her parent.'

'Oh God, Ma, if you go on any longer I'll have to go to confession next quarter with nothing to confess because I'll believe I'm a paragon of virtue.'

'We won't go that far.'

We ate lunch in semi-silence and decided to continue our splurge with ice-cream at Darling Harbour where we sat on the pier watching the activity around us. There was a jazz band playing and further along a busker was doing a comedy act, grabbing people who were walking by to assist him. Everyone seemed to be enjoying themselves and basking in the atmosphere.

'Michael has a girlfriend,' I decided to tell Mama.

'Really.'

'But he didn't sleep with her while I was there. No way. I was with him every minute.'

'I hope you weren't snooping or driving him crazy, Josie.'

'Of course not. I just reckon he mustn't love her at all if he doesn't feel the need to make love to her. You said he was sex-starved when he was young.'

'I'm sure he's learnt how to control himself now. Maybe you should butt out of his affairs.'

'He really loved you once, you know,' I said watching for a sign on her face.

'Josie, life is not a *Mills and Boon* book. People fall out of love. People disappoint other people and they find it very hard to forgive. We both were so young and Michael having to move to Adelaide upset his life just as much as it upset mine. But we survived and we've both got on with our lives and we're different people. You're the only thing we have in common.'

'He calls me an "obnoxious creation".'

Mama tried to keep a straight face but failed.

'Let's go home, Miss Obnoxious Creation. We'll do Jane Fonda and ease our guilt about this splurge.'

'As if you need your guilt eased.'

So we went home and did the *Jane Fonda* exercise tape easing our guilt. But I just couldn't get the idea of Mama and Michael being together out of my mind.

I wish life was a *Mills and Boon*. The idea of them as a couple is nicer than the idea of them with other people. I almost feel optimistic, because I'm the very thing they have in common, and I know that I will always keep them together somehow.

23

I don't know what it is about nostalgia and the past that can make you feel so depressed, yet so drawn to it. Nonna seems obsessed with it. She'll talk about it constantly. Maybe when I'm her age I'll speak about my past constantly. I know that when I'm with my friends all we seem to say is 'Remember this and remember that'.

I guess it's the photos that I'm really drawn to. Mama always says that if we ever had a fire the first things she'd grab would be me and our photo albums. Because photos are a testimony that someone did live. A reminder of a past we may have loved or hated. A piece of our lives.

Nonna's photo of Marcus Sandford fascinates me. That look about him. The 1940s' Australian look. That he could today have wrinkles and be old seems unbelievable.

'He was in love with me,' Nonna told me quietly on Wednesday afternoon.

She didn't boast about it. Neither did she giggle.

I looked at her and nodded. 'Were you in love with him?'

'Don't be silly, Jozzie. I was married.'

'It's funny that this man in the photo exists more to me than Nonno Francesco did. I feel as if I know Marcus Sandford more.'

'I did see him again after Robertino died,' she said quietly.

'It was when Zia Patrizia and Zio Ricardo and the children moved to Sydney and during my last Christmas in Queensland. Zio found a building job. He was doing so well for himself that he wrote to Nonno and asked him to come down to work wit him. That way Patrizia and I could be together. Nonno had bought half of a sugar-cane farm by then and a lot more Italians and Europeans were being allowed into the country so North Queensland was full of Italians. I had no children, so I could work. I was secretary for the Italian cane cutters' organisation.'

'Did many Italian women work?'

'No, not really. Francesco left in November to go to work on a farm further north so we would have enough money to settle in Sydney and he came back in February and we went straight down. I was alone for four months.'

'You were alone for Christmas?' I asked horrified.

She nodded.

'Francesco couldn't afford to come home and then go away again. It was a very busy time. I was sad without Patrizia and the kids.'

'But you had Marcus as a friend.'

'But, Jozzie, it is not like friends of today that you can have over and nobody talks. Oh no. You could not be friends with Australian men. Not even Italian men. Women were friends with women,' she said with a definite nod of her head.

'One woman,' she whispered, (Italians are so used to bitching about people that they tend to whisper a lot even when the person is one thousand miles away or even dead) 'they talked about so much that she killed herself.'

I looked at her disbelievingly and she nodded solemnly.

'Just because of a bit of talk?'

'Talk could break you, Jozzie.'

'I wonder if those people who talk and mind other people's business go to hell,' I said.

She shrugged.

'He came to see me though. He said it would break his heart if I would leave. I could see it in his eyes. But I knew that if I stayed I would break my heart.'

'That's so romantic. I wonder if he ever married.'

She shrugged and told me more.

It was the time of the proxy brides. A number of Italians were married by proxy back then. Some to sweethearts they had left behind and wanted to bring out to Australia, and others to people they didn't know. Nonna told me horrible stories of men who sent their photos over to Italy and then when the girls got off the ship they would find themselves married to much older men who had deceived them with younger photos of themselves. Or else the Italian proxy wife would have too much fun on the ship coming over and arrive lacking something very important to the old-fashioned Italian male.

The stories, like most of the things Nonna has told me in the last couple of months, are really interesting. Stories of another way of life. Stories of another person who I know but I don't know. Katia Alibrandi, what happened to you?

Just sitting there patiently listening to her made me realise how much I had changed. I would have been bored by it all a year ago and because of my past feelings towards her, I would have ignored every word she said. Whereas I'm beginning to realise that my feelings are changing and we're establishing quite a good relationship. I like that a lot.

So Nonna found that the world had grown smaller. She moved to Sydney and lived with Zia Patrizia and the kids but after a while they bought a house in Leichhardt and that's where my father's family comes into it.

Leichhardt was at its prime in the 1950s. The gates of immigration had opened and relatives and friends from the same Italian towns found themselves bumping into each other in the streets of Sydney.

Communities started up: the Italians in Leichhardt spreading to Haberfield and Five Dock. The Greeks went to Newtown and Marrickville. A different Australia emerged in the 1950s. A multicultural one, and thirty years on we're still trying to fit in as ethnics and we're still trying to fit the ethnics in as Australians.

I think my family has come a long way. The sad thing is that so many haven't. So many have stayed in their own little world. Some because they don't want to leave it, others because the world around them won't let them in.

So with all this information I've gathered from Nonna and Mama, who was a child of the sixties, I'm going to try to remember it.

So one day I can tell my children. And so that one day, my granddaughter can try to understand me, like I'm trying to understand Nonna.

24

When I got off the bus on Thursday afternoon Jacob was waiting for me. He had his sports clothes on and his hair tied back in a little ponytail. When I looked down at my long uniform, black stockings and black shoes, starched blazer and conservative tie, I wondered if we'd ever find a niche together.

He wrapped his arm around my shoulder and waited till we were off Parramatta Road before he kissed me.

'You smell sweaty.'

'Soccer,' he explained.

'When I was in Adelaide I had to watch the soccer. My father is a fanatic. It's the only time I see him lose control.'

'You should see Anton. I think it's his European blood. He runs around hugging and kissing us.'

I laughed at the thought of Anton kissing another man.

'So how are things going with your old man? Does he still ask questions about me?'

'My father says you have sex on your mind,' I told him truthfully.

'And how does he know that?'

'Because he said at your age he had sex on his mind.'

Jacob laughed at that and kissed my ear. 'He's right about that.'

I felt embarrassed like I did every time Jacob expressed sexual tendencies towards me, which was quite often. But at the same time I felt great.

'He has a girlfriend, you know. I heard him speak to her on the phone yesterday,' I told him trying to steer the conversation along. 'I haven't met her but Michael says she's attractive, intelligent and well-spoken.'

'Worried?'

'Kind of,' I said, truthfully, looking up at him. 'He's going to go back to Adelaide next year. Just when we're beginning to get on really well. It'll never be the same. We'll become really stilted with each other and awkward. For the first time in my life I feel cheated by his absence.'

'You'll see him for holidays, Jose. I'll drive you down myself.'

'I think my parents are attracted to each other, Jacob. I mean I haven't seen them together a lot, but when they are together it's a look here and a look there. Michael even blushes.'

'Why shouldn't they be attracted to each other? They were once.'

'It's weird, I've never shared my mother with anyone. Could you imagine if she ever got married?'

'I can't believe you would never expect her to get hitched. I mean she's pretty hot for a mother.'

'My mother? Hot?'

'I'd go for her if I was in my forties.'

'Do I remind you of her?'

'God, no.'

'Thanks,' I said drily. 'Does that mean I'm not hot and you wouldn't look at me if you were in your forties and I was in my thirties?'

He shook his head, grabbing my arm and pulling me closer.

'You're different. You come across all tough and fearless while deep down you're a softy. She comes across a softy, whereas deep down she's tough and fearless. I mean a lot of single parents botch up and she didn't. In fact she did a great job.'

'Meaning I'm perfect.'

'Not quite,' he laughed.

I stopped outside the terrace and cursed.

'God, my grandmother is here.'

'So? I get to meet her finally.'

I shook my head against his shoulder. 'Not now, Jacob. Another time.'

He looked angry, folding his arms stubbornly. 'What's the big deal?' he asked.

'There's no big deal. I just haven't told her about you and we're beginning to get on. She'll be angry with both Mama and I.'

'You haven't told her about me?'

'She wouldn't understand why Mama's letting me out with someone she hardly knows.'

'What's wrong with that?' he asked exasperated, throwing his hands up in the air.

'It's not their way. I'm young as far as she's concerned. Girls just don't go out with anyone just for the sake of it.'

'You're seventeen, Josephine, not five.'

'My grandmother wouldn't understand, Jacob. Give it time. She was brought up in another time and place. I know it's hard for you to understand. It's hard enough for me.'

'No,' he said shaking his head and pushing me back. 'I understand what you're saying, Josie. If I was an Italian there wouldn't be a problem, would there? Or maybe if I was John Barton.'

'That's not true,' I shouted. 'Well, about John

anyway. Of course she'd understand more if you were Italian. That's the way older people think.'

'Let me meet her. You might be surprised.'

'Are you listening to me? It doesn't matter whether I'm seven, seventeen or seventy. She won't want me walking into the house saying "Meet my boyfriend". Jacob, she's been confiding in me so much lately. If I spring you on her she'll wonder why I haven't been confiding in her.'

'Why haven't you been confiding in her about it? We've been going out every weekend for the last month or two, Josie. Do I mean that little to you?'

'Give me time. I'm so unsure of things, Jacob.'

He shook his head in disbelief, turning away.

'You know something? I had no hassles in my life before I met you. Now everywhere I turn I face a brick wall. I'm always giving you time. I can't sleep with you because you need time. I can't meet your grandmother because you need time. What the fuck are you waiting for?'

'I knew it,' I shouted angrily. 'This is why it'll never work between us, Jacob. We live two different lives and you can't understand that. Why can't you understand my life? Things aren't as easy for me as they are for you. You can do whatever you please but I can't because there are some things that could offend people I love. You live with such freedom, Jacob. You live without religion and culture. All you have to do is abide by the law.'

'You think you're the first person to ever suffer. You think your life is so difficult. But it's *you* who makes it difficult. Break away from those rules, Josie. Make your own.'

'That's so easy for you to say and so difficult for me to do,' I told him quietly.

'I want to meet your grandmother,' he said stubbornly, looking up at the terrace.

'Why?' I said through clenched teeth. 'I had to drag you to meet my mother. Are you doing this to spite me?'

'If you introduce me to her I'll know you're not ashamed of me. Your grandmother is one of the most influential people in your life. I want her to know that I'm another person in that same life.'

'Not today, Jacob.'

He looked at me, nodding with rage.

'Then I can go back to my normal happy life again. Thank you.'

I watched him walk away, hating him so much for not understanding and yet when I thought about it again I couldn't understand it either. What was my hesitation? Maybe I was unsure about Jacob as much as I loved him? I knew Nonna would take one look at Jacob and be unimpressed with the way he dressed, the way he spoke and the way he didn't fuss. To girls my age Jacob is impressive. To grandmothers he represents the downfall of their granddaughters. I didn't want to go back to the way things were between Nonna and I, yet I didn't want to lose Jacob.

The next afternoon I went to his place. It was the first time I had done this and I was nervous about someone else answering the door and nervous about him answering it. I had no speech prepared. No feelings to express to him. I just didn't want us to be apart.

I had never walked through Redfern before. A lot of people looked at me because my uniform seemed out of place. They sat on their front porches watching me closely and because I was ignorant about them I was scared. Until I saw some girls my age. They were dressed in a uniform too and were sitting on a front step. They

could easily have been Lee, Anna, Sera and I. I smiled
and they smiled back.

He answered the door, still in his school uniform, and
looking as unaccommodating as I thought he would.

'Let's not be angry with each other, Jacob.'

'I'm angry with you, but I can't understand why you
could possibly be angry with me,' he said.

'Listen, be thankful that I swallowed my pride and
I'm here,' I said angrily, taking the wrong approach.

'Thankful,' he spluttered. 'Give me strength.'

'Can I at least come in?' I asked, trying to look past
him.

'No. I'm not ready to introduce you to my father.
I haven't told him about you. He could be offended that
I'm going out with a non-Australian.'

'Very funny.'

'But you understand, Josie. It's his way.'

'How can you mock what I was trying to say yesterday,
Jacob.'

'Oh, you were trying to say something constructive
yesterday, Josephine? I thought you were babbling as
usual.'

I stood looking at him with such anger.

'Forget it, Josephine. We'll both be happier. I can
associate with my kind and you won't have to put up
with some cultureless Aussie with no heart and soul.'

'Jacob, you have more heart and soul than anyone
I know,' I told him.

'Eh, what's going on out there,' I heard someone
shout.

I looked past Jacob to see a tall lanky man walking
down the hallway towards us.

'What's going on, eh? Are you shouting at this little
girl, Jacob?'

'Dad, this is Josie,' Jacob introduced me reluctantly.

'Josie? *The* Josie? Come in, come in. You're all he talks about,' he said taking my hand and pulling me in.

Jacob has inherited his father's eyes, but apart from that I didn't see any resemblance until he smiled. That twitching smile that is always followed by a mischievous grin.

'He's been dying for me to meet you,' he said with a wink.

I felt like such a bitch then, but I knew that I wasn't ashamed of Jacob. I just needed time before I introduced him to Nonna. In a way my fascination with Marcus Sandford was because he reminded me of Jacob. They both took an interest in women whose backgrounds weren't similar to theirs. They were both tolerant. I knew in my heart that Nonna would see that too.

I sat down in his kitchen while Mr Coote made a cup of tea.

'And what are you going to do with your life, Josie?'

I looked at Jacob and then his father and shrugged. 'I don't know.'

'She wants to do law,' Jacob snapped, eyeing me.

'Law? And you're wasting your time with this airhead,' he laughed, tugging Jacob's hair.

Jacob stood up and stormed out of the room and I ended up having afternoon tea with Mr Coote who treated me like a queen.

'Moody little bugger,' he said, tilting his head in Jacob's direction.

I smiled because I could imagine Jacob saying those words.

'No, it's me who puts him in those moods.'

He looked amused at that and shook his head.

'Naw, Jacob is different to others. He's aware of more around him. Of what he can and can't do.'

I nodded and put my tea-cup in the sink, asking him where Jacob's room was.

He was lying on the bed reading *Popular Mechanics*, flicking the pages and ignoring me.

I walked to his mantelpiece and saw a photo of his mother.

'She was pretty.'

'She was the most beautiful woman in the world. If she was alive I'd probably be a better person.'

I sat on the floor next to his bed and leaned against it.

'You're good enough, Jacob,' I whispered.

I lay there for a while and then I felt his hand on my hair. 'I'll take you home. It'll get dark soon.'

I sat up on the bed and put my arms around him, kissing him slowly. I felt his hand come up across my cheek and I realised that was what I loved about him. He was a loving person. His need to touch my face or hair made me feel closer to him than if we were making love.

'You've never made the first move before,' he said. 'I liked that you did.'

'I wish I could make you happy and me happy,' I whispered against him.

We lay down holding on to each other, touching each other's faces.

'I suppose your grandmother wouldn't understand this?' he grinned.

'We'd have to take her to the hospital because she'd have a cardiac arrest,' I told him soberly.

We both burst out laughing, holding each other as tightly as we could and I felt comfortable with the freedom he had. I would never have been able to do that in my home.

His hand came up under my school shirt and I felt calloused flesh rub against me. I was embarrassed. Just say he felt a bit of flab and it turned him off. I wished my skin felt like silk, just like the heroines in the novels. I wondered what he thought about the size of my breasts. But he didn't seem to care.

He pulled me on top of him and put an arm around my waist. I kissed his neck and it felt weird going over his Adam's apple, because it bobbed up and down. I felt his leg push itself between my legs and flinched.

'What's wrong?' he asked quietly.

'I just don't trust people who have bodies that change with their moods,' I told him, feeling his hand on my breast and cursing myself for wearing my worst bra.

'Well, then you'll never trust the opposite sex again.'

He unbuttoned his shirt and took my hand and I was surprised that he had hair on his chest. Jacob with his shirt off was white-skinned and bigger than I imagined and I leaned forward and kissed a clear patch on his chest.

He shuddered and it fascinated me that I could do that to him. When I think of it now I can't remember clearly what happened then, except that I was bolder than I ever imagined I would be and at one stage we kissed for so long that I felt my lip bleeding.

But then when his hands went up my uniform and I felt them between my thighs and I looked up to see a poster of a motor bike that said 'Get something between your legs' on it, I realised that I could be losing my virginity in Jacob's bedroom with his father in the other room, completely without thinking.

'No more, Jacob,' I said trying to catch my breath.

'Oh, come on, Josie. It'll be okay.'

'I just think we should stop now before we go too far.'

'What's wrong with going too far?' he asked, kissing my neck.

'A couple of things.'

He helped himself up on his elbows and looked down at me.

I felt his breath on my face.

'I've got something.'

'What?'

'Something to take care of things, dummy.'

I shook my head and pushed him away, trying to pull my skirt down.

'Look at me, Jacob. Look at us both. We're in our school uniforms. Your father is in the other room. My mother expects me home in five minutes. How romantic can this be?'

'Josie, we're going to sleep with each other eventually.'

I fixed up my blouse and sat up with my arms folded.

'Not today. Not now,' I said, not looking at him.

'Not ever. Is that what you're saying?' he asked angrily.

'We're going to have another fight, aren't we? God, Jacob, that's all we do.'

'Josie, I want to make love to you. I like you more than I've ever liked anyone in my life.'

'Liking doesn't give us grounds to have sex. I could get pregnant or catch AIDS or something.'

'I told you I've got something,' he yelled, exasperated.

'A condom is not going to solve all our problems, Jacob.'

'Do you plan on being a virgin for the rest of your life?'

'No. Until . . . maybe until I'm engaged. Or maybe when I'm twenty or something.'

'I'm going to throw up,' he said shaking his head. 'Now I've heard it all.'

'Well, what's wrong with that?'

'Welcome to the nineties, Josephine. Women don't have to be virgins any more.'

'No, you welcome to the nineties, Jacob! Women don't have to be pushed into things any more.'

'What is it? A prize or something?' he scorned.

'No. It's not a prize and I'm not a prize. But it's mine. It belongs to me and I can only give it away once and I want to be so sure when it happens, Jacob. I don't want to say that the first time for me was bad or it didn't mean a thing or that it was done in my school uniform.'

'But you're almost eighteen. You're old enough. Everyone else is doing it.'

'And next year someone is going to say to someone else "but you're only sixteen, everyone else is doing it". Or one day someone will tell your daughter that she's only thirteen and everyone else is doing it. I don't want to do it, Jacob, because everyone else is doing it.'

'How about let's do it because we want to. I want to anyway,' he said grabbing my hands together.

'But I don't know if I love you enough and I don't even know if you love me enough. We don't even love each other, Jacob.'

We lay there in silence until he nudged me.

'I do a bit, you know,' he said gruffly.

'You do what a bit?'

'You know. Like you . . . whatever . . . love you a bit.'

He seemed a bit flustered and I hugged him.

'I think I kind of love you too, Jacob.'

'I really missed you when you were in Adelaide that time and sometimes when I don't see you for a couple of days I think I'll go crazy,' he said honestly, looking at me as if he needed for me to understand.

'I missed you too.'

'I won't push for it any more, okay,' he sighed. 'We'll stick to clever conversation.'

I laughed and hugged him hard.

'A bit of this and that won't hurt.'

'Yeah, it won't hurt you,' he said drily. 'It'll drive me bloody crazy.'

He drove me home later, but first we parked a few streets away kissing each other so much my mouth felt bruised.

I think Mama realised what we had been up to, because she kept looking from one of us to the other, but she didn't say a thing. She just gave Jacob some leftover lasagna to take to his father at nine-thirty, which meant she wanted him to go home then.

'Ring me,' I called to him from the top of the stairs.

'No, you ring me. I like you taking the initiative when it comes to us,' he grinned.

I nodded and sat at the top of the stairs. Every problem I felt I had blew out the window.

25

I'm sitting here in my room confused, angry, and so disorientated. After spending a lifetime trying to fit in somewhere in life and almost getting there I'm back at the beginning again. Today it was Mama's birthday. She turned thirty-five and Nonna and I made a cake and we had a little party.

We invited Zia Patrizia and her family, and altogether there were about ten of us at Nonna's place.

'October the first, conceived on New Years Day, eh, Zia Katia?' Robert said kissing her from behind.

'That's what I've always thought,' Mama laughed after she blew out the candles. 'Exactly nine months, isn't it?'

'Since when is a baby born exactly nine months later?' my cousin Louisa scoffed.

She's studying science at university and thinks she knows everything on the subject.

'Okay, so she was conceived the week before which was Christmas Day. Even kinkier. Merry Christmas, Katia, he would have said just before he . . .'

'Robert!' we all shouted together.

'Robert, I remember my father. I don't think he was a romantic,' Mama said.

'Oh, he was romantic,' Zia Patrizia said. 'Christina was born during their first year in Sydney and Francesco was working way up north from Ingham at Christmas time so he would have had to come home a few times for Christina to be conceived.'

I laughed with them all and then suddenly stopped.

Laughter still rang around me. People stuffed themselves with cake. Louisa argued with Robert on how long a woman really carries a child, Mama danced around the room with my Zio Ricardo who we all love and adore. Zia Patrizia broke up a fight between little Joseph and Kathy who were pulling each other's hair out. Everyone was doing something, except two people. Nonna Katia and myself. We were just watching it all. My mind was ticking. Her face was reflecting. At that very moment I knew something that could have changed our lives.

I stayed after everyone left. I told Mama I would walk home so she went to her cousin's place for dinner.

As I watched her leave I thought I would never see anyone so beautiful. Not traditionally beautiful, but beautiful from the inside. She glowed. All I could think of was that this woman deserved so much more than any other woman in the world.

Nonna Katia came from behind me and kissed my head but I pulled away.

'You're a liar,' I said to her, walking into the kitchen.

'What are you saying, Jozzie?' she asked, following me.

I turned around furiously. I wanted to hit her in rage.

'You-are-a-liar,' I whispered hoarsely. 'All our lives you've told us what to do, when to do it. You trained us to be respectful so people would think we were perfect and nobody would comment about what Mama did. You wouldn't let Michael in your house after you found out he was my father. You let your husband kick my mother out of the house when she was seventeen years old and pregnant. You've made her feel inferior all her life . . .'

'Why are you saying this, Jozzie?' she shouted in distress.

'You slept with him. You slept with Marcus Sandford.'

She whitened and stepped back, putting a hand to her throat.

'Jozzie, what are you saying?'

'Oh God, Nonna, don't be even more of a hypocrite. You were the one who told me about the four months you had to spend on your own. Four months in summer, from November to February. When you told me I felt so sorry that you had to spend Christmas and the festive season away from people you loved. But then today when everyone was joking about Mama being conceived on New Year's Day, I thought it was impossible. How could Mama possibly be conceived on New Year's Day when Nonno was up north?'

'She was premature,' she sobbed.

'She was not. She always tells me what a fat baby she was. Nine and a half pounds when she was born. Premature babies don't weigh that much.'

'Jozzie, stop . . .'

'No. You slept with him. You had the hide seventeen years ago to treat Mama the way you did when all the time you had done worse. You were married. You slept with Marcus Sandford while you were a married woman. You've gone on about Australians all our lives. Don't get involved with them, Josie, they don't understand the way we live, you'd say. What about you, Nonna? Did he understand the way you lived? Did he understand what marriage was?'

I was shouting and she was crying, but I was too shocked to care. Maybe I was wrong. Maybe my grandfather had come home for a weekend during that time.

I wanted her to tell me that. I wanted her to say that my grandfather came home for one weekend and they made love and conceived my mother. But she didn't. She just cried.

'I hate you,' I shouted. 'Not because of my life. But because of my mother's. I'm never going to come and visit you again, unless Mama is here. If you complain to her and she forces me to come here, I'll tell her everything.'

'No,' she shouted. 'Don't ever tell Christina.'

I pushed past her and felt her trying to grab my hand, but I shrugged free and ran to the door. I'm not quite sure why I hate Marcus Sandford and Nonna Katia for what they did. I had thought their story was romantic. I had thought that nothing had happened. It was like he was a myth I could always dream about.

My mother, though, is the reality. Her reality was living in a house until she was the age I am now. Living with a man who detested her for something her mother did. Living with indifference, if not hate.

I wonder about life if Nonna had married Marcus Sandford. If Mama had been Christina Sandford, daughter of Marcus Sandford and not Christina Alibrandi, daughter of an Italian immigrant. Would life have been different for her? Would she have depended on Michael so much and would she have slept with him like she did which was more out of loneliness caused by her parents than pressured sex?

Why can't it seem romantic any more?

Why does it feel like the end of the world because of what they did?

Now it seems that my illegitimacy is child's play compared to all of this. Marcus Sandford, a policeman and army officer, had an affair with a married immigrant in the 1950s. They had a baby and that baby had a baby.

People would have a field day. Our lives would be ruined.

I think I've always dreamt of being someone really impressive and famous. Someone people could sit back and envy. Growing up the granddaughter of Marcus Sandford, whoever he is today, could have brought me that feeling. It could have brought me a completely different way of life.

But now all I want to be is an insignificant Italian in a normal Italian family where there is a father and a mother and grandparents who have all stayed married to one person because it's the thing to do. I want a boring life where there is no excitement or scandal. No illegitimacy, no scandalising affairs. Nothing. Just normality. But we're not normal.

Katia Alibrandi, Christina Alibrandi, Josephine Alibrandi. Our whole lives, just like our names, are lies.

26

It took me a week to realise that I was no longer angry about what Nonna did thirty-six years ago. It's funny that all my high-school life I've been worried about what people think of me and say about me behind my back. Yet all of a sudden I realised that I didn't care what they thought and I even began to doubt that anyone, give or take a few gossips like Sera, gave a damn either. I thought of Michael and my mother, who didn't seem to worry about people's opinions. And by the looks of things, Nonna didn't have the right to. Jacob didn't give a damn who I was either, John accepted me the way I was and Lee and Anna had never made me feel different. So that covered all the important people and I'd be a pretentious hypocrite if others were more important to me than those who loved me.

That doesn't mean I wasn't angry at Nonna, because I was. She lived her life as a lie. She missed out on having a wonderful relationship with her daughter because that lie allowed her to be trapped.

She dominated our lives hypocritically and made herself look the victim when in actual fact it was Mama who was the victim. I fully realised how I felt on the way to Sera's place on Friday afternoon. The four of us were going to catch up on last-minute studying for the HSC and Sera was crapping on as usual about things that weren't her business.

'Thank God your father's a barrister,' she said. 'It's respectable. Could you imagine what the community would think if he was just a labourer or something?'

I looked up seeing the bus approaching behind her.

'My community wouldn't give a shit what my father does for a living, Sera. Only your stupid community does.'

'Well, touchy, touchy,' she sneered disdainfully.

They got on the bus but I hesitated and stepped back.

'Count me out, okay. I need to see someone,' I said with a wave.

I ignored their protests and walked towards the city and suddenly I began to cry. I must have looked pathetic walking along, clutching my haversack and crying my head off. But I think I cried more out of relief than self-pity. Relief because I was beginning to feel free.

From whom?

Myself I think.

So I jumped on the first bus that would take me to Nonna's place.

Maybe thinking of your grandparents as un-passionate people is wrong. I tend to think that passion is only for youth, but maybe older people can teach us a thing or two about it. Okay, so the thought of Nonna Katia having sex makes me sick to the stomach, but one day my grandchildren will feel the same and I'll say to them 'Why? I once felt passion for a boy. I was once young. I was once in love'.

So I knocked at her door and when she answered I hugged her and like all grandmothers and mothers and people who love you no matter what you do to them, she hugged me back.

'Why?' I asked her when we were seated in the lounge room.

'Because I was young, Jozzie,' she whispered hoarsely. 'Because I was beautiful and for all those years nobody treated me like I was beautiful but him. Marcus Sandford made me feel special,' she said fiercely.

'Didn't Nonno Francesco?'

'Your grandfather Francesco treated me like one of his farm animals,' she spat.

I closed my eyes wondering how she would have felt.

'I dreamt too, Jozzie. I did it because I had dreams just like you dream now. I was not always old.'

I hugged her hard and cried my guts out. More than I've ever cried in my whole life because I had never thought her capable of dreaming like me.

'When did it happen?' I sniffed.

She took out a hanky and wiped my eyes. 'He came to bring me a letter from my sister,' she said holding me against her. 'After I had told him not to come to me again he still came. So I took the letter from him and asked him to go. He shook his head and touched my face and told me I was so beautiful. He said that he could take me away from the life that I hated so much but I . . . I pushed him out of the door, Jozzie. Pushed him.'

There was anguish on her face as all the feelings and memories that she had buried in the past were brought to the surface. I almost felt cruel asking her to bare her soul in such a raw way.

'I . . . I pushed him because he was saying someting that I had dreamt of him saying for so long and by pushing him out I was trying to . . . to push my own feelings, Jozzie. Push them away. But he just grabbed my arms and shook me and I could not fight him any more. Do you understand?' she asked me.

I nodded because I knew that she needed me to understand.

'I was so sick of fighting him and fighting me. And for what? For Francesco who never could make me happy?'

There was so much I wanted to ask, but there would be time for that later.

'It was not like being wit Francesco,' she said, no longer looking at me. She clutched her hand to her heart and I noted the tears in her eyes. 'He undressed me . . . careful . . . careful as if I was special and he laid me down on the bed . . . my marriage bed, Jozzie, and he loved me. Not like Francesco who would lie on me for two minutes and then roll over and go to sleep. He loved me, Jozzie, for more than two minutes. When I was wit Marcus I was so angry wit Francesco because I realised then how much he hadn't given me. He just took all the time . . . it was as if I had no rights, but wit Marcus I had rights.'

'Why didn't you stay with him forever?'

'We stayed together for two months and he would beg me over and over again to leave Francesco. He would say that he'd take me some place where there were no Italians who knew me or Australians who knew him.'

She shook her head and kissed my forehead.

'But I couldn't, Jozzie. I was still an Italian girl in my heart and I could not disgrace Francesco and especially my sister and her family. I could not disgrace the memory of my Mama and Papa. People were talking enough.'

'People tend to talk about us a lot, eh?' I tried to joke.

'I suppose that we have kept the gossips well entertained for over forty years.'

'So you left him and he let you go?'

She nodded.

'He is still in my heart. I can still close my eyes and

see him today, but I did the right thing, Jozzie.'

'I don't understand. I wouldn't have gone back to Francesco,' I whispered.

'That is what is different today from my days. Today if a man gets on your nerves you divorce him. If he says someting you don't like, you divorce. In my day when you marry someone, you marry them for good. Richer and poorer. Better or worse.'

She looked at me and smiled.

'I was married to Francesco in the eyes of God. I did not want to hurt God any more than I did.'

'What happened when you got to Sydney?'

'Well, by then I knew I was pregnant so I thought that when the baby came I would say it was premature. I would work it out somehow. So when the time was right I went to Francesco and told him we were going to have a baby. I thought he would be happy after ten years. I remember the way he looked at me. He hit me in the face.'

She touched her face as if she was living it again.

'He called me bad names and I thought he would kill me and I wondered how he could possibly know.'

'How did he know?'

She shook her head.

'He told me he could not father children. When he was a young boy he had the mumps. He married me and tricked my parents and me all those years. All I ever wanted in my life was to have babies, Jozzie and he married me knowing that. So I hit him and hit him,' she said. 'Because I was so angry. Angry for ten years of tinking that maybe life was not good wit him, but I would have babies soon to make up for it.'

'Why didn't you leave him then?' I said, shaking my head in confusion.

'Oh, Jozzie, you still do not understand,' she sighed. 'Could you imagine how life would be for me if I married Marcus? Could you imagine what life would be for my sister? People are cruel. They would make our lives hell. But mostly, Jozzie, tink of Christina. Back then, tink of the way my darling Christina would be treated. It is not like these times, Jozzie. She would have had no one. No Australians, no Italians. People would spit at her and say she was nuting.'

'So you stayed with him?'

She nodded. 'He agreed to it. I tink he would have been embarrassed if people found out that it took another man to give his wife a baby. He promised me he would bring her up as his if I didn't embarrass him any more, so I stayed to protect my baby. Nobody ever knew. Francesco kept his promise.'

'But both you and Mama paid,' I said shaking my head. 'I would have left him, Nonna. I would have been selfish and thought of myself.'

'No. One day you will understand, Jozzie. One day you will have children and you will understand what sacrifices really are.'

'I would have gone with Marcus Sandford,' I told her stubbornly. 'How could you never have seen him again?'

'I see him every time I look at Christina. Do you ever wonder where her gentleness comes from, Jozzie? That serene soothing feeling about her. She got that from her father. It comforts me.'

'I wish you would tell her. She'd understand so much.'

'When she got pregnant my heart broke. Not for me or Francesco. For her. I wanted to take her in my arms and hold her. If I could have carried her on my back for nine months I would have. But he looked at me wit so much hate and I knew if I tried to help her he would ruin her life. So I said "Yes, Francesco. Anyting you say,

Francesco." When she did someting while she was growing up that he didn't like I would say "Yes, Francesco. She is wrong, Francesco". Oh, Jozzie, for years I had been waiting for God to punish me. Those years without Christina or you when you were a baby were my punishment. After he died, Christina came home, but she resented me and tings would never be right.'

'My mother loves you,' I cried against her. 'I know she does. She's just so confused about the way you feel about her, Nonna. You've both just built up so much resentment, but I know if you try you'll both be happy. Think how happy Francesco would be and how sad Marcus would be if we were all miserable.'

She nodded and held me close.

I stayed with her that night. I know Mama thinks I'm crazy because in the past I've had to be bribed to stay with Nonna Katia but I wanted to stay with this woman I didn't really know. She hadn't lived life the way I'd thought. She hadn't stuck to rules and regulations. Hadn't worried about what other people thought every second of her life. She had taken chances. Broken rules. If she hadn't, Mama wouldn't have been born and I wouldn't have been born. That freaks me out.

Just like I made a promise to her not to tell, I made her promise me that she would accept Michael and let him in her house again. She agreed.

I prayed and cried that night, harder than I ever had in my life. I prayed that the blessed 'one day' would come so I could welcome it with open arms. And I cried because I was loved by two of the strongest women I would ever meet in my lifetime.

27

Watching rugby union is probably at the end of my list of things I'd like to do on a Sunday afternoon before exams, but my cousin Robert was playing and I had promised to watch his grand final.

Stupidly I had taken my economics book with me thinking that I would get a few minutes of reading, but every time someone scored, one of the hysterical people around me would hit me on the back and send my book flying.

'You'd do anything to beat me in the HSC wouldn't you?'

I looked up in surprise at seeing John Barton and moved over for him.

'Thank God for another sane person. Everyone's gone beserk,' I said.

'What are you doing around these mad people?'

'My cousin bribed me. If I came to this he'd take me to the St Anthony's graduation.'

'Oh yes, where only the privileged can attend. I promised Ivy when we were about twelve I think.'

I laughed, thinking for the first time that I wasn't envious of Ivy.

'You two are very similar, you know,' he said taking the economics book out of my hands. 'I wish you could be friends. I really want you to be there for each other, okay.'

I shrugged, confused. 'We're very different, John.'

He shook his head, tapping me on the head with the book.

'I've known her since I was five. I thought she was the most confused being until I met you. Maybe that's why I get on with both of you.'

'Because you're confused?'

He shook his head at the thought and laughed.

'No confusing talk, okay. We will be gay and light-hearted today,' he said, theatrically.

I liked John this way, but he was different. There was a euphoria about him that was catching. We were loud and obnoxious throughout the whole game, standing on the seat and singing the St Anthony's anthem.

After the game I stood around while the boys threw beer in their hair and all that macho stuff they do when they win a game. Robert, I'm proud to say, won Man of the Match and when it was all over John walked me home.

'So how is my competition at Cook High?'

'Jacob Coote?'

'Still with him?'

'Most certainly am,' I said proudly.

'Can you try not to be offended if I tell you something?' he said looking at me earnestly.

'Please don't tell me that Jacob and I aren't suited, John,' I pleaded.

'No,' he laughed. 'Don't be so paranoid. It's just that I had a big crush on you in Year 10. I wanted to ask you out but I was scared you'd say no.'

I laughed and hugged him.

'I had a bigger crush on you.'

'Really? I'm touched,' he said grabbing my hand and swinging it as we walked along.

'Jacob's a bit funny about you and all. He's got his

own demons in a way, but you're a friend, John, and we're probably going to be in the same university taking the same classes and I want you to always be my friend. Which means that you and Jacob will have to be friends. If we survive the HSC, let's all try to go out together. Maybe even Ivy, if I can stomach it.'

'If we survive? Are you planning on dying or something?' he asked as we stopped at the Parramatta Road lights.

I turned to him and he was looking at me questioningly, his forehead creased.

'I just want it to be over. I want this year to be over, but another part of me is so petrified. God, John, we're never going to be at school again. We were top dogs here in a way. At university we'll be nobodies.'

'Just make your decisions and follow them through, Josie. That's what I've done. I've got my whole future planned out the way I want it to be and there is nothing anyone can do to take that away from me.'

'You're not going to follow in your father's footsteps?'

He grinned, shaking his head. 'No way, Josie. My father lived his life his way. I should have the same choice. The future is mine, to do whatever I want with it.'

He hugged me, swinging me around and I thought that all I needed was Jacob to drive past and see us.

'You're a psycho today, John,' I laughed as we crossed. 'I wish I had your attitude. I'm almost there, but I don't think I've come to my emancipation yet.'

'Good word. "The Emancipation of John Barton",' he said looking pensive.

'So what will the emancipated John Barton do with his life?'

'Anything he wants, Josephine,' he said looking straight through me. 'Anything he damn well wants.'

I couldn't help thinking that everything was working out well with our lives which had seemed so complicated at the beginning of the year. We chatted all the way to my place and by the end of our walk I was feeling as optimistic and positive as John.

'Look after yourself, Josephine,' he said hugging me.

I felt relieved walking up the stairs. The thought of law didn't scare me so much with John there and I knew that he and Jacob could be friends, hopefully.

I rang Jacob that night and we stayed on the phone for two hours. I even told him about being with John that day and he didn't go crazy. He just said that educating him wasn't going to happen overnight so I had to be patient.

Thinking of the six years ahead of me at university I figured that patience was something I was going to need plenty of, but somehow having John and Jacob, Michael, Mama, Nonna and my friends, I couldn't possibly go wrong.

So I slept without having nightmares that I was reading an HSC paper I knew nothing about, or that Dante's *Inferno* was no longer written in Italian but in French. I slept with the knowledge that my life was going somewhere good because of good people around me. And no HSC failure could take that away from me.

28

The next day I was walking down the corridor towards the steps that led to the home room when I noticed Ivy sitting there with her head in her hands. When she looked up and saw it was me she stood up quickly, wiping her tears and taking my hand.

'Oh, Josephine. What are we going to do, Josephine?'

I thought to myself, how like Poison Ivy to work herself up so much about the first HSC exam.

'What's happened?' I asked, thinking that maybe the school had given us the wrong novels to study this year.

'John's dead. John Barton is dead.'

I looked at her in numb shock. My mouth opened to say something but not a sound came out.

She sank back down on the step and began crying again.

'Don't be ridiculous,' I whispered, beginning to feel sick inside. 'I saw him yesterday.'

I wonder now why I thought it wasn't true. Maybe because people I knew didn't die. Other people did. People I read about in the paper and could forget the next day.

'He killed himself.'

My hands started to shake first and I wanted desperately to vomit but I tried to keep it down. I sank down in front of her, grabbing her shoulders. 'Don't be stupid, Ivy. Don't be stupid,' I shouted. 'Who told you that lie.'

'He swallowed tablets and they found him this morning.'

'This is a joke, isn't it, Ivy,' I said angrily, shaking her. 'A real sick one. John's not suicidal. Some dickhead is having you on.'

'For God's sake, Josie, he's dead. My father wrote the fucking autopsy report.'

I remembered thinking how weird it was hearing Ivy say 'fuck' and I knew hysteria was coming on because I wanted to laugh uncontrollably when she said it.

I shook my head, walking up the steps in a trance.

No, I kept telling myself. He tried to and at that moment they were trying to pump out his stomach. But he wasn't dead because people I knew didn't die.

'I know how you feel, Josie,' Ivy cried after me. 'He was my best friend.'

Anna came towards me with a worried look on her face.

'Oh, Jose, how terrible,' was all I heard her say.

I couldn't keep it down any more so I rushed to the ladies and threw up nothing in particular. I sank down on the ground closing my eyes and wanting to cry but I couldn't. I just felt so scared. I'm not sure of what. I couldn't remember what he looked like. I couldn't remember anything he had said to me or what he was wearing the last time I saw him.

All I could remember was telling him that if we survived the HSC we'd all have dinner together. I wrapped my arms around my knees for warmth, desperately wanting to go home to Mama. Instead I went to the home room and sat for my economics HSC paper.

When it was over I rang my father to pick me up. He didn't ask any questions. I think he could tell by the sound of my voice that I wanted him there.

'It's only an exam,' he told me when I got into the car.

I nodded, not looking at him.

'You want to talk about it? I know I'm not ready to handle your big-league problems, but I want to try,' he said gently.

'You can't help,' I said flatly.

'Not even a bit.'

I looked at him and I realised then that I couldn't cry because I was so angry.

'John Barton killed himself last night.'

He expelled a breath, shaking his head.

'What?'

I shrugged, trying to control my fury as much as I could. I tried to clench my mouth as tight as possible because I was afraid I was going to cry and I didn't want to.

'Josie, I don't know what to say to you.' He seemed desperate to get me home, looking over at me whenever he could.

He stopped in front of the terrace but I didn't get out.

'I hate him,' I said as controlled as I could. 'He's a bastard.'

He turned to me, waiting.

'Do you know something? I hated being illegitimate. I always did until the other day when I realised it was nothing. I never admitted it out loud because I was scared to hurt Mama so I hated you instead because I didn't know you.'

I looked out the window and leaned my head on the glass.

'In primary school I was so confused because kids will always be cruel and there was always some shithead who knew about me so they'd tell me what their mother said. Children are so honest. I swear to God, it drove me crazy at times. Sometimes I wished I was dead. I wanted to kill myself.'

I looked at him wanting him to understand.

'Do you know how many Italian girls weren't allowed to play at my house, Michael? They wanted to, I know that, but their mothers wouldn't let them. The Australian girls were the worst. They'd come up to me and say "What nationality are you, Josie?" and because I spoke Italian at home and I ate spaghetti and I lived like an Italian I'd say "I'm Italian" and they'd put on a reprimanding voice. "No you're not. You were born in this country. You're an Australian." So the next day the same girls would come up to me and ask "What nationality are you, Josie?" and I'd think to myself that these smart asses weren't going to get me twice so I'd say "I'm an Aussie" and they'd say "No, you're not. You're a wog." And I wanted to kill myself because I was so confused.

'But then I reached high school and I think that it's no big deal that I don't have a father and I think it's no big deal that I'm on a scholarship. Then I hear someone saying that their mother reckons that people who can't afford the school fees, smart or dumb, shouldn't be allowed into the school, especially if they don't know who their father is. I'd get so depressed because I was confused and I felt like killing myself. But I didn't . . . and he did.'

I looked at him, taking his hand and shaking it.

'How dare he kill himself when he's never had any worries! He's not a wog. People don't get offended when they see him and his friends. He had wealth and breeding. No one ever spoke about his family. Nobody needed to because everyone knew that his father was the man they wanted down in Canberra. Nobody ever told their kids they weren't allowed to play over at his place. Yet he killed himself. How could somebody with so much going for him do that?'

'A person doesn't necessarily have to be happy just because they have social standing and material wealth, Josie.'

'How could he do something like that, Michael?' I asked, almost begging for an answer. 'You're an adult, tell me.'

I felt tears in my eyes, but I refused to cry. My hands shook as I wound down the window.

'I'll walk you up,' he said quietly, opening the door.

We walked up in silence. I felt him take my hand and only when he squeezed it did it stop shaking.

'He was my friend,' I whispered as we walked in.

He closed the door behind me and looked around.

'Chris, can you come out here?' he sighed, looking down at me.

Mama poked her head out of her room and smiled until she looked at me closely. 'Josie, what happened?'

'Mummy?'

She hugged me and I grabbed her as closely as I could. 'I don't want you to ever die,' I cried.

'What happened?'

'John Barton died,' I heard Michael tell her.

'Oh my God,' she gasped. 'Oh, Josie,' she said cupping my face. 'Oh, darling, I'm so sorry.'

'How about you get her into bed and I make her something warm to drink?' Michael said.

'What happened? How?' she asked.

'Just get her to bed, Chris,' he said.

'He killed himself, Mama. I saw him yesterday and he was happy.'

'Oh my God. His poor mother. His poor family.'

I lay in bed and she lay next to me and I wanted her to hold me, because whenever she didn't I felt petrified.

'I'm scared to die,' I whispered as Michael walked in.

'He was scared to live,' he said kissing my forehead.

'He said to me once that life was shit. But I said it wasn't.'

'And you were right.'

'I should have realised.'

He sat down on the floor leaning against the bed. 'Josie, Josie,' he said. 'You can't think for other people. Nor can you feel for them or be them. They have to do that for themselves.'

'But you have to be there for them,' I said angrily. 'You have to look for the signs.'

'How can I make you understand?' he argued.

'I don't want to understand. I want to talk to John Barton now. I want to see him and tell him that he's a dickhead. I want to debate against him and graduate with him and beat him in the HSC and I want to be a law student with him. I want to know him in ten years time,' I cried. 'But I don't want to go to his funeral. What am I going to do, Michael? What are we all going to do?'

'You're going to go on living. Because living is the challenge, Josie. Not dying. Dying is so easy. Sometimes it only takes ten seconds to die. But living? That can take you eighty years and you *do* something in that time, whether it's giving birth to a baby or being a housewife or a barrister or a soldier. You've accomplished something. To throw that away at such a young age, to have no hope, is the biggest tragedy.'

I squeezed my eyes shut trying to block everything out.

'I'm so scared. I keep on wondering where he is. I can only think of him lying in a morgue, dead,' I sobbed.

'I feel cold and I want to vomit, but I want to hate him.'

He leaned over and kissed me.

'Josie, I would rather die than ever see you suffering this way. I don't want you or any child I ever have or any woman I ever love to go through or feel what you're going through, but it's happened and I don't know what to do.'

'Stay here. I'm scared.'

'I'm here, Josie.'

'Try to sleep, darling,' Mama said.

I felt a kiss across my brow and clung on to her for dear life.

'How does it feel to have a daughter, Mr Andretti?' I heard her ask him.

I didn't hear the answer. I just closed my eyes and dreamt of the worst things possible.

■

I woke up suddenly during the night. It was as if I had been shaken awake and I lay there taking deep breaths to get over the shock. Then it hit me and I leapt out of bed, stubbing my toe on my shoes and hopping to the jewel-case.

The white sticky-taped paper which contained John Barton's thoughts lay exactly where I had placed it months before. My hands shook so much. I wanted to throw it away. To tear it up or burn it. But I didn't. I pulled off the sticky tape, tearing a bit of the paper and walked to the window where the street-lights showed up the writing. It was a poem written in beautiful small handwriting.

■

Can you see what I see?
No I don't think you can

I see images of nothing
and I attempt to make that
nothingness mean something
As hard as I try there is
still nothing and that nothing
is meaningless
I am somewhere else now, outside
I am surrounded by people and
the sky. I see the people and the
blueness of the sky
but still nothing has changed
Everything remains the same
I am still alone.

■

I sat on the floor under the window trying to remember what I had written to him. But I couldn't. I couldn't remember one word of it. I wondered if I had forgotten because what I had written was so unimportant. Slowly I stood up and tore up the poem. I tore it once, twice, three times and then four. I opened the window and held my hand outside, opening my fist and letting the morning wind take the pieces away. As soon as I did it I wanted to run outside on to the street and put the pieces back together, but I realised that was impossible. So I watched them fly away. One lone piece flew back onto the window pane. I took it and I wondered if, like that piece of paper, John Barton was still alone.

■

Jacob took the death worse than me. We sat in the park near his place the next day on the merry-go-round and I could tell he was upset.

'We had someone in common, him and I,' he said, looking pale.

I put my arm around his shoulder and stayed close to him.

'Why did he do it, Jose? What have the rest of us got to look forward to if he had nothing?'

'They're saying he was schizophrenic,' I told him.

I was scared to let go of Jacob. I had dreamt that it was him who was dead and not John and all morning I felt unsettled until I saw him again.

'I'm glad you're not dead, Jacob,' I whispered against him.

He kissed my lips and hugged me hard.

'You know something, Jacob, I'd hate to be as smart as John. I mean he was really, really smart and to be that smart means you know all the answers and when you know all the answers there's no room for dreaming.'

He nodded.

'There's nothing to look forward to any more if you don't have dreams,' he said. 'Because dreams are goals and John might have run out of goals. So he died. But we're alive and one day I want to own my own garage and you want to be a hot-shot barrister and it's not going to happen today or tomorrow, it's going to happen in years and it's something to look forward to. Promise me you'll never stop dreaming.'

I nodded, stunned by the passion of his words.

'You promise too.'

'I promise.'

He kissed me and we held on to each other. I didn't realise until those few days how much a hug meant. To have someone hold you could be the greatest medicine of all.

■

The funeral was packed with people, young and old. I wanted to stand up and scream 'See, John, see all these people who loved you'. Ivy stood on the pulpit and gave a small eulogy and I remembered then what John had said to me the day he died. 'I want you to be there for each other'.

Later on, when eight St Anthony's boys carried the coffin out of the church, I cried. It wasn't just a physical burden on their shoulders, it was an emotional one. The pain and grief on their faces was indescribable.

Sometimes an hour has gone by and I haven't thought of John. Sometimes two, but then I remember that not a minute will ever go by when his mother won't think of him.

The teachers have all gone berserk and we've had special talks with them regarding the HSC. They seem to think the pressure killed John, but I know it didn't. John, I think, knew for years that he was going to die. That's why he never committed himself to Ivy or myself. Maybe he didn't want to drag us down with him. Maybe it was the strongest thing he ever did.

Sometimes I feel like a junkie. One minute something happens in my life and I'm flying. Next minute I take a nose-dive and just as I'm about to hit the ground with full force something else will have me flying again.

But the day John died was a nose-dive day and I hit the ground so hard that I feel as if every part of me hurts. I remembered when we spoke about our emancipation. The horror is that he had to die to achieve his. The beauty is that I'm living to achieve mine.

29

I suppose Speech Night was pretty emotional.

HSC was almost over and it was really one of the last times we'd ever wear our uniform for a school function. I received three awards that night for English, Italian and Science. Ivy was Dux, but then I never doubted that. Simply because I guess she deserved it more than me.

I met her at one stage in the ladies and I realised that she wasn't Poison Ivy any more. She was just Ivy. As scared as I was of what it meant to be out of our uniform. She smiled hesitantly and I smiled back, and I saw tears in her eyes.

'I'm only Dux because I didn't want you to be,' she told me. 'I worked harder because of you. You got on my nerves a lot.'

'Yeah, well, I only excelled in English to beat you.'

She laughed and wiped her hands.

'I'm a bit scared, you know. My father really wants me to be a doctor.'

'Yeah, well, my grandmother wants me to marry one, so we have heaps in common,' I tried to joke.

We stood looking at each other and I wanted to say so much to her and that surprised me. Because in the past I had to make up things to say.

'I feel lost without . . . John as a friend. I always felt he was going to be there pulling me up when I was down,' she blurted out.

'I really wanted him to be with me while I did law. I don't think I can make it without him now,' I confessed.

I wondered why we were standing there just babbling out all our fears and then I remembered what John had said about us being similar.

'It wasn't our fault, Josie. Not yours or mine. It was John. But I feel like crying because people will always remember the way he died and not the way he lived.'

'But we'll remember.'

She nodded and started to walk away.

'Ivy?'

'Yes.'

'If we go to the same university and we bump into each other one day, let's have a cappuccino and talk.'

And she hugged me and it was with her and not my best friends that I could cry about what had happened in the last few weeks.

Michael took me for a pizza that night.

'I was proud of you tonight,' he told me looking at my certificates. 'So was your mother. I thought she was going to stand up on her chair and chant "Josie, Josie, Josie".'

'But that doesn't count. You're my parents.'

'Yes, I like the sound of that.'

I looked up at him and smiled.

'We never say it out loud, do we?'

'No, because we're both stubborn people,' he laughed, reaching over to touch my face. 'When you were saying your speech, I know I was pretending to sleep, but I thought you were poetic. Just like your mother used to be.'

'My mother poetic?'

'She loved poetry. Elizabeth Browning was her favourite. She was going to go to university and study English literature and become a poet.'

'How embarrassing. My mother was going to do an arts degree,' I joked. 'Come on, Michael, my mother has never had a desire to go to university.'

'What do you know of your mother's desires? She wanted to be the greatest poet around. She'd recite to me constantly. I hated it.'

'Then why didn't she tell me?'

'Maybe she thought you'd blame yourself. I mean the reason she didn't go was because of me and you.'

'Why, why, *why?*' I asked. 'I would have gone. Why don't people do things they want to do? I'd never let anyone or anything stop me.'

'How the hell do you know that, Josie? You haven't begun to live life. Come back to me when you're forty and tell me that you've done everything you've wanted to do. When I was seventeen I wanted to be a pilot, but we moved to Adelaide and the move depressed me and I forgot everything I had wanted in my life. People change. Circumstances change them.'

'Were you passionate about being a pilot?'

He looked pensive.

'I've been passionate about two things in my life. One was Christina Alibrandi. The other is Josephine Alibrandi.'

'How sad that you're no longer passionate about Christina Alibrandi,' I said.

The food came and we began to eat.

'How about we get contacts?' he asked me after a mouthful.

'Contact lenses? But then we'd be good-looking. I couldn't handle that.'

'If you get them, I'll get them.'

'We'll be twins.'

He put down the pizza, looking pretty nervous which was weird, because Michael Andretti is always in control. He took my hand and squeezed it.

'I've discussed this with your mother.'

'Oh my God,' I shouted with joy. 'You've been seeing each other behind my back and you're getting married?'

'Be serious for once,' he said. 'What I discussed with her is that I'd like you to be . . . an Andretti.'

'By marriage?'

'Can you calm down. God, Josie, what do you think life is? Easy? I want to adopt you. I want you to have my name.'

'And Mama?'

'I can't adopt her.'

'I could suggest one way of changing her name,' I said slyly.

He looked at me, shaking his head in amusement.

'Don't be offended if I ask you for time,' I said honestly. 'It's not just me involved here. It's Mama and Nonna. But if it helps, I'd be so proud to be an Andretti . . . Dad.'

Reaching over the table, I hugged him hard, thinking of what my name would sound like, over and over again. Although I had no real ties to the Alibrandi name it belonged to Mama and Nonna and I belonged to them.

'I'll miss you when you go back to live in Adelaide.'

'I'm not going back. I've bought a house in Balmain.'

'Balmain?' I screeched.

'Everyone is looking,' he reminded me.

'Oh my God. When did you buy it?'

'The sale is going through now.'

'Oh God, this is great. It's so close. I can stay over and we can re-furnish it and everything.'

He rolled his eyes, biting into a piece of garlic bread.

'Does Mama know?'

'I think I've mentioned it.'

'On one of your secret dates?'

'You are so obnoxious.'

'What about the accountant in Adelaide?'

'Mind your own business.'

'Well?'

He sighed, shaking his head.

'You'd have to be the nosiest person I know. We decided to split up. It was amicable.'

'Oh gosh, I'm devastated to say the very least.'

'You sound it,' he said drily. 'It was a hard decision, but I had to get my priorities right. I ran away from commitment eighteen years ago. I should never have done what I did to your mother. I can't run away again. Because I'm older and I run slower. I want to have my time with you now.'

'So this has nothing to do with your great passion for my mother?'

'Jos-ie,' he said in frustration.

'The accountant wasn't your type. You said she ate spaghetti with a fork and spoon.'

'I told you good things about her as well.'

'Oh, like what?' I scoffed. 'That she was attractive, intelligent and successful. For God's sake, there's more to life than that.'

'I'm blocking my ears.'

We ate the rest of the meal without me tormenting him and he then drove past his house to show me what it looked like from the outside. Balmain has the loveliest pubs, bookshops and inexpensive restaurants and there's a strong sense of history attached to it. Michael's house was a small sandstone terrace, even tinier than ours, with a room added on top that Michael said would be mine when I stayed. It had the most enchanting garden and I pictured being able to do so much with it.

He dropped me off at home. I was walking towards my gate as he was leaning against the car and I turned around and walked back to him.

I hugged him and felt his arms come around me.

'I love you, you know.'

'That's because I'm lovable,' he grinned, pinching my face.

'That's something *I'd* say.'

We sat on the doorstep for a while that night. Not saying much. We didn't need to. I remembered the same time, last year, when Michael wasn't in my life. It was the scariest feeling in the world.

■

Mama was watching TV when I came in. I sat beside her without saying a word and we just cuddled up for a while.

I didn't know how to approach the subject of the adoption or my change of name. Mama, not knowing about the Marcus Sandford story, had no idea how little the Alibrandi name really meant to us all.

'Have you made a decision?' she finally ended up asking when there was a commercial break.

I looked up at her and shrugged.

'What did you first think?' I asked.

'I cried.'

'I feel that by accepting the Andretti name, I'm rejecting you and Nonna,' I told her honestly.

'But I know in my heart that you would never reject me, Josie. So I know that it's not a rejection and seeing Nonna has now accepted Michael, she knows it's not a rejection. So I can accept any decision you make, but it'll still make me cry. Because you've been all mine for so long and now you're his as well.'

'If I do it,' I said looking at the images on the television set, 'I think I'll be doing it more for him.' I looked up at her. 'I think it'd make him feel so much better about what he did if I'm an Andretti by name. Last year I would have said, who cares what he wants. But now I'd like to ease his guilt. I know Michael, Mama, I know he crucifies himself.'

'Whatever you want,' she said.

'But I don't want to be adopted,' I said adamantly. 'Changing my name is one thing, Mama, but I don't *need* to be adopted. People get adopted because their mother can't look after them or because they don't have anyone. But I have you and I can still have Michael without him adopting me.'

'He's a very lucky man,' she said taking my hand.

I sat back against her and sighed.

'We all are, Mama. We're all very lucky people.'

30

Jacob Coote and I are finished. I know I've spoken about our fights before, but this time it's definitely over because he came over here to tell me it is. I've been crying for ten hours and thirty minutes now. I think the fact that I've been listening to the CD *Twenty Great Tear-Jerkers* hasn't helped.

He came to see me during the day because we've both finished school. I somehow thought something was wrong because Anna told me he was at Speech Night yet he didn't come up to speak to me.

But still he hugged me so I lived in hope of a great explanation.

'It's not your fault,' he told me.

'What's not my fault, Jacob?' I asked alarmed.

He sighed, shaking his head.

'I think we should have a break.'

That to me does not have a future. People say that because they don't want to hurt their partner. What he really meant was that we were never going to be together again.

'Why?' I asked grabbing his shirt. 'What did I do? What happened?'

'It's not your fault.'

'Stop saying that,' I shouted.

'Look,' he said, through clenched teeth. 'I just don't

want to get serious with anyone.'

'Jacob, where has this come from? You never told me that before.'

I wanted so much not to cry. I wanted to be such a liberated woman about it. I didn't want to grab on to his shirt and plead.

'We're so different. You're an intellectual. I'm an idiot.'

'Don't say that,' I yelled. 'You're not an idiot, you stupid idiot.'

'I was at your Speech Night, you know. You won about one hundred awards.'

'I won three.'

'Yeah, same difference. That means you were the best out of all those girls for three different things, Josie. I don't even think I passed my HSC.'

'I can't believe you. Since when have you been into self-pity? You've always been the most together person I've met. You've never had any illusions or delusions about yourself. Why are you doing this?'

'Because I've been fooling myself all this time. I used to be proud of not getting good marks. "Who cares?" I used to say. Because I'm going to be a mechanic I didn't care what kind of marks I got. But since I met you it's got to me. I'm aware of more things. I'm aware that I will never ever be as good as you or as smart as you. I feel like such a failure when I'm around you and I hate myself for that. I need to work things out. Decide what I want out of life. But I don't want you to blame yourself.'

I looked at him incredulously.

'You've just told me that I make you feel like a failure and I make you feel inadequate and then you tell me not to blame myself? I think you're lying. I think you're looking for something better to come along. Someone more your type who you can feel proud of in front of your friends. That's what it is, isn't it? You never once took me out with your friends. I only know Anton and that's because he's crazy over Anna.'

'Bull,' he yelled. 'How about you and your grand-mother? Still haven't met her have I, Josie? I'm not good enough. You're the one waiting for something better to come along. Maybe someone who wants a degree. Maybe a reincarnation of John Barton.'

I gasped in shock.

'How dare you bring up poor John? He hasn't even been dead a month. Haven't you heard of mourning periods?'

'No. Remember me? No rules, no regulations. No culture. Nothing. I just have to abide by the law. I have no guidelines. I'm not an Italian . . .'

'That's it,' I yelled. 'That's it, isn't it? It's not because of how I make you feel. It's because of what I am. Or maybe what I'm not.'

'You're so emotional. Honestly it drives me crazy. Pull yourself together,' he snapped, shaking me.

'I like being emotional. Italians are always emotional. You Australians are cold.'

'Be rational. You're an Australian too.'

'I'm emotional remember, Jacob. Emotional people can sometimes be irrational and I'm not an Australian. I'm a wog. I'm only an Australian when you people want to label me one and when you don't I disappear or I go back to limbo. That's what this is all about, Jacob. My blood is too foreign for you.'

'I'm not a racist,' he argued angrily. 'Don't you dare label me one. You're just so confused about who you are that you feel that everyone is labelling you. I like that culture in you, Josie. It makes you different to people I've been around and that's why I felt attracted to you. Because I've never met anyone like you. As bad as I said I feel when I'm around you, that doesn't mean you made me feel that way. It's my fault. You've opened my mind so much.

'Sometimes I'm with my friends and I feel as if I don't fit in because of you. Because you opened me up to this whole new world out there. I don't want to become a mechanic and work all day long and then at night go to the pub and marry someone just like me and have two children and whinge about housing payments and petrol prices and the economy. I wanted that last year. No, that's not true. I thought that's what life was all about last year. But this year I realised, because of you, that there's more to life. I still want to be a mechanic, but I want to step outside my circle and look at the other options. I don't want to do what other people think I'll end up doing. I don't want to be stereotyped because of the school I attend or the district I live in. I want all the things in life that John Barton gave up because he was scared to step out of his circle. But I have to do that on my own.'

'What if we'd made love that afternoon?' I cried. 'You said we'd be together for a long time. You said you kind of loved me.'

'I did . . . I do,' he whispered. 'You were right not to let me make love to you. Because you're you. Out of some misguided thinking you would feel the need to stay with me for the rest of your life, because you probably think that the first man you make love to is the man you have to marry. I've thought of that and it seems pretty freaky, but beautiful. My father was the only man my mother ever made love to, but she was sure of herself. You're not. Jose, I'm not saying we haven't got a chance. We have a great chance. But now is all wrong.'

I cried in front of him, past embarrassment. The funny thing is that he was crying too.

'I'll still take you to your grad,' he said quietly.

'Just go,' I sobbed in convulsions.

'I'll ring you.'

'I won't come to the phone. Just go.'

He tried to hug me but I pushed him away. So he left.

I spent the rest of the afternoon crying. When my mother came home I cried even more. She found the need to ring Michael and when he came over I cried again.

'Maybe it's for the best,' she said to me as I sat between them.

I looked at her in dismay.

'I feel so terrible, Mama. I'm more upset now that I've split up with Jacob than I was when John died. What kind of person am I?'

'You're at a very emotional time in your life, Josie. Don't question it,' Michael said, handing me a hanky.

'You know what devastates me the most? He's going to marry someone else one day. Someone is going to be his wife and it's not going to be me,' I sobbed.

'One day you'll get over it, Josie.'

Did she have to say 'one day'?

I know deep down I will never get over it. Jacob Coote is not going to be in my life any more. I will never fall in love again.

31

I found it very cruel that the sun shone and the weather was perfect during the darkest of my days. I sat in front of the fan in my T-shirt and undies and adopted the European lifestyle of taking siestas at two in the afternoon for five days when the exams ended, until I noticed that even my mother had a tan compared to my pasty tear-blotched face. So I finally emerged from the house and had pizza with Lee, Anna and Sera. To celebrate the end of the exams. Not that I was in any mood to celebrate.

The four of us went for pizza at Harley's where I was bombarded by unwanted sympathy that made me feel even worse.

'If it helps, Angelo and I aren't really going strong any more,' Sera said.

'I think your situations are a bit different,' Lee said, looking over at me.

'He hasn't rung?' Anna asked sadly.

'Don't talk about it,' I whispered, because I could hardly talk.

It had been a week since my big confrontation with Jacob and I had almost lost my voice from all the crying.

'It'll work out one day. Maybe when you're older,' Anna reassured me gently, handing me a tissue.

'This from the girl who still leaves a sack at the end

of her bed on Christmas Eve,' Lee said. 'There's a good chance that things won't work out so don't spend the rest of your days thinking he'll come back.'

I shook my head and sat up, blowing my nose.

'Forget it,' I sniffed. 'So what's going on with you, Anna?'

'Oh, Josie, Anton is Jacob's best friend and all. I don't want to upset you.'

'What are you going to do? Wipe out Jacob and everyone he knows from existence?' I asked.

Anna shrugged, giving a small smile.

'Well I'm going to Anton's formal and I'm taking him to ours.'

'Has your mother met him?'

'Adores him.'

'My mother adored Jacob,' I cried into the tissue.

'Oh, Josie.'

I wiped my tears again and tried to control myself.

'I'm sorry. I promise I won't cry again.'

'What's happened so far, Anna?' Sera asked.

'Yeah, tell us all the nitty-gritty details,' Lee said sarcastically, looking at Sera with a scowl.

'Just a few kisses,' Anna said going red.

'Did he slip you the tongue?' Sera asked.

We all groaned just as the pizza came and the waiter looked offended.

'He's not as tough as he'd like people to think. He's gentle really. He said I had nice skin and I don't even need all that junk women put on their faces.'

'That's what they all say and then when you try looking natural they'll puke at the sight of you,' Sera said patting Anna on the hand.

We all looked pensive for a while as the pizza cooled.

'Well, I've got news,' Lee broke the silence. 'I slept with Matt last night.'

'What?'

'Where?'

'Was he good?'

We all spoke in unison.

'I slept with Matt,' she said with a shrug. 'It was no big deal.'

'Where?' I asked.

'In his friend's flat.'

'Did . . . did it hurt?' Anna asked.

'Not really. Weird actually. I thought pleasure was what sin is all about. I don't see the pleasure in sex so I can't see the sin in it.'

'You mean you didn't like it?' I asked.

'It was nothing like the books,' Lee said, thinking. 'No rising above the clouds or things like that.' She shrugged. 'No big deal.'

'I don't think pleasure is supposed to be a sin,' I said. 'I think guilt is a sin.'

'Why should she feel guilty?' Sera snapped. 'Maybe if you'd slept with Jacob you'd still be with him now.'

I remembered what Jacob had said and ignored her.

Lee gave a humourless laugh, picking up a piece of pizza.

'What do you think?' I asked her. 'Would sex have changed things with Jacob and I?'

She shrugged.

'Men are different. They satisfy themselves easier than we do. One poke and they're happy.'

'So you think, Sera, that I should have let Jacob use my body for his own pleasure?' I asked her.

'How about your pleasure? What makes you think you wouldn't enjoy it?' Sera asked scornfully.

'Lee didn't enjoy it.'

'I didn't say that,' Lee spoke up. 'I just said it wasn't as great as people make out and to answer your question,

Josie, you would've felt guilty now if you'd slept with Jacob. You were too unsure for one thing. You think that guilt is a sin and when you think you're sinning you don't enjoy things as much.'

I nodded. 'If I slept with Jacob, maybe I would still have him. But I probably would also need a therapist.'

We all had a bit of a laugh and Sera hit the table a few times.

'Listen, first times are never great. The guy has to be fantastic for it to be good. But it gets better,' she explained to us between mouthfuls.

'I always think, what happens if I get married and I'm not good in bed,' Anna blurted out.

'That's why I don't believe you should be a virgin when you get married,' Sera said. 'You should experiment. Men do.'

'Yes, but only if you're in love with them,' I said.

Sera nudged Lee as if they were now part of a secret society.

'That one believes in Santa Claus and this one believes in the tooth fairy.'

We finished our pizza and paid the bill and decided to walk to Anna's house instead of taking a bus.

'You did right,' Lee said quietly to me as we walked alone, while the others walked ahead.

'What do you mean?'

'Not sleeping with him. You're different to me. Different to Sera. You're the type who'd suit being a virgin until she's in love, or even until she's married. You could probably make it look trendy. Anna will probably be a virgin six months after her wedding night from fear of not being good in bed.'

We laughed and I looked at Anna.

'I don't know. Not if she keeps on with Anton.'

'I'll give them two weeks and it'll be over,' Lee sighed.

'So you think that even if I did sleep with him I wouldn't have been able to hold on to him?'

'Jose, your loss of virginity will be written in a diary and you'll probably go to confession on its anniversary every year for the rest of your life. Losing mine was just a page in my life. No big deal.'

'You keep on saying that. You've convinced me it was a big deal,' I said looking at her. She looked pensive.

'It is a loss of innocence you know,' she said thinking about it. 'Just like everyone says it is. I think it's the only thing you have left that belongs to you and that belongs to that cocoon of childhood.'

'Are you going to see Matt again?' I asked.

Lee shrugged.

'You know what I wish?'

'What?'

'I wish I was a little girl again,' she whispered quietly.

'So do I,' I whispered back.

We put our arms around each other's shoulders and followed the others home.

32

My emancipation didn't happen like I expected it to.

I thought maybe I'd wake up one morning and see the light. Feel liberated from everything. Or maybe one particular incident would see me through it. But it happened while I was hysterically crying – again.

It was after receiving a birthday card from Jacob which I threw in the bin. I just sat there thinking back on the year and I realised that I was emancipated long ago. It wasn't at one particular point either, it was at several. The hang-ups I once had were superseded, but not with other hang-ups as much as with a few sorrows.

I remembered feeling socially out of it at St Martha's, yet when the fiasco of the walk-a-thon happened, I realised I wasn't. I thought my birth circumstances were a cross I'd bear for the rest of my life, but what had happened between Nonna and Marcus Sandford made me realise that it had never been my cross. I had only made it mine.

And the different cultures thing?

Well, I'm not sure whether everyone in this country will ever understand multiculturalism and that saddens me, because it's as much part of Australian life as football and meat-pies. But the important thing is that I know where my place in life is. It's not where the Seras or the Carlys of the world have slotted me.

If someone comes up and asks me what nationality I am, I'll look at them and say that I'm an Australian with Italian blood flowing rapidly through my veins. I'll say that with pride, because it's pride that I feel.

A lot has changed at home. I'm not sure why. Maybe because I've changed. Michael has moved into his home at Balmain and I stay with him a lot. The funny thing about it is that Mama will sometimes come over for dinner and the both of them amaze me. They just seem so tuned in to each other.

They talk for hours without embarrassment or awkwardness and I wonder what is stopping them from getting closer. Maybe they're both terrified of how strong their feelings really are.

I fight with Michael a lot. Expecially now that I see him so much. He can sometimes be such a male chauvinist and he doesn't think twice about criticism. Though he expects of me, not what he wants, but what he feels that I want. If I cheat myself, he says, it makes him furious. We clash because there is a generation gap.

He watches current affairs programs and considers them entertainment and he goes absolutely berserk when he catches me watching American sitcoms. He detests them.

But I love Michael Andretti more and more every day. I love him double to what I did maybe a month ago yet I see his faults now too.

And Jacob?

Well, I don't think it is my Italian background and his Australian one that is keeping us apart. I think, at the moment, we're too different. We haven't figured out what we really want from ourselves, let alone from each other.

I think that during the year Jacob got a bit more

ambitious than he used to be and I became a bit less. Sometimes I'm not even sure that I want to be a barrister. But I'm not going to make that a problem or a hang-up. When my results come out I'll make my decision then. But I'm optimistic. I do believe in my heart that one day I will be with Jacob Coote again. So I took the card out of the garbage and put it on my mantelpiece.

It's my birthday today. I'm not seventeen any more. The seventeen Janis Ian sang about where one learns the truth. But what she failed to mention is that you keep on learning truths after seventeen and I want to keep on learning truths till the day I die.

Just like I'll know who I am till the day I die. I'll believe in God and I won't let any church rules take that away from me. I'll believe in my world. A world where an Irishman told us to feed the poor and we fed the poor.

Where musicians asked us not to 'Sing Sun City' and we supported them against the segregation between blacks and whites.

A world where Sting asked if the Russians loved their children too and we knew the answer was yes.

I know there is a lot that is bad with the world, but too many people are ready to give up on it. But I'm not. Because I honestly believe in the goodness of the individual person and especially the youth.

So I'm sitting here listening to U2, to the words written by, perhaps, a modern-day poet. And tonight I'll be with friends and family, which is what life is all about. I will sit between two women. The two most influential women in my life, whose relationship was almost destroyed by one man who has been dead for fifteen years.

I will sit between them and be a link and I'll fight with all my might to see that nothing tears my family unit apart. I'm not saying my life will be easier now because I finally feel free. I'm not saying that people will stop whispering about me behind my back. Because I think that if I lived life like a saint and walked with two feet in one shoe; if I wore the clothes of St Francis of Assisi and suffered like a martyr; if I lived by the rules and never committed a sin, people would still talk. Because human nature is like that. They'll always, like me, find someone to talk about.

I've figured out that it doesn't matter whether I'm Josephine Andretti who was never an Alibrandi, who should have been a Sandford and who may never be a Coote. It matters who I feel like I am – and I feel like Michael and Christina's daughter and Katia's grand-daughter; Sera, Anna and Lee's friend and Robert's cousin.

You know, a wonderful thing happened to me when I reflected back on my year.

'One day' came.

Because finally I understood.

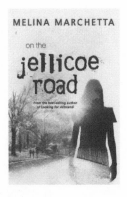

Taylor is leader of the boarders at the Jellicoe School. She has to keep the upper hand in the territory wars and deal with Jonah Griggs – the enigmatic leader of the cadets, and someone she thought she would never see again.

And now Hannah, the person Taylor has come to rely on, has disappeared. Taylor's only clue is a manuscript about five kids who lived in Jellicoe eighteen years ago. She needs to find out more, but this means confronting her own story, making sense of her strange, recurring dream, and finding her mother – who abandoned her on the Jellicoe Road.

The moving, joyous and brilliantly compelling new novel from the best-selling, multi-award-winning author of Looking for Alibrandi and Saving Francesca.

SAVING FRANCESCA

**From the multi-award-winning bestselling author of
Looking for Alibrandi, comes a memorable story
told with humour, compassion and joy.**

Francesca is at the beginning of her second term in Year Eleven
at an all boys' school that has just started accepting girls. She still
misses her old friends, and, to make things worse, her mother has
had a breakdown and can barely move from her bed.

But Francesca had not counted on the fierce loyalty of her new
friends, or falling in love, or finding that it's within her power to
bring her family back together.

**Shortlisted for the 2004 South Australia Festival Awards for
Literature – Young Adult division and the 2004 YABBA –
Older Reader's section. Winner of the 2004 Children's Book
Council of Australia Book of the Year for Older Readers and
the 2004 WAYRBA – Older Reader's section**

BYE, BEAUTIFUL
Julia Lawrinson

She thought of Billy, and how he would never say 'Bye, beautiful' to someone like her, that likely no one would ever say anything like that to her in her life, and how she could not do anything to change any of it.

Sandy does not know if she would fit in anywhere, but she feels like a complete outsider in this hot wheatbelt town where her policeman father has just been transferred.

And then she meets Billy, the part-Aboriginal mechanic's apprentice and town heart-throb.

Sandy's feelings for him are overwhelming her, but she is about to find out that her greatest rival is her own sister, the alluring, confident Marianne.

Set in Western Australia in the 1960s, this is a story of secrets and heartbreak, of families and changing times, by rising star Julia Lawrinson.

COME EXPLORING AT

www.penguin.com.au

AND

www.puffin.com.au

FOR

Author and illustrator profiles

Book extracts

Reviews

Competitions

Activities, games and puzzles

Advice for budding authors

Tips for parents

Teacher resources